STON

Mike Jefferies was bo... early years in Aust... Goldsmiths School of ...ght art in schools and prisons. A keen rider, he was selected in 1980 to ride for Britain in the Belgian Three Day Event. He now lives in Norfolk with his wife and three stepchildren, working full-time as a writer and illustrator.

SCIENCE
FICTION
FANTASY

MIKE JEFFERIES

Stone Angels

HarperCollins*Publishers*

HarperCollins Science Fiction & Fantasy
An Imprint of HarperCollins*Publishers*
77–85 Fulham Palace Road,
Hammersmith, London W6 8JB

This paperback edition 1994
1 3 5 7 9 8 6 4 2

First published in Great Britain by
HarperCollins*Publishers* 1993

ISBN 0 586 21527 1

Set in Stempel Garamond

Printed in Great Britain by
HarperCollinsManufacturing Glasgow

Contents

CHAPTER ONE

Midwinter 1140

A BONE-HARD frost glittered on the dark inner walls of the cathedral, ghosting the medieval stone carvings, etching the forest of rickety, wooden scaffolding that marched away into the darkness with countless, feathery patterns of ice. Reed lamps set in iron fire-baskets burning on each of the soaring columns cast a dim, smoky, guttering glow across the nave. There was a sudden noise, a scraping of stone upon stone, from somewhere in the darkness. It woke with a start Geothrick, the apprentice stonemason, who had been sleeping high up in a corner of the narrow, north clerestory upon a bed of straw. Shivering, he listened to the frozen silence as he gathered the meagre hessian sack that served both as his coat and blanket tightly around his shoulders, and crept hesitantly forward, feeling for the single wrought-iron guard rail on the edge of the narrow walkway before peering down into the gloomy darkness below.

There had been something unnatural about the sound that had awoken him, something so different from the normal night sounds of the cathedral that it had set his teeth on edge and made his spine tingle with fear. He shivered, wondering if it was the fragment of a nightmare, the echo of ghosts or demons come to haunt him in the darkness. Anxiously he listened for the familiar rustle of straw, the scrape and clatter of hooves on stone and the grunts and snorts of the Bishop's animals that had been herded and tethered into the nave to shelter them from the bitter mid-winter weather. He caught the sounds of the restless animals and mingled with them he heard the reassuring coughs and snores and slurred dreamy murmurings from the group of pilgrims who were sleeping upon the wooden pews in the central aisle, wrapped up warmly in their travelling rugs.

'I must have dreamt it.' Geothrick yawned as he crawled back to his meagre scattering of straw amongst the huddle of apprentices and serving boys who slept in the clerestory. But as he was about to burrow underneath his hessian blanket he faintly heard the sound again. It was different now, closer, and it sounded as if it were directly above him in the vaulted roof.

Geothrick sat upright, tilting his head from side to side and trying to make sense of the faint whirring, grating noise. It wasn't like anything he had ever heard before. A sudden frozen draught of air ruffled his hair and made him look up. Birds! That must be what the sound reminded him of, a large bird, perhaps a swan or a goose beating its wings to rise. Geothrick felt a cold shiver of fear knot up in his stomach as he remembered that the Bishop's geese and swans had their wings clipped and that the owls that roosted in the tower flew and hovered without making a sound. It couldn't be a bird.

Curiosity inched the young, trembling apprentice back to the edge of the clerestory to dare another look. Despite his fear he had to find out what was causing that persistent low humming, grating sound. He crouched down and pressed himself hard against the guard rail. Craning his neck he looked up and searched the dark forest of frost-glittering scaffold poles below the stone ribs that supported the vaulted roof high above his head. The sound seemed to shift, to rise and fall as softly as the waves breaking on a summer beach. Slowly and uncertainly he let his gaze travel the length of the cathedral from the shimmering points of starlight that he could see through the west window to the dark, secret shadows beneath the soaring arches of the ambulatory. But there was nothing to see. Nothing unusual in the smoky, dying glow of the flickering lamps. Geothrick yawned and was about to retreat to his bed of straw when a movement beneath the lantern of the tower caught his eye. A huge, winged shadow momentarily engulfed the choir screen and then vanished up across the roof. He gasped and clutched at the guard rail as he stared down to see a dark figure, larger than a man, with a feathery arch of wings slowly fly out from beneath the lantern of the tower. Geothrick watched, transfixed with awe and terror, as the figure glided past him and he realised that it was an angel, a vision from heaven. Its nakedness glistened in the torch light and every feather of the great curve of the wings that grew from its shoulder blades seemed etched in perfect detail.

The noise grew louder and he realised that it was the beat of the angel's wings that had awoken him.

'So beautiful. So beautiful,' he whispered, stumbling over his words as he made the sign of the cross in the air above his head.

Cold beads of sweat were forming on his forehead and he glanced anxiously at the indistinct shapes of the other apprentices in the gloomy darkness. He listened for a moment to their ragged sleeping breaths. He didn't want to share this miracle with anyone, or startle the angel and scare it away. He crouched lower and pressed himself back into the shadows of the walkway, smiling as he watched the angel make a slow and almost lazy arch above the centre of the nave. Quite suddenly it vanished with a whirr of feathers. Geothrick gave a cry of dismay and crowded forward to peer down in time to see the angel sweep in a tight circle over the central rows of high-backed wooden pews in the nave. It hovered erratically and then darted between the stone columns as quickly as a giant dragon-fly, disappearing in and out of the darkened aisle in a rush of frosty air.

Geothrick realised that the angel was moving out of sight from where he crouched, that each graceful, soaring arch was taking it back toward the choir stalls. He couldn't bear to lose sight of his beautiful vision and he scrambled between the sleeping bodies that crowded the clerestory, running as fast as he dared toward the small spiral stairway close to the north-west door that would take him down into the north aisle. He peered down to his left, through the passing archways, as he ran and caught glimpses of the angel flying in and out of the gloomy shadows. He reached the stairway and flung himself down, taking the slippery steps two at a time. On the bottom he paused, widening his eyes against the darkness of the north aisle, and listened. His breath hung in the air around him in frost-white vapour streams. Faintly he caught the sound of the angel and he knew it must have reached the choir stalls or even flown over them into the lantern of the tower.

Geothrick ran as fast as he could along the north aisle, tripping and stumbling over the groups of half-seen pilgrims and artisans who were sleeping huddled around the last glowing embers of hot ash that choked the heavy iron fire-baskets in the aisle. A string of startled grunts, oaths and mumbled curses followed Geothrick through the inky shadows. Breathlessly he reached the fluted stone columns closest to the choir stalls and hesitated. The whirr and beat of the angel's wings was suddenly loud again and almost directly in front of him. He edged forward as far as he dared and, looking up through the archway, he saw that the angel was descending to hover above the lines of dark, wooden stalls, stirring up a gale of icy wind that ruffled Geothrick's untidy hair and made the guttering reed torch light dance madly and throw leaping, hideous shadows up across the walls.

'Don't make so much noise!' Geothrick wanted to shout, to warn the beautiful vision. He didn't want any of the clerics or singing men waking: he knew they were sleeping off the effects of their evening jugs of ale between the choir stalls. His warning cry came out as a gargled, paralysed whisper, and it came too late.

A fat monk, spread out on the front stall, felt the draught of the angel's wings and he grunted and snorted in his sleep, turning awkwardly away only to slide off the narrow wooden seat with a crash. Rudely awakened, the monk tried to scramble to his knees, a curse puffing out his cheeks. He glared upwards, his angry curses turning to a startled cry of terror as the shadow of the angel enveloped him. A hand reached down and gripped him around the throat. Geothrick looked on helplessly, his gaze of adulation turning into a cry of horror. He watched the fat monk stagger as the angel lifted him to his feet with one brutal jerk. The monk gasped and choked, his face blackening, tears streaming down his face, and he clawed at the strangling fingers that tightened around his neck.

The angel's beautiful, pale face contorted into a hideous snarl as it stabbed at the monk's chest with its right hand, tearing through his coarse robes and smashing through the thorax with a sharp crack of bone. Its face lit up with a look of triumph as it ripped out the monk's still-beating heart and held the pulsating organ high above his head and squeezed the heart dry of blood.

'Awaken Sammeal!' it cried.

Rivulets of blood splattered and trickled down through

its tousled curls and ran as dark, glistening rivers across its forehead, hissing and bubbling as it soaked its way into its stone skin.

'Sammeal! Sammeal, it is I, Abaddon, your servant of darkness!' Urgently it smeared the congealed streaks of blood and livid tissue from the ruptured heart across its cheeks and neck. Then it threw its head back to look up through the dark forest of scaffolding to the glistening, frosted stone ribs that formed the vaulted roof.

'Sammeal?' It called softly, slowly turning as if searching for someone, its folded wings casting elongated shadows across the nave.

'I will wet the bloodstone again,' it hissed impatiently, snatching up the quivering corpse of the monk from where it had been discarded at its feet. With a snarl it tore open the shattered sternum and plunged its face into the oozing wound. The cleric's body convulsed, his feet danced wildly, treading empty air as his hands opened and closed in helpless spasms. The rosary of jet-stone beads that he carried slipped from his dead fingers as Abaddon gorged, sucking out the monk's bodily fluids.

Geothrick sank down in the safety of the shadows feeling dizzy and sick with the horror of what he had just witnessed. He couldn't comprehend what had happened. Angels were messengers from heaven, not hideous, murdering monsters. He clutched at the cold, stone column for support. He was paralysed and unable to tear his gaze away as the angel withdrew its bloody face from the inside of the monk's chest. Its lips were swollen now and dripping with blood, the pale pink skin of its face a translucent mass of red, glistening veins. It lifted its head again and called out.

'Sammeal, I have performed the sacrifice. I command you to arise!'

The angel's demanding voice echoed away into the flickering lamplight to be swallowed by the frozen silence. The clerics sleeping in the choir stalls began to stir, disturbed by the noise. Abaddon spun round toward the stalls and lifted the now-withered corpse of the monk high above its head. It seemed possessed with rage, its eyes contracted into glowing pin-points of fury, its lips split open as if to issue a screaming hail of curses at the waking clerics. But the angel hesitated and lowered the body, gathering it carelessly beneath its left arm as if it were a limp rag doll. It swept its piercing, pitiless eyes across the dark archways that flanked the nave as if it feared someone might have witnessed the sacrifice. It was as if it sensed a watcher in the shadows.

Geothrick cowered down, pressing himself onto the cold flagstones. He felt naked and exposed, his heart pounding in his chest with the terror that the angel might see him. But the angel's gaze passed over him without a blink. A gust of icy air touched the back of his neck and Geothrick looked up in time to see the angel rise, its huge, feathery arch of wings outspread as it vanished into the shadows of the lantern of the tower. Sleepy figures half-rose amongst the choir stalls. Voices grumbled and muttered, unsure of what had disturbed them.

'It was probably only last night's ale and a hard, wooden bench for a pillow,' yawned one of the singing men.

'More likely to have been Ethelred's pottage.'

'I thought I saw an angel,' murmured a sleepy monk.

Voices laughed away what visions they might have seen and bodies subsided back into the blankets and cloaks which were gathered up more tightly against the bitter cold as the group of clerics settled back to sleep.

Geothrick rose trembling to his feet and listened to the deepening silence. A moment before the clerics spoke he was going to call out, to warn them of the murdering angel, to tell them what it had done. But now he feared they would not believe and they would merely curse him and beat him for waking them again. But it wasn't a nightmare; he knew it had really happened, but how was he to convince them? Beyond the choir screen from somewhere in the gloom of the south transept he caught the faint sound of something heavy being dropped.

'Of course, the body of the monk. If I can find where the angel put it, I could convince everyone.'

Summoning up the last threads of his courage he crept silently between the sleeping figures in the choir stalls and, hugging the shadows cast by the four massive stone columns that supported the tower, he edged his way into the south transept. The sound of stone grating harshly against stone brought him to a sudden stop. It was darker and echoingly empty in the transept with only the last dying embers of the two reed lamps burning on either side of the huge oak doors, casting their soft illuminating pools of light across the end of the vast building.

Geothrick hesitated to move forward as he felt his courage evaporate. What if the angel had been a dream, a nightmare so real that he only thought he had really seen it? What if the new sound that he could hear was a phantom, something terrible waiting a hand span in front of him in the darkness? He shivered and was about to retreat and creep back to his place in the clerestory when he heard the harsh grating sound again, and it seemed to be coming from somewhere along the far wall. He tilted his head and listened. It didn't sound anything like the beat of the angel's wings or the shriek and howl of phantoms. He thought that it might be the frost making the stones crack.

'I've got to find that monk's body: then I can prove that I wasn't dreaming,' he whispered aloud to give himself the courage to edge slowly forward between the haphazard rows of benches and high-backed stalls that crowded between the tower and the south transept. He reached the last high-backed stall and paused, peering anxiously into the gloom for the monk's body. Geothrick caught his breath in a stifled gasp as he picked out the outline of the angel against the far wall. The body of the monk was sprawled on the floor near its feet. He hadn't expected to see the angel again, he had assumed that it had simply vanished into thin air after dropping the corpse of the monk somewhere in the transept.

Geothrick's forehead wrinkled into a bewildered frown as his eyes became more accustomed to the darkness and he watched the angel repeatedly stoop and claw with its fingers at a crack in the stone floor. It seemed to be trying to lift up and drag aside one of the enormous flagstones that lay across the entrance to the transept chapel. He couldn't understand what the angel was trying to do or why it hadn't vanished. He forgot his fear and curiosity made him abandon caution as he inched closer, moving round in front of the stall he had been hiding behind. The angel was digging, clawing at the thick layers of dirt and dust that had filled the cracks between the stones. With a cry of triumph it managed to grasp the far corner of the heavy stone slab closest to the wall with the fingertips of both hands. The muscles of its arms bulged and knotted with effort, its face contorted into a snarl of bared teeth, its wingtips beat and thrashed wildly against the columns of the low archway that led into the chapel.

The stone slab moved and lifted an inch. Abaddon threw his head back and called out a whispered chant, a ribbon of names and words that Geothrick couldn't understand, as it pulled the stone free. It lifted another inch and began to twist, rising up upon the stone next to it.

Abaddon chanted faster.

'Zahrim, Akkabal, Gibel, Ishtaz.'

It was invoking the demons of the pit to help him, but the flagstone snagged and tore free from its grip as it slipped back with the harsh sound of stone grating on stone, the sound that Geothrick had heard when he first crept into the transept.

Abaddon cursed the stone and struck it violently with its fist, sending up a shower of stone splinters and making it rock slightly from side to side. The angel lifted its arm to strike the stone again but then hesitated, touching it with an outstretched finger instead. It rocked again and Abaddon realised that it now lay slightly askew with one bevelled edge riding up proud against the one that lay next to it. With a cry it gripped the raised edge and struggled to lift it clear. It moved, jarring and binding on the uneven edges of the flagstone that lay on either side of it and then it became wedged, stuck fast between them.

Abaddon issued another string of curses and spat a bloody gob of boiling spittle at the heavy stone slab. Then it clenched its fists and sank to its knees. It folded its wings tightly across its shoulders before bending forward to press its swollen lips against the narrow, black crack that it had managed to open between the flagstones.

'Guardians of Hell's Gate, you must awaken. Come to me and gather the gift of this sacrifice!' the angel cried with an urgent, demanding voice.

Geothrick felt the stone floor of the transept tremble beneath his feet as Abaddon's voice echoed away below him in the bowels of the earth. The wooden benches and pews rattled and a sudden gust of hot foul air that stank of death and corruption wafted up through the crack. It carried with it a faint sound of demonic voices, shrieks and cries of pitiless laughter and the growing rush and scrabble of clawed feet. The breath of foul wind stirred the dying embers of the reed lamps making them flare up and explode in a blaze of bright sparks that momentarily flooded the transept with light. It sent the crouching angel's shadow fleeing up amongst the forest of scaffold poles into the vaulted roof. It etched the tall stone columns and rising arches in stark relief. The bright sparks crackled and then went out, plunging the building into utter darkness. But in that moment of searing light Geothrick glimpsed a mass of fingers and claws reach up through the black crack between the flagstones and prise it apart, widening the gap. Small, hideous demons, dwarfed creatures that must have been spat from the pits of Hell, creatures with claws and cloven feet, swarmed up into the transept and began to clamber all over the monk's carcass. They were as thick as a nest of ants, biting at his fingers, tearing off strips of skin from his arms and legs, fighting and squabbling amongst themselves as they did so. Slowly they began to pull and drag the mutilated body toward the edge of the black hole in the floor.

Geothrick shuddered with horror as he watched the door-crack to Hell yawn open only yards in front of him. It had to be a dream, a hideous nightmare, it couldn't be real. He savagely pinched his left arm to wake himself up but the burning pain that shot up his arm and the two angry red weals on his soft skin proved he wasn't dreaming. The visitation of the angel and the demons who were now devouring the monk's body were horrifically real, and so close to him he could almost reach out and touch them. A voice inside his head screamed out, shouted at him to escape, to get out of the transept as fast as he could before those monstrous creatures discovered he was watching them. Before . . . before . . . his mind froze with the terror of what they might do to him. His legs became as weak as jelly and he found he couldn't move, couldn't take a step toward escape. He was trembling uncontrollably from head to foot.

Abaddon hissed impatiently at the feasting demons as he

roughly dragged the monk's body toward the open lip of the crypt before pushing it over the edge, cursing as the shrieking creatures swarmed after it. Geothrick caught sight of the monk's disfigured head jerking back before it disappeared, dragged into blackness down a flight of barely seen steps.

'I will awaken you, Sammeal. I will try again when the summer moon is in the seventh house,' the angel whispered into the dark hole as the demons' voices grew fainter. Slowly he began to pull the flagstone back into place.

The harsh rub of stone upon stone broke the paralysing terror that had gripped Geothrick. He stumbled backwards and turned but in his haste to flee he collided with the tall wooden pew that he had been crouching in front of and sent it crashing to the ground. Abaddon leapt to his feet, a snarl of startled anger hissing through its lips as its eyes searched in the direction of the fallen pew. It caught sight of a youth, a ragged mason boy, struggling to his feet before he fled, dodging between the forest of wooden scaffolding and rows of benches and tall pews that filled the archway and escaped into the lantern of the tower.

'There was a watcher, a witness to the sacrifice, a mason's brat who must have heard me utter Sammeal's name. You must seize him before all our secrecy is undone!' Abaddon called into the dark mouth of the crypt.

The squabbling shrieks of the demons fell utterly silent as the angel's voice echoed amongst them, then they cast aside the body of the monk and clambered up the steep stone stairway in a rush of clawed feet. Dozens of fire-hot red eyes reappeared in the entrance to the crypt searching, following the vanishing footsteps of the apprentice.

'He runs toward the presbytery!' Abaddon cried. 'Light! Give me light to find him, he must not escape to tell what he has seen, Sammeal is not ready yet. The boy must be buried alive in the crypt of torment, his tongue silenced forever!' the angel hissed, sending up a gale of frozen ice particles as he beat his wings and rose in pursuit.

Behind him the hideously deformed Bokwoys and Kibozus, the guardians of the Gate of Hell, shrieked with rage that their secrecy had been violated and swarmed forward, lighting up the transept with livid tongues of phosphorescent fire. The flames billowed and roared out of their snarling mouths and ran in zig-zag, leaping lines across the floor, cracking the stone and charring the pews it touched. The fire melted the feathery patterns of frost that covered everything, sending up clouds of boiling steam and leaving nothing to mark its passage save finger trails of soot and hot, wet spidery threads of bubbling condensation.

Geothrick heard the howls of pursuit and felt the heat of the livid flames crackle and singe his heels. The beating whirr of the angel's wings was now almost overhead and getting closer and closer, sending an icy down draught against the back of his neck. The scrabble of monstrous claws sounded only a footstep behind him as he reached the centre of the tower and looked desperately for somewhere – anywhere – that he could use to escape this legion from hell that was swarming after him.

'Capture him. Tear out his tongue and silence him!' the angel hissed from somewhere in the darkness overhead.

Geothrick realised he must wake everyone in the cathedral. He must scream and shout until his lungs burst. He must warn them that the Gates of Hell had opened in the transept.

'Help me! Help me!' he screamed. 'I'm being attacked. The devil . . . the devil is on my heels!'

He dodged blindly sideways as the angel swooped down and tried to seize him, colliding with the bronze lectern that stood in the centre of the tower and sending it crashing

23

noisily to the ground. Throwing his hands out to stop himself falling, he stumbled and caught sight of the two lighted candles that stood upon the high altar beyond the presbytery in the eastern apse.

'The altar is a holy place. Evil cannot touch it – I must reach the altar,' he gasped, scrambling and leaping up the broad stone steps in one bound. Concentrating every ounce of his strength he reached the two, softly flickering flames that were haloed by the frosty air.

Above him Abaddon swooped down again, twisting between the forest of poles, a string of curses pouring through his lips. Geothrick dodged to the right, crying out as the angel's fingers tore out a fist full of his dirty matted hair. Screaming and shouting he sprinted the length of the presbytery. The demons were overhauling him, gaining on him with every stride. Their outstretched claws were scratching and tearing at his legs and ankles as he leapt over the low altar rail and threw himself forward up the three wide stone steps of the high altar.

'Sanctuary – I seek sanctuary from all the foul demons and monsters of the night!' Geothrick shouted, trying desperately to kick off the biting, snarling creatures that were clinging to him and fighting to drag him away from the altar.

He reached out and managed to hook his hands around one of the central pillars supporting the heavy slab of marble that made up the top of the altar. Inch by inch, screaming with every breath, he fought to scramble beneath the altar.

The cathedral was in uproar, woken by Geothrick's screams. Sparks were struck in the darkness and lamps were rekindled, bolts were drawn and doors thrown open. A gathering rush of footsteps began to converge on the presbytery and close around the wildly dancing flames of the altar candles.

Abaddon cursed the ragged mason's boy and tried to land on the altar and pull him away from it, but the candle flames flared up, scorching its wings, making the finely carved arch of feathers shatter and break into a thousand jagged splinters and sending a searing bolt of pain through its black heart. The angel shuddered and leapt away from the altar. No matter how it tried to approach it the candle flames bent and flared toward him, driving it back.

'Blind him! Tear out his tongue! Silence him before he utters a word!' the angel snarled in rage at the swarm of demons as he rose into the air.

'Sanctuary! I seek sanctuary. You cannot touch me here!' Geothrick shouted in terror as the Bokwoys' jabbering chants began to diminish the power of the altar.

Geothrick's shouts turned to screams of terror as the biting demons began to scramble up his legs, biting and clawing at him.

Suddenly they were everywhere, scratching his skin to ribbons, scuttling up toward his head. He let go of the altar and frantically tried to tear them away from him and beat them off. He rolled over and over in an effort to crush them but they overwhelmed him, pinning down his arms. All at once they were on his face, their cruel claws cutting through his eyelids. With shrieks of triumph they dug deeper, gouging out his eyes. He threw back his head with a tormented scream, twisting and contorting his face in pain. Another demon with a mouth of razor-sharp teeth hooked its claws into Geothrick's hair as his mouth opened and forced his head inside and savagely bit off his tongue, gulping it down with one swallow.

Geothrick's scream ended in a gurgling, choking retch, blood oozing from his raw eye sockets and filling his mouth. The demons scattered, vanishing through the shadowy archway with a rattle of sharp claws on the hard, stone floor moments before the first of the advancing clerics reached the altar rail.

'No, not rats, they could never have disfigured young Geothrick's face like that.' The voice of Bishop Elmphric was so emphatic that it made the other members of the investigating council turn expectantly toward him.

'But I saw their fleeing shadows. There were hordes of them escaping through those archways,' insisted the choirmaster. 'They came up from the river searching for food during the cold spell.'

'I thought I saw something else, a huge figure like an angel, it rose up and flew away,' one of the monks on the edge of the council muttered to his neighbour.

'Well, I wouldn't be heard saying that. They'll call you a heretic – or worse!'

'I don't like any of it. Rats or not it smells of the Devil to me. It's a miracle the boy survived.' The monk nodded grimly.

Geothrick lay in the infirmary in a black river of despair. He was oblivious to everything except the burning agony, the long, howling nightmare of pain that raged inside his head. Visions and hideous images screamed at him in the darkness, making him flinch and strike out wildly against every hand that tried to tend his horrific wounds. He cowered away from every touch that penetrated his searing flames of pain fearing them to be the cold, pitiless, strangling fingers of the dark angel come to seize him. Even the monks' soft, whispering voices became the shrieks of demons inside his head and the quick clatter of their wooden clogs upon the stone-flagged floor a rush of scrabbling claws that made him sit bolt upright upon his mattress of straw and thrash his legs as he twisted and turned his blind, bleeding head from side to side. The legions of the Devil were everywhere, he could hear them closing in, filling his claustrophobic darkness, swarming through the cathedral.

He had to warn the Bishop. He had to scream and shout until his lungs burst. He had to wake everyone up before it was too late. He had to tell them of the murderous angel and the yawning doorway into the pits of Hell that lay beneath the transept. But all he could do was gurgle and stab helpless, trembling fingers at the empty air while dribbling strings of bloody spittle which escaped silently from his ruined mouth. He was frantic to warn everyone, to make them understand the danger that was hiding in the shadows of the cathedral, but the monks misunderstood his wild jibberings and gesticulations and saw it as a tragic madness brought on by whatever had savagely attacked him as he clung to the altar. They did what they could to soothe him and heal his wounds but they ignored the spidery scratchings that he drew blindly in the dust. Everything he did to communicate with them was scuffed out by their hurrying feet.

Time and the monks' care gradually healed the gouges and tears that disfigured Geothrick's empty eye sockets and sealed the suppurating stump of his tongue, but the need he had to reveal the presence of the evil, to make even one of the monks who had nursed him understand what he was trying to tell them, became more and more desperate to him. Winter had drawn to an end and the sounds and scents of spring and blossoms were drifting in through the open doors of the infirmary. The words the angel had hissed to the demons as they had dragged the mutilated body of the monk down into the pit kept screaming and echoing inside his head. They wouldn't stop or give him a moment's peace.

'I will awaken you, Sammeal. I will try again when the summer moon is in the seventh house.'

Geothrick's sense of foreboding increased as the days

grew hotter. He didn't altogether understand the angel's words but he was convinced they meant the creature would reappear to murder again. He became afraid to sleep in the cathedral amongst the somnolent mutterings and snorings of the clerics, fearing that in every groan and creak of the huge stone building as it settled onto its foundations he could hear the reawakening scrabble of demons' claws and the whispering hum and beat of the angel's wings.

Fear drove him to flee from the infirmary before the finger-nail Easter moon had risen. He vanished in the dead of night, blindly feeling his way out across the dew-wet cloister fields toward the water gate, crawling and stumbling. Unseen branches scratched his hands and face as he followed the sounds of the water fowl that roosted on the canal. He had to escape and find somewhere to hide, somewhere the angel and its demons couldn't find him. He paused and lifted his blind head as he listened. He heard the whisper of the wind in the tall reed stems and felt with his hand for the towpath that lined the bank. When he found it he knew he must be close to the mason's yard, the place of his childhood, where the huge blocks of stone were hoisted from the barges and stored before they were worked and then hauled up to be set in the cathedral.

He reached the boundary of the yard and ran his finger-tips over the rough, cold stone slabs. A silent breath of relief ghosted his dribbling lips. Here amongst the giant blocks of marble and granite and the mounds of rubble he would surely find a place to hide, to escape from the demons that haunted him. Moving slowly forward around the edge of the yard he began to search for the entrance, tracing the massive contours of each silent monolith with his hands, sensing the hidden beauty, the soaring arches, cusps and intricate chevrons, the recumbent effigies and monumental sculptures that lay waiting beneath the rough, uncut surfaces of the stone for the mason's skills to reveal. Eventually he found a gap, little more than a narrow crack between two towering blocks of Purbeck marble, but it was a road he could follow. He squeezed into it and began to work his way forward. He snagged his toes on something that lay in his path, something that, as he accidentally kicked it, moved and clinked dully against something else with the ring of metal striking metal. Geothrick stopped abruptly, a shiver of fear, of anticipation of what he might have stumbled upon, tingled his spine. Gingerly, he moved his right foot and finding the objects he explored them with his toes. He caught his breath: they felt like mason's tools.

He dropped to his knees and spread his trembling fingers, brushing them quickly, backward and forward, across the cold, damp earth. His heart was pounding in his chest as he touched and found the pitted head of a dummy hammer, its wooden handle splintered and riddled with worm holes. Beside it he discovered three rusty bull-nosed chisels, each one blunt and missing a tooth. They lay half-buried in the wet earth and a hand span from them lay the worn-out fragment of a dreadnought rasp. He bent forward with tears of joy coursing down his cheeks as he gathered the discarded, rusty tools in his hands and hugged them to his chest. It didn't matter that he could never use them, to have found them and be able to hold them in his hands was blessing enough.

Clutching the rusty tools beneath his arm Geothrick crept forward, moving deeper and deeper into the vast maze of huge blocks of stone. Blindly he crossed and re-crossed his tracks. It was as if the hand of Fate guided his footsteps, drawing him into the furthest, disused corner of the mason's yard where, too weary to crawl another step, he collapsed in the shadow of a slab of pure white marble. The bundle of tools clattered to the ground beside him and, as he slept, he dreamed that he carved a white angel. He dreamt that it grew out of the stone as his hammer rose and fell, it grew, despite his blindness, into a most beautiful, powerful sculpture. In the moment between sleep and waking a soft voice on the morning wind whispered to him in his darkness and called out the angel's name. It told him it would protect him and drew its pure white wings around him as it urged him to wake and pick up his hammer and chisel. The voice told him to carve 'Shateiel', the white angel of silence.

CHAPTER TWO

The Incarnadine Angel

DARK, INDIGO thunderclouds were piling up over the city. Lightning crackled in the air and distant rumbles of thunder trod the horizon. The hot breath of summer had stolen away into a moment of electric silence.

Jarvin Mandrake was late for his appointment but the sheer beauty of the huge cathedral made him pause in the shadows of the Erpingham Gate to stare up at the soaring spire etched in albescence against the impending storm. The dark, racing cloudscape gave the cathedral, with its sheer tower and needle spire, the impression that it was moving toward him, a vast ship of stone relentlessly ploughing its way across a wild sky.

Jarvin shivered and involuntarily stepped back a pace. Images of his accident in the Temple of Isis crowded into his mind, cold beads of perspiration prickled at his forehead and the palms of his hands. Claustrophobia began to wrap itself around him and he was back in that lower burial chamber, trapped beneath tons of subsiding rubble. The stifling darkness was swallowing him up. He shuddered and blinked to break the illusion that the building was bearing down upon him and forced the spectre of what had happened back beneath the fragile surface of his sanity. He concentrated his gaze on the gnarled shapes and shadows cast by the avenue of ancient yew trees bordering the gravelled pathway leading toward the high Norman arch that framed the West Door. He looked toward the tall, blank arches that flanked it where he was to meet his guide.

He spotted the young priest who had been sent out to meet him strutting impatiently backward and forward in front of the West Door. His long, frocked robes flapped about his ankles each time he spun round and glanced irritably from his wristwatch up into the thunder-dark sky overhead. Jarvin half-lifted his hand to wave and reveal his presence but he hesitated, swallowing his words, shutting his mouth with a snap. Instead he raked his stubby, trembling fingers through his shock of pure white and untidy hair as he fought down the impulse to turn on his heel and run.

It was too soon after his accident in the tomb. It was too soon to be away from the safety of the hospital and it made him feel naked and vulnerable. He shivered and strove to push the spectres of that stifling darkness back beneath the surface, cursing his uncle under his breath for refusing to listen to his doubts, for brow-beating the doctors into prematurely releasing him into his care.

Those persuasive, forceful words echoed in Jarvin's head. 'What possible harm can come to the boy? He'll be working in the cathedral: he will live in the hostel and we will look after his every need. It will be just like being here, he'll want for nothing. In fact it will be better for him because he can absorb himself in work that interests him and forget that accident. Yes, I'm sure the post I have secured in the cathedral will be the best cure. In fact I'm convinced of it.'

Uncle George, the Bishop of Rochester's words faded from his head. He had over-ridden every objection and secured Jarvin's release from hospital. He had bought him a railway ticket to Norwich and put him on the train and now he was alone, clutching his small, battered suitcase against his chest, his stomach knotted with panic as he stood in the shadows of the Erpingham Gate. The worst of it was he had a nagging suspicion that the post of Ecclesiastical Archaeologist that had been secured for him was little more than an elaborate charade to get him away from the Beckonsthorpe Psychiatric Institute before anyone in the media connected him with Uncle George.

Jarvin had protested that his knowledge of church architecture and archaeology was very sketchy; that since he had left university he had specialised in Egyptology. But Uncle George had swept his doubts aside and assured him that he was the perfect choice and in fact the accident was a blessing in disguise and had simply freed him to do the job. He would not be hidebound by a wealth of religious beliefs and he could view the cathedral with a fresh eye which made him exactly right for the post. Jarvin had almost believed him, until those last, few hurried instructions had been flung through the carriage window as the train pulled out of Beckonsthorpe station.

'Jarvin, I must insist you don't talk to anybody, not a soul, about your stay here at Beckonsthorpe. Especially about the effects of that . . . that unfortunate accident. Remember, it wasn't easy securing that post at the cathedral, you won't get another opportunity like that again.' Uncle George had suddenly smiled and reached into the carriage to pat his arm before whispering conspiratorially, 'I'm sure you'll find plenty to interest you in the cathedral without getting in anybody's way, but you will make sure you stay out of trouble, there's a good boy.'

Jarvin had sensed a hidden threat behind the smile that had set him wondering if his uncle hadn't used his clerical powers to quash any rumours of mental instability in the Mandrake family before they threatened to ruin his chances of becoming the future Archbishop.

The distant rumbles of thunder were getting closer,

pressing in around the cathedral and making his head ache. The outer edge of his vision began to shimmer almost imperceptibly, slowly darkening as black, formless shadows ate it up. His throat tightened as he realised he was about to suffer his first attack since leaving the Institute. His breathing shortened, developing into irregular gasps of panic. He caught the dry, musty odour of his claustrophobia as the howling, shrieking sounds of the phantoms that had attacked him in the tomb echoed inside his head.

'No! No! Keep away from me! Keep away!' Jarvin shouted, staggering dizzily forward and flinging his suitcase aside as he frantically fumbled in his jacket pocket for the bottle of tranquillisers that the doctor had given to him before he left Beckonsthorpe.

He knew he had to follow the procedure, do exactly as the doctors had taught him. It was the only way for him to overcome the terrifying attacks of claustrophobia, tear open the blackness and silence the inhuman voices that raged at him inside his head. Gulping down two of the sedatives, he clamped his hands over his ears, pressing so hard that he made his head throb with pain. His ears buzzed as though they were full of angry wasps and the noise blotted out the nightmare sounds that haunted him. He screwed his eyes so tightly shut that his eyelids burned and white flakes of light broke up the blackness. Cursing and swearing he collapsed onto his knees, oblivious to the sharp, gravel chips that cut into him. He twisted his head from side to side as though in torment as he fought against the swallowing darkness and gradually overcame it.

The tranquillisers quickly took effect. Calmness welled up, the screaming phantoms receded and eventually vanished: his breathing slowed. It had worked! For the first time he had beaten it on his own. He grinned as he licked his dry, trembling lips and swallowed. God he needed a drink to calm his nerves. He needed it so badly after that attack he could almost taste the hot bite of its oblivion at the back of his throat. Blinking, he took his hands away from his ears and looked up to see the young priest who had been sent out to meet him and who was now standing a pace away. He had stooped to retrieve his battered suitcase and was reading the name printed on the front.

'Mr Mandrake, are you all right? I heard shouting beneath the gate arch and I thought you must be in some kind of trouble. We get some very unsavoury characters . . .'

The priest hesitated, his voice trailing away as he let his eyes travel over the sprawling figure who was looking up with a drunken and foolish grin spread broadly across his stubbly face. The priest stepped quickly backward, his face tightening into a rigid mask of disgust. It couldn't be the young archaeologist who Bishop Mandrake had described to him on the telephone, although he did have a shock of untidy white hair. The person kneeling before him looked more like one of the vagrants or drunks they were constantly forced to evict from the cathedral grounds. No, surely this couldn't be the nephew of the Bishop of Rochester who he had been sent out to meet and asked to give a brief introductory tour before settling him into his lodgings in the West Gatehouse.

The priest's eyes narrowed suspiciously. 'Where did you get this suitcase?' he inquired coldly, strengthening his grip upon the worn leather handle as he prepared himself to deal with a drunk.

'It shmine! It . . . it's mine!' Jarvin answered, unaware of the effect the powerful tranquillisers were having on him as he tried to scramble to his feet.

He staggered slightly and swayed in an effort to keep his balance. He felt light-headed and dizzy and his voice sounded different, sluggish and remote, as he slurred his words. The priest's face swum in and out of focus, his thin, bloodless lips were pinched together with disdain.

'You're drunk! You had better give me an explanation of how you got this suitcase and get out of here before I call the police!' the priest demanded angrily.

'No, you have it all wrong. The suitcase is mine, I'm Jarvin Mandrake.' He tried to reply but the jumble of words that slurred off his tongue sounded nothing like it. His lips tingled with a painful numbness just like they did after he had been to the dentist and he didn't even feel the dribble of saliva escape out of the corner of his mouth and trickle down his chin. He tottered helplessly sideways and struck the cold stone wall of the gate arch forcefully with his shoulder.

Through the buzz of noise inside his head he faintly heard the rumbling crash of the thunderstorm breaking overhead and through a maze of light and leaping shadows he could see the priest advancing toward him just as the first lightning strike lit up the thunder-dark sky behind the cathedral spire. Suddenly he realised what must be happening to him. It had to be the drugs, the new tranquillisers that he had just swallowed. Vaguely he remembered the doctor warning him that there might be some strong side effects but it was too late now, they had already rendered him hopelessly incapable and given him the appearance of a debilitated drunk. He knew he had to stay calm and try to convince this priest that he wasn't under the influence of alcohol, that he really was Jarvin Mandrake. And he had to do it without revealing that he had just been released from the Beckonsthorpe Institute for the Insane. Uncle George would never forgive him if he blurted it all out before he had even reached the blasted cathedral. He sucked in a shallow breath and concentrated his whole effort on speaking slowly and clearly as he conjured up a plausible excuse and remembered what his uncle had told him.

'I . . . I'm afraid there seems to be a misunderstanding. I really am Jarvin Mandrake. Look, look here, I can prove it,' he slurred.

The priest hesitated as Jarvin fumbled and delved in the inside pocket of his jacket for the sealed, crumpled letter of introduction. Finding it at last he held it out in a trembling, unsteady hand toward the priest who snatched it from him and tore it open before scanning the short paragraph. He read of Jarvin's appointment as archaeologist to the cathedral followed by a brief résumé of dates and other details of Jarvin's career.

'You could have stolen this letter along with the suitcase. It proves nothing, unless you can tell me its contents.' The priest looked up at Jarvin with suspicious, doubting eyes. He'd had to deal with dozens of drunks before. He folded and crushed the letter firmly against his cassock and waited for Jarvin's answer.

Jarvin swayed and clutched at the cold stone wall for support. The effect of the drug was anaesthetising his mind, he was losing the thread of his answer even before he opened his mouth. 'I . . . I haven't read the letter but I'm sure it's about my appointment here.' He paused, trying to remember where 'here' was as he swept a vague wandering hand across the Cathedral Close.

A peal of thunder crashed overhead and a searing flash of lightning lit up the gloomy archway. It made Jarvin jump, sharpening up his focus and making him remember. 'The letter probably gives details of my career, my degree at Oxford and my work in the Egyptology department of . . . of . . .' He lost the thread again and stuttered to a halt, but it had been enough to convince the priest that he was who he said he was, a very, very drunk Jarvin Mandrake.

The priest's sneer showed his disgust. He despised drunks. He thrust the suitcase and the crumpled letter roughly back into Jarvin's hands, almost pushing him over and abruptly turned away. 'You had better follow me.' He flung the words icily over his shoulder as he strode away toward the Great West Door of the cathedral.

Numbly Jarvin regained his balance and staggered after him along the gravelled path. The thunderstorm had passed over the cathedral and it had begun to rain. At first it was only a smattering of large, irregular raindrops but it quickly became a cascading torrent, striking his face and making him shiver. The effects of the tranquillisers began to wear off and he felt cold, empty, desolate and alone as he reached the West Door.

The small, heavy portal set into the Great West Door of the cathedral sighed shut behind him, muffling the roar of the torrential downpour that was battering at the avenue of ancient gnarled yew trees outside. The rain was gurgling in the gutters, streaking long, wet finger-marks across the outstretched stone arms and down the weathered, blind, empty faces of the monumental sculptures and gravestones that peopled the neatly-mown lawns surrounding the cathedral. Jarvin stumbled forward and dropped his suitcase just inside the door, shaking himself as violently as a wet dog and scattering raindrops from his hair as he rubbed a hand across his forehead, smearing the trickles of water that were running into his eyes, making them sting and blur his vision.

He was soaked to the skin and his head was throbbing from the after-effects of the tranquillisers. He felt wretched, wretched enough to turn on his heel and walk out of the cathedral right then and put an end to this ridiculous charade. He wanted to be rid of Uncle George's unwelcomed intrusion into his life forever. The idea of running away, of vanishing amongst the crowds that he had threaded a path through on his way from the station, began to crystallise.

'I'll get out of here now,' he muttered under his breath as he bent down to retrieve his suitcase and began to turn around and stretch out a hand toward the door handle. But the priest's firm hand on his elbow stopped him.

'This way, Mr Mandrake. Or have you forgotten that I have promised your uncle I would give you a brief tour of the cathedral before I show you the way to your lodgings.'

The priest paused and crowded closer. It didn't matter whose nephew he was: he needed to check how drunk Jarvin Mandrake was before he took him any further into the cathedral. He sniffed cautiously at the air between them, hunting for the tell-tale reek of alcohol that he expected to find on his breath. He sniffed twice and then moved so close that his beak-sharp nose almost brushed against Jarvin's lips. Frowning, he stepped back and straightened up. He couldn't understand it, there wasn't the slightest trace of alcohol on his breath yet only ten minutes ago he had found him roaring drunk beneath the Erpingham Gate. He had been barely able to stand up and couldn't string a dozen words together.

'I'm not drunk. I haven't touched a drop today,' Jarvin insisted.

He hesitated, the truth was on the tip of his tongue but the priest merely shrugged his shoulders dismissively at his denial.

Before Jarvin could blurt out the truth the priest had turned and beckoned him to follow. Perhaps the sudden drenching had sobered the young archaeologist up enough for the briefest of tours.

'Keep close to me, Mr Mandrake. And please try not to blunder into anyone,' he called coldly across his shoulder, descending the wide, stone steps as he turned right and hurried into the nave.

'I'm not drunk, damn you, why don't you believe me?' Jarvin muttered miserably under his breath as he followed the young man down the steps and turned past the first of the soaring stone columns that supported the roof.

'Damn! Damn! Damn!' Jarvin muttered again as he reluctantly turned into the nave, knuckling his free hand into a tight fist of frustration. Why should he care if the priest thought he was an alcoholic or people judged Bishop Mandrake on the fragility of Jarvin's own sanity? But he knew that deep down inside it did matter, it mattered a whole lot to him: it was the thread he had to cling to and strengthen if he was ever going to find a way out of the labyrinth of claustrophobic shadows that had been cast by that accident in the tomb.

'Wait! Wait for me!' he called out to the hurrying priest as he looked up through the mirage of his own misery.

The whispering, brooding silence and the sheer beauty of the vast ancient cathedral brought him to an abrupt halt. It had been years since he had visited the cathedral as a child and he had forgotten the breathtaking beauty, the light and shadow cast by the fourteen pairs of rising columns capped by their intricate arches. He gazed round at the forest of stone ribs and their pattern of carved, lierne bosses that spanned the vaulted roof, a solid tunnel of stone that marched away in diminishing perspective beyond the choir screen and through the lantern formed by the tower to end in a blaze of light that flooded through the tall stained glass windows above the altar.

'I had forgotten how beautiful it all was!' Jarvin breathed softly, sensing the priest rather than seeing him, realising that he had come back to where he stood as he craned his neck and let his eyes travel slowly across the hundreds of carved and painted bosses in the vaulted roof seventy feet above his head.

He could just pick out Noah in his ark, a white swan and a golden eagle; he could see Moses' mother putting him into the basket and Solomon on his throne before his head began to spin with dizziness. He blinked and staggered as he clutched at the priest's arm to keep his balance.

'That isn't the original roof is it?' he asked as he noticed the plain Norman round-headed arches and capitals that supported the intricate stone ribs of the vaulted roof.

The priest shrugged off his question impatiently. 'No it isn't. There was a fire some time during the fifteenth century that destroyed the original wooden roof. But I'm sure you'll find all the details about it in the official guidebook, it's very concise. You see there isn't much in this cathedral's past that the historians haven't uncovered already, Mr Mandrake.' His lips thinned into a hard, tight smile of disdain as he pressed his fingertips piously together. 'I'll make sure there is a copy of the guidebook in the Dean's office for you to collect in the morning. I'm sure you'll find it most helpful in your work.'

The priest glanced down at his watch and muttered something under his breath. 'We're running rather late, we'll have to hurry. If you will follow me I have just enough time to show you the ancient Bishop's throne and then I will take you across to your lodgings. Then I'm sure you'll want time to sober . . .' He paused and coughed shallowly to disguise his slip of the tongue. He continued, barely concealing his contempt for Jarvin: he hated drunks no matter how well they managed to hide their addiction. 'I mean you'll want to change out of those wet clothes and get a good night's rest before you start your work here.'

Jarvin nodded bleakly at the cleric's back as he followed

him along the gloomy South Aisle before they turned sharply into the choir toward the central altar. The barb, intentional or otherwise, had struck home; convincing the priest that he wasn't an alcoholic seemed an impossibility. Jarvin glanced up at the intricate medieval carving on the rich, dark wood on the canopies of the stalls and momentarily forgot the priest's hasty judgment as he caught sight of at least half a dozen beautiful misereres carved on the undersides of the monastic stalls that had been left upturned for visitors to see. He had barely stooped to examine them and glide his fingers over their swelling, chiselled contours, touching the wood carvers' interpretations of the medieval angels, birds and mythical beasts that had been worn as smooth as darkened glass by the rub of countless hands, when the priest's impatient voice hurried him on. Sighing, Jarvin straightened up and then smiled to himself. He would come back the next day, perhaps the job was a blessing in disguise after all, there was so much hidden away in the wood and stone, carvings of the cathedral, everyday things that would reveal the lives of the ordinary people, the medieval craftsmen who had built it. Yes, there was so much to absorb him while he recovered from the effects of that nightmare accident.

'I'm coming!' he called out to the priest, moving on through the choir stalls and into the area beneath the tower.

A peal of distant thunder made him look up. His eyes travelled up over the rising round-headed arches with their plain mouldings to the pillars and blank arches and circular windows that formed the lantern of the tower. Yes, there were so many threads of history for him to unravel. Jarvin hurried around the central altar, hugging his suitcase to his chest to stop it from knocking against the neat rows of stalls. He was about to cross to the pulpit where the priest was waiting impatiently when a dark sculpture of an angel, partially hidden by a pillar a few yards along the right hand wall of the South Transept, caught his eye. Jarvin shuffled to a halt and absently dropped his case onto the stall he was standing by. There was something about the half-seen, life-sized figure that had made the hairs on the nape of his neck instantly prickle. He shivered and found himself slowly moving forward, drawn irresistibly toward it. Each hesitant, reluctant footstep revealed more and more of the dark angel crouched down on one knee upon a marble plinth. Its left hand was gripping a mass of broken chains and shackles that spilled over the edge of the dais; its right hand was clenched into a raised fist. Its wings rose in a feathery, spreading arch high above its head.

Jarvin halted directly in front, his breaths coming in short, shallow whispers. He had never seen such dark wood before, or was it stone? Its shadows were so dark, a black, bottomless void of despair. The statue seemed so real, its surface texture had the dull sheen of skin. It was so frighteningly lifelike; every muscle, vein and wrinkle etched in such fine detail that he hesitated to touch it. He swallowed and turned his head to break the overwhelming feeling that the angel was watching him and he called out to the priest. 'I've never seen anything like this sculpture before. The texture and colour is so unusual. What is it made of?'

The priest threw his hands up in exasperation and retraced his footsteps across the central area beneath the lantern, gathering up Jarvin's discarded suitcase as he did so. 'I'm going to be late for that service in the Jesus Chapel if you don't stop wandering aimlessly about,' he muttered under his breath, forcing a brittle smile onto his lips as he stopped beside Jarvin and realised that the quicker he answered these pointless questions the quicker he would be rid of him.

'Ah, so you've noticed our incarnadine angel,' he said

45

with a dismissive wave of his hand that took in the sinister crouching figure. 'It's carved from one solid piece of pink marble. The guidebook says it was probably quarried from a rare vein of pink marble somewhere near Rome and originally brought over to England by the Romans to be used as an altar in one of their pagan temples. Of course, the colour has darkened since then, especially on the angel's hands and face. It has turned a blackish, blood colour with age but there are still traces of the paler pink stone if you look closely on the undersides of its arms and on the feathers of its wings.'

The priest paused and glanced at his watch adding, as he impatiently turned away, 'I believe there are a few fragmented references to the statue somewhere in the cathedral archives. I think the earliest one appears in 1119, the year the founder of the cathedral, Herbert de Losinga, died. But you'll have to look them out for yourself. The guidebook says it's one of the finest examples of medieval sculpture in England. Now please will you follow me, I'm running awfully late.'

'But . . .' Jarvin frowned, about to disagree with the cleric. There was nothing remotely medieval in the style of the carving, except perhaps the way the folds and creases of the scant robe had been draped across the angel's loins and chiselled in the stone, but there was something ominously sinister and compelling about the blood-dark, crouching figure that made him hesitate. He wanted to touch it, to feel the texture of the angel's skin, to plunge his hand into its swallowing darkness. His fingers inched closer, trembling as they stretched out.

'Almost everybody who visits this cathedral wants to touch the angel, Mr Mandrake, that's why there's a notice forbidding it.' The priest's icy voice cut right through the compelling desire and made Jarvin jump. The bold letters of the sign leapt sharply into focus directly in front of him.

'No, no, it was the mass of rusting iron chains around the angel's plinth that caught my attention. It's most unusual, I didn't think medieval masons had ever used marble and iron together. And look at the way some of the links seem to have oxidised, in places they have fused into the stone.'

The priest shrugged. 'I'm sure there's a perfectly simple explanation to it. Now please, follow me.'

Jarvin silently shook his head. For him it would need much more than a simple explanation to unlock the secrets hidden beneath the surface of that dark and sinister sculpture. But he realised that it wasn't the time to press his questions, the priest was becoming more agitated and more impatient as he strode away ahead of him.

'I'll come back,' he whispered as he glanced up into the inky shadows that shrouded the incarnadine angel's face. Suddenly he gasped and staggered backward before quickly turning, stumbling, almost dropping his case in his haste to escape. 'It's ridiculous . . . impossible!' he stuttered. 'I'm jumping at shadows, no . . . it must be the tablets.' He tried to shake off the overwhelming sensation that the angel had opened its eyes and for an instant stared directly at him out of the shadows.

He shivered and fought to regain his composure but his skin tingled as if icy cold fingers were touching him as he hurried up the broad stone steps into the presbytery and past the high altar. Once he looked fearfully back over his shoulder, dreading to see that the angel had lifted his head or risen to pursue him and he let a breath of relief escape from between his trembling lips. The figure was now partly obscured by the thick stone columns and arches that supported the tower and it was still crouching, engulfed in its own petrified shadows.

'Jarvin, you're definitely losing your marbles if you

imagined that the statue moved!' he whispered angrily to himself. 'People will be convinced that you're mad if you believe that! Remember, you're an archaeologist, a scientist, for Christ's sake!'

He fell silent as he reached the apse and the short flight of wooden steps that led to the ancient throne. The priest was standing on the top step looking down at him with a mixture of contempt and disdain.

'The Bishop's throne, Mr Mandrake, is our most interesting relic; not that gloomy stone angel.' And he swept his hand back emphatically toward a simple wooden chair resting on two worn stone supports.

But as he began to recite the history of the throne his voice was drowned out by a sudden loud rumble of thunder. The wind had changed, the storm was turning, moving rapidly back across the city. The cleric paused, his eyebrows arched with irritability as the sound of the thunder echoed along the length of the vaulted nave. He counted the seconds as the rumble subsided into fragmented whispers between the soaring columns which magnified the interval of silence before a crackling flash of lightning lit up the west window sending leaping shadows fleeing across the vast gloomy cathedral. Peals of thunder rolled across the roof, fresh rain squalls lashed the windows and gurgled throatily in the gutters.

The priest suddenly clapped his hands together. 'I think I'd better get you to your lodgings before the weather worsens!' he shouted out against the rising clamour of the storm. 'Come along, Mr Mandrake!' He hurried down the wooden steps past Jarvin and strode past the altar into the shadows of the presbytery, his frocked robes flapping noisily at his ankles.

Jarvin shuddered. It seemed suddenly cold and inhospitable – and echoingly empty in the summer darkness of this huge cathedral. The edges of his claustrophobia began to tighten in his throat and swallow him. In the enfolding hall with its half-circle of gloomy arches that surrounded the Bishop's throne, the dry parchment smell of the Egyptian tomb prickled in his nostrils and haunting voices were beginning to whisper inside his head. He had to get out of there, get out from beneath that roof of stone fast.

'Wait! Wait for me!' he almost shouted in panic, leaping down the steps after the disappearing cleric.

On Jarvin's right he glimpsed a blur of soft, rich light high up through an archway, an impression of silver and gold in the darkness. It held his gaze and he almost collided with the priest who had stopped at the top of the broad stone steps to wait for him.

'Relics, Mr Mandrake,' he muttered irritably as he steadied Jarvin and prevented him from stumbling down the steps. 'The lighted chamber that caught your attention beneath the reliquary arch houses the cathedral's treasures; but you'll have plenty of time to examine them another day. Now, please try and stay close to me.'

Jarvin mumbled his apologies and fell into step with the hurrying cleric. Continuous peals of thunder rolled across the roof, echoing along the nave. Lightning flashed and crackled as they descended the stone steps and began to cross the transept. Suddenly Jarvin stopped and stared wildly about him and then grabbed the cleric's sleeve. 'The floor! I felt a tremor – it's going to collapse!' he cried in panic.

The priest smiled and shook his head as he untangled Jarvin's fingers from his sleeve. 'You probably did feel a slight vibration but it's nothing to worry about. The cathedral is quite safe, it acts as a natural amplifier to sudden loud sounds like thunder. It has something to do with the layout of the columns and the intricate patterns of the stone ribs that form the vault of the roof. Bishop Hugo was quite worried about the vibrations some hundred and fifty years ago and he had Roche, the famous French engineer, do exhaustive structural surveys. He said that the foundations of the cathedral were built on solid medieval rubble, that it was structurally sound and that it would withstand at least another thousand years of violent storms like this one without falling down.'

Jarvin hesitated and fought to control his panic, rubbing with the back of his hand the beads of ice cold sweat that had ghosted his forehead. He had felt that self-same tremor beneath his feet moments before the floor of the Temple of Isis had collapsed and buried him alive. He wasn't convinced about the solid foundations of medieval rubble.

'But surely there are cellars and crypts beneath the cathedral?' He frowned as they hurried toward the North Aisle.

The cleric shrugged. 'No, not as far as I know. I'm sure it stands firmly on its original foundations. But . . .'

A violent thunderclap drowned out the priest's voice and made the flagstones of the central tower vibrate beneath their feet.

'Jesus! I've got to get out of here!' Jarvin cried as the terror of being trapped as the roof or the floor caved in overwhelmed him.

A vivid flash of sheet lightning illuminated the tall, stained glass windows above the door of the South Transept. Something made Jarvin glance back across his shoulder as the searing light flooded the cathedral. He caught his breath in a stifled gasp. The crouching stone angel was momentarily etched in livid crimson hues against the light. Its elongated shadow was reaching menacingly out toward him from amongst the petrified glade of stone columns. The lightning flickered and faded into rumbling, rainwashed silence and the dark stone angel melted back into the shadows.

'This place gives me the creeps,' Jarvin hissed, almost breaking into a run in his haste to reach the West Door.

'Your lodgings are in the West Gatehouse. We have to leave the Cathedral Close by going out through the Erpingham Gate to reach the entrance!' the cleric shouted against the roar of the rain which was beating patterns on the gravel pathway.

'Follow me!' he called, gathering up the loose hems of his robe and holding them in an untidy knot above his knees before sprinting away through the avenue of yew trees, their bent and dripping branches brushing wet fingertips against his shoulders, as he headed for the distant, dark shape of the gate arch.

Jarvin turned up his collar and hunched his shoulders against the downpour. Clutching his battered suitcase tightly against his chest he followed at a shambling run. The high, gabled archway of the Erpingham Gate loomed indistinctly through the curtain of rain. Jarvin hesitated as he drew closer. He could hear the harsh voice of the cleric raised in anger. He was beginning to dislike this brittle representative of the clergy. Slowing, he moved into the shadows beneath the archway to find the priest gesticulating at a group of figures who were sheltering there.

'Out! Out, do you hear? I want you out of here the moment it stops raining or I'll call the police!' The priest paused and glanced round angrily at Jarvin as he picked his way through the jumble of feet and legs to where the priest stood.

It was too dark beneath the archway to see clearly who the cleric was shouting at but there was a strong smell of wet, dirty clothes and the odour of stale bodies rising from the figures who were sitting and lying against the rough stone walls. A voice laughed and then cursed the priest;

there was the clink of glass on stone followed by a sweet, almost sickly, smell as a bottle was passed amongst them. Gradually Jarvin's eyes grew accustomed to the gloom and he found that he was staring down into at least a dozen bearded, dirty and hostile faces.

'Vagrants! Dropouts, Mr Mandrake. I'm afraid we are constantly plagued by them,' the priest muttered with disgust as he moved through the archway and beckoned Jarvin to follow him.

'But they are only sheltering from the storm. Surely they're not doing any harm,' Jarvin protested loudly.

'Yes, that's right, vicar!' A chorus of jeers broke out. 'We're not doing any bleeding 'arm. What do you think we're gonna do, turn this stinking archway into a squat?'

Shrieks of laughter and a string of curses echoed on Jarvin's heels as he hurried through the arch, but a soft female voice on the edge of the crowd called out to him.

'Thanks, father, you're a decent priest. You're the first one who hasn't tried to have us thrown out.'

Jarvin paused and looked down into the blue eyes of a thin, pale face framed by tangled, dirty strands of blonde hair. There was a softness he hadn't expected to see, a haunting look of regret that made him want to stop when a coarse voice amongst the crowd sneered and shouted at him. He felt the priest's fingers tug at his sleeve and he heard his voice urging him to come away.

'Come on, quickly, before there's any trouble,' the priest insisted. 'I think they've started drinking, I can smell that revolting cocktail of methylated spirits and cheap sherry they mix. I'll telephone the police for help when we get to the Gatehouse before they start rampaging through the Close. Let the police move them out.'

Jarvin hesitated and for a moment he resisted the pull of the cleric's hand. He couldn't so easily act as judge and jury on this group of wretched-looking people who were sheltering from the storm. He couldn't so easily subscribe to them being swept away out of sight because they were littering the entrance to the cathedral. He agreed they had been hostile but the priest had shouted at them and they hadn't actually committed any crime by seeking shelter. Surely the church was supposed to be there to give help and shelter to these casualties of society.

Jarvin was about to ask the priest where charity began when a large, close-cropped figure dressed in a tattered overcoat and clutching the neck of a bottle in a brown paper bag, rose from where he had been crouching on the far side of the gloomy archway. 'Bloody priests! Always poking their noses in where they're not wanted.' He snarled, staggering and then lurching purposefully toward Jarvin.

'What the fuck do you want?' He spat the alcohol-reeking words directly into Jarvin's face, raising his left fist. The hand was knuckled and ready to strike. Jarvin clearly saw the words 'Hate and Death' tattooed in spidery letters on the skin before he stepped quickly backward.

'Nothing! Nothing at all,' he managed to mumble as he hastily retreated.

'Come on!' the priest hissed, virtually dragging him away from the gateway and into Tombland.

'What were you trying to do? Do you want to get yourself beaten up?'

They hurried the dozen or so yards through the pouring rain along Tombland and quickly climbed the two worn, stone steps to the entrance of the West Gatehouse where the cleric rang the bell.

'No, no, I didn't,' Jarvin slowly replied as he regained his composure. 'I just thought you were a little harsh back there, they were only sheltering from the storm.'

The priest laughed but there was no humour in his voice.

'Harsh, Mr Mandrake? You don't know the half of it. I'm pretty sure that rabble you're about to defend are part of the group of vagrants who have repeatedly broken into the old Dean's Hall on the other side of the Erpingham Gate and turned it into a squat. They're giving us no end of trouble and every time the police turn them out they break back in again. We're at our wits' end to know what to do next. Harsh with them indeed! We do have a couple of real vagrants who visit us from time to time when their wanderings bring them into the city and they do receive our charity. We even let old Mary sleep in the inner porch rather than turn her out into the streets whenever she calls at the cathedral.'

The priest fell silent. The creak of floorboards and slow footsteps sounded beyond the door. There was a moment's pause and the scrape of a key in the lock before the priest's face broke into a smile, the first one Jarvin had seen since their meeting, and his voice softened as the door swung open to reveal a short, frail, white-haired woman of about seventy.

'Mrs Sibson! I'm so sorry to disturb you but I've brought along Mr Mandrake. He's to lodge with you.'

'Why yes, of course, Bishop Mandrake's nephew.' Mrs Sibson paused, her smile stiffening a little as she observed Jarvin's dishevelled and untidy appearance. 'Yes, now I remember, he's the archaeologist who is coming to work in the cathedral.'

With that thought her face softened as if being an archaeologist explained away the state of his clothes. Her gaze shifted past Jarvin and focused for a moment on the drifting curtain of rain, the shimmering reflections of the cars in the water and she listened to the swish of the traffic in the roadway. A loud rumble of thunder made her blink and jump as sharply as a sparrow.

'What am I thinking of? Come in both of you before you catch your deaths in this awful downpour.'

A series of shouts and the sound of breaking glass from further along Tombland, probably from beneath the Erpingham Gate, made Mrs Sibson crane her neck anxiously forward and she took a step into the road to peer out.

'I shouldn't go out if I were you.' The priest spoke quickly, placing a restraining hand upon her shoulder. 'I'm afraid it's those squatters who have invaded the Dean's Hall; they're drinking and causing a nuisance in the Erpingham Gateway. May I use your telephone to call the police?'

Mrs Sibson drew back and firmly slammed the heavy front door. 'Yes, of course, go ahead.' She waved an agitated hand toward the telephone on the hall table.

'Squatters!' she muttered crossly under her breath as she turned toward Jarvin and cast a more critical and curious eye over his shabby, soaking clothes, unshaven face and battered suitcase which he was still clutching to his chest. 'I really don't know what the world is coming to with the youngsters of today.'

She frowned and stared down at the widening puddle of rain water on the carpet where Jarvin stood and then she looked up sharply into his face. 'You don't hold with squatting, with trampling on other people's privacy? You don't believe with taking what isn't yours, do you, Mr Mandrake?'

It sounded more like an accusation than a question and it was said with a voice that seemed as sharp as granite splinters.

'We . . . well . . . I think . . .' Jarvin hesitated and felt his cheeks redden beneath Mrs Sibson's unflinching gaze.

Before the accident in the tomb he would have smiled and voiced his opinions on the plight of the homeless and the dispossessed. He would, perhaps, have turned her point of view or at the worst broadened it a little, but now he felt unsure. His ideas were confused and he wished he had never left the Beckonsthorpe Institute, but the front door of the Gatehouse was shut fast and there was no immediate escape.

'No . . . no . . . of course not,' he stuttered to fill the silence as the priest dialled the Police Station.

He shuffled awkwardly from one foot to another and felt a squelching, wet sensation between the toes of his right foot. His embarrassment deepened as he remembered the large hole in his shoe that he had forgotten to have repaired. His misery seemed complete.

'But how rude of me.' Mrs Sibson's voice cut through his discomfort. 'You're almost soaked to the skin and I'm keeping you here in the hall. Let me show you to your room at once so that you can change into some dry clothes. There's no need for you to wait down here for the police to arrive, I'll call you if they want to speak to you.'

Her whole manner had changed as she smiled and headed toward the staircase. Jarvin gave a silent sigh of relief and quickly followed the old lady up the broad, ornately carved stairway. He heard the priest's voice in the hall below him as he spoke to the police in urgent, pressing tones.

'Yes, there were at least twenty of them. Yes. They were violent, and drunk. You must come at once.'

Jarvin glanced down over the balustrade. A part of him wanted to shout out, to tell the police there were only a dozen of the poor wretches and they were only sheltering from the storm but instead he silently shrugged his shoulders and hurried after Mrs Sibson. She led him up another, narrower, twisting flight of stairs.

'Mind your head!' she called out as he reached the twist and almost grazed the skin of his forehead on a low wooden beam.

Stooping, he climbed the last half dozen steps and reached an oblong landing with ancient and steeply gabled rafter beams of gnarled oak. Mrs Sibson was waiting for him beside an open door.

'I've put you up here in the gods, Mr Mandrake. It isn't very large I'm afraid but it does have a remarkable view of the cathedral. I'm sure you would rather be up here after grovelling around all day digging things up!'

This was said in a voice that crackled with hoar frost; as a statement of fact not as an apology for lodging him in the attic. However Jarvin managed to manufacture a smile at her definition of archaeology. 'My Christian name's Jarvin,' he offered as he squeezed awkwardly past her into a tiny, musty room.

'The bathrooms are two floors down,' Mrs Sibson continued crisply as if he hadn't spoken at all. 'And breakfast is at half past six sharp. If you should want anything else be good enough to leave a note on the hall table. I will attend to it as soon as possible.'

The priest's voice floated up to them, calling out that the police were on their way.

'You will enjoy your stay with us, Mr Mandrake, I'm sure of it,' she announced before turning abruptly on her heels to hurry back down the stairs.

Jarvin crowded the small doorway and watched her grey head of hair briefly bob up and down before it disappeared from his sight. He wanted to call out to her and ask a dozen questions, but most importantly he wanted to ask for a key to the front door. He hated the thought of being locked in anywhere since the accident, but he could imagine her reaction to such a request. He could see her withering gaze and frosty lips pursed for her reply.

'Issuing keys is most irregular, Mr Mandrake. None of my other lodgers have ever requested them. In fact, beyond their duties in the cathedral they have found no need to venture out.'

Jarvin shrugged his shoulders helplessly and retreated slowly back into the small cupboard of a room. It had a tiny slither of leaded glass to form an excuse for a dormer window. So this was to be his new home. Pulling the door shut behind him he despondently tossed his suitcase onto the sagging iron-framed bed. The sudden weight of the case made the rusty springs creak and rumpled the simple red counterpane.

Wearily Jarvin let his eyes travel over the threadbare scrap of carpet that lay upon the bare floorboards beside the bed. He glanced around the yellowing, crumbling plaster walls which were divided into irregular oblongs by wormy, wooden studs. He noticed a rickety card table, its green baize top torn and scalded by countless coffee cup rings, standing at the foot of the bed. Beside it was a broken Windsor chair, a towel neatly folded upon it. The attic felt cold and very gloomy. He looked around and found a brass light switch beside the door jamb and flicked it on. He blinked at the sudden glare from the naked bulb above his head and glanced up past it into the steeply raked ceiling with its sturdy purlins, heavy cross ties and a forest of rafter beams. He knew for sure that he was lodging in the roof of the Gatehouse with the sparrows and the starlings. He listened and faintly, above the noise of the city, he heard the soft rattle of the rain beating on the weathered tiles a few feet above his head.

He shivered, remembering that his clothes were soaking wet, and he kicked off his shoes before peeling off his jacket and trousers. He used the towel from the chair to dry his hair and rub some life into his arms and legs before snapping open the locks on his case and rummaging through his clothes for a pair of jeans and a warm sweatshirt. Absently Jarvin ran his fingers through his damp hair and tried to push it out of his eyes before crossing the room to the window. He stooped and rested the palms of his hands on the narrow sill before looking out across the rainswept city. The grey slate roofs glistened and shimmered, reflecting the rows of chimney pots and pencil thin spires. The distant hills were shrouded, hidden beneath low, wet clouds, but to the west there was a finger of light on the horizon that gave a hint that the storm would pass by evening.

The clamour of police sirens, shouts and the rush of footsteps from the direction of the Erpingham Gate made Jarvin jump. He leaned forward and pressed his nose hard against the cold, leaded pane of glass as he tried to look down into the cathedral grounds. There were figures running, scattering in every direction. From his viewpoint high up in the Gatehouse it was difficult to see exactly what was happening. Jarvin heard the front door slam and then he faintly caught the sound of the priest's voice as he joined in the pursuit. He had seen enough and was about to move back from his uncomfortable eyrie when he caught sight of the girl who had spoken to him when he walked beneath the archway. He had the briefest glimpse of her tangled mass of blonde hair streaming out behind her as she disappeared beneath the spreading foliage of the avenue of yew trees. She was running toward the north-west door of the cathedral. There was a policeman barely yards behind her, gaining on her with every stride. Seconds later she burst out through the line of trees and ran across the wet lawns toward the serrated row of monumental sculptures and ancient headstones that peopled the grass. She sprinted headlong amongst them and then momentarily seemed to hesitate at the foot of a white, stone angel. It was as if she was unsure which way to go to escape. A shout from behind her and a short blast on a police whistle made her glance desperately back at her pursuer. She leapt forward, colliding with the angel's plinth. She flung her arms up around its feet to stop herself from falling. And then she disappeared.

Jarvin blinked and rubbed his eyes in disbelief. He stared down at the solitary stone figure as the policeman momentarily slowed before reaching the angel and then ran in a widening, uncertain circle, searching for the girl. After the policeman had moved away she reappeared and ran swiftly toward the West Door and slipped into the cathedral.

'No, that's just not possible. People can't just disappear like that. It must have been a trick of the light, or raindrops on the windowpane,' Jarvin muttered aloud as he fingered the stubble on his cheeks with his thumb and forefinger. He glanced darkly at the huge bulk of the cathedral. There was something about the place that made the hairs on the back of his neck prickle.

CHAPTER THREE

Chance Meetings

JONI FROST fled along the gravel pathway with her mane of blonde hair streaming out behind her and the rain stinging her face. She was desperate to escape from the policeman who had singled her out beneath the Erpingham Gate and was now pursuing her through the cathedral grounds. She skidded on the gravel, kicking up a wave of tiny chippings as she dodged to the right, ducking her head beneath the low branches of the ancient yew trees in an effort to shake him off, but he seemed to anticipate her every movement and turned when she did. By cutting through another, larger gap in the avenue of trees he emerged right behind her and almost caught her.

'Get away from me!' she shouted, sprinting out into the curtain of rain that was drifting across the grass and searching the bleak, unbroken, high brick walls and the blank, reflecting windowpanes of the houses that stood shoulder to shoulder making a boundary of the cathedral grounds, desperate for a way out. There was no gap, nor an open back gate. There was nothing.

'Damn!' she gasped, knowing that the police would probably be waiting to catch her and her friends at the other two main gateways. She needed to find somewhere to hide until the hunt had died down.

The shrill blast from the policeman's whistle sheared through her racing thoughts. It sounded so close, as if it was at her elbow. He must be about to overtake her. She gasped, expecting the clutch of fingers on her arm at any moment. She looked to the left toward the dark bulk of the cathedral and saw in front of it only grey and white shapes, blurred in the drifting rain. She changed direction toward them and they sharpened into focus. Tall, lichen-speckled gravestones leaned conspiratorially toward each other; dark, silent obelisks and solemn monumental sculptures with outstretched, rain-streaked arms crowded the naked grass. It was a graveyard. She must have wandered through its forgotten avenues a hundred times without ever really noticing it was there. Now it loomed through the pouring rain as a blurring ribbon of possible hiding places, a maze of crumbling, weathered stone slabs and blind, empty-faced, petrified figures. If she could just reach them before the stretching hand of her pursuer grabbed hold of her she might evade capture. She might keep the closely-guarded secrets from her past away from their prying eyes.

Throwing back her head she raced through the first row of graves only to almost trip, skid and stumble on the broken headstones and fragments of effigies that lay scattered and half-hidden in the grass. The policeman cursed and stumbled to his knees behind her. Joni ran on, picking a twisting route toward the centre of the graveyard hoping it would slow down her pursuer while she searched out somewhere to hide.

She skirted a huge, black marble vault with broken, rusty iron railings and crossed three more neatly-mown avenues in her search. She was getting desperate. Every possible hiding place looked open, too exposed. She ran on into a broader avenue where the headstones were even more spaced out. Ahead of her in the centre of the pathway the statue of a white angel beckoned with outspread wings. It stood upon a plinth of grey-veined stone. It seemed that she must have already passed through the more densely crowded area. She hesitated, remembering the black marble vault that she had skirted earlier. That was probably the best, no, the only place.

She half-turned to look for it when a shout from immediately behind her made her almost jump out of her skin. She glanced frantically back and saw the policeman's red-veined face, his eyes furious and bulging from the effort of the chase. He was less than ten yards away and bearing down on her like a raging bull. For those brief, lung-bursting moments of effort after he had stumbled she had dared to believe that she was going to escape, that she had a chance, but all the time he must have been gaining on her, catching up with every stride. Now her anger at being caught so easily boiled up inside her. She clenched her fists and leapt away from his reaching hands.

'Leave me alone, you bastard . . .' she began to shout across her shoulder, the words pouring from her mouth in a raging gasp.

But as she made that last desperate evasive dash for freedom she collided with the grey marble plinth of the white angel. She had forgotten that it was directly in her path. She juddered to a halt. The words, the breath, everything but the blinding stab of pain from the sudden impact was knocked clean out of her. She reeled and staggered, her head snapping brutally forward, striking hard and bloodily against the cold, wet stone of the angel's leg. Her knees buckled beneath her and black shrouds of unconsciousness spread numbing fingers over the pain.

Somewhere outside the opening tunnel of darkness she heard a laughing shout of triumph from her pursuer as he surged forward to grab her falling body. She flung up her arms to cling onto the angel, her limbs flailing wildly, her fingers grazing and instinctively grabbing the long, flowing folds of the angel's robes where they fell about its feet in frozen pleats and tucks of stone.

Joni's world abruptly changed colour. The falling curtain of rain became a shifting kaleidoscope, a sparkling arena beneath a deep azure sky. The shrouds of darkness melted away and she could see the dark, burly shape of the policeman towering so close to her that if she breathed, their bodies would touch.

His triumphant shout evaporated and, breathing hard, he came to a sudden stop. He wiped a slow hand of disbelief across his sweating face. His eyes were wide open with startled surprise. He reached out, sweeping his fingers through the air only inches from her face, then stepped back away from her. He looked uncertainly up and down the broad avenue of gravestones.

'Where the fucking hell did she vanish to?' he muttered angrily, casting a hard, penetrating glare at the statue and the area of grass around it.

He was about to examine the plinth more closely when he caught sight of two of his colleagues emerging through the avenue of yew trees.

'I lost sight of the girl I was chasing. She's in amongst these gravestones. Have you seen her?'

They shook their heads as they moved toward the South Gate.

'Well, I'll just have a look around and I'll meet up with you in a minute,' he called to them as he moved in a slow, widening circle, peering behind each headstone.

Joni shivered and silently let out the pent-up breath that was burning in her lungs. She looked anxiously at the receding policemen. She couldn't understand what had happened. Why hadn't he reached out and grabbed her? Why had he looked right through her as if she wasn't there? It was as if she had melted into thin air.

It was then that she noticed that all around her had changed. The colours, the sounds, everything, felt wrong, different. She imagined she could hear the rub of stone against stone, the creak of timber, as the cathedral settled onto its foundations. She could see buildings appear and disappear, seedlings sprout where the ancient avenue of yew trees stood; she could hear the murmur of buds opening, the rustle of leaves unfolding and the creep and sigh of worms burrowing through the deep, black earth.

She glimpsed shadowy, indistinct figures moving through the cathedral grounds, a shifting pageant of history that washed over her, and with it the low hum of centuries of time shifting in and out of focus in one long, continuous melodic whisper.

She looked up at the weathered face of the angel and in its blind eyes she saw images of the life she had escaped from, the suffocating self she had tried to destroy. She saw her mother, distraught, crying amongst the toys of her childhood. She saw the empty void, the endless vacuum of guilt, that filled her father's heart, the gnawing pain they both suffered not knowing whether she was alive or dead after she had vanished from the university six months ago. She saw for one, fleeting moment the catastrophes her selfishness had created and tears of awful regret and shame coursed down her cheeks.

Joni sobbed as she fought to swallow the welling tears. She didn't want to be reminded, to have the raw scab of her guilt torn open. She could never be the person her parents had wanted her to be and the bitterness of their refusals to acknowledge her failings, the way they had remained deaf and blind to her arguments, still tasted harshly on her tongue. That was why she had run away and tried so hard to bury all trace of her past amongst the shifting population of street people, because . . .

'Damn you for making me remember!' she muttered angrily, trying to shut out the arguments, the justifications for what she had done as she stepped away, releasing her grip on the base of the statue. But the feel of it still persisted and burned and tingled in her fingertips. She rubbed them furiously together as if to wash them clean.

A shiver of cold fear ran down her spine and she felt as if the angel was silently watching and judging her. Slowly she tilted her head back and looked up into the soft, weathered contours of its damp shadows, half afraid of what she might see. But the eyes were blind, empty, crumbling hollows. The statue looked so old and forlorn towering above her. Its rain-scalded wings were leprously white against the thunder-dark clouds, its outstretched hands catching and spilling the deluge of raindrops, but she knew there was something magical or supernatural about the angel. There was some hidden power that had cloaked her in invisibility and triggered those buried memories, without it she would have been herded into a police van by now.

Frowning, she took another backward step, gathering and closing the loose ends of the collar of her ragged denim jacket against the persistent trickles of rain water that were running down her neck. She stared up at the petrified figure. There was something else, something more frightening than the idea of magic within this figure. She had the distinct impression that it had tried to communicate with her, to warn her of some terrible catastrophe. Whether it had already happened or was a glimpse of the future she didn't know but it had been a brief sequence of silent images, clouded, half-seen, demonic shapes. Feathered wings that beat against the moonlight, disquieting images that flickered through the shadows of her own imagination leaving a gnawing knot of anxiety, a persistent ache in the pit of her stomach.

A movement away to her right made her instinctively duck down behind the statue's plinth. The strange magical effect the angel had over her had made her momentarily forget about the policeman. Careful not to touch the plinth she raised her head and watched him reach the edge of the mass of headstones and monumental figures that crowded the grass. His face looked dark and troubled as he cast a long, uncertain look back. He muttered something to himself and slowly shook his head before shrugging his shoulders and hurrying away through the drifting grey curtain of rain toward the South Gateway.

Joni let out a sigh of relief. She wanted to laugh with relief that she had escaped, she wanted to clap her hands and set the startled pigeons flying from their roosts in the cathedral, but instead she hunted the rainswept lawns with silent eyes. She searched the shadows beneath the avenue of yew trees and the blank, blind windows that bordered the cathedral grounds. The police knew she was in there and they might at any moment begin another, more thorough, search to find her. She would have to find somewhere to hide until they drove away. She glanced up at the angel and inwardly shrank away from touching it again. She caught the sound of rainwater gurgling in the gutters of the cathedral and let her gaze travel up across the steep, leaded, gabled roof of grey-white to the soaring spire of the building. Of course there must be a thousand places in there, dark corners and dusty cubbyholes where she could hide out of the rain. Casting a last, quick look around her she hurried across the wet grass to the West Door and slipped inside.

Two stern faces belonging to volunteers from the Ladies' Fellowship viewed her entrance and dishevelled appearance with disdain and suspicion. The last thing Joni wanted if the police entered the building was for these two doorwardens to point a finger at her. She tried to smile and give the nonchalant appearance of a student visiting between classes rather than that of the fugitive that she was. She paused in front of the visitors' table, conscious of the widening puddle of rainwater that was dripping from her sodden clothes and keeping well back from the piles of leaflets and tour brochures.

'There's a couple of important notes that I forgot to write down the other day.' She tried to speak casually and act naturally, as if she popped in and out of the cathedral every day before she moved away from them toward the nave.

Joni realised as she hurried down the broad, stone steps that she didn't have anything with which to take notes, she wasn't even carrying a shoulder bag. Some student! She felt her neck prickle and imagined the two old women watching her, their thin, wrinkled necks stretching slightly as their heads moved conspiratorially together, their eyes following her, as they made a special note of when she had entered the building and what she looked like. A thin, dry cough from the table behind her made her almost jump out of her skin.

'You had better hurry up and make those notes before you catch your death of cold, dear!' one of the women called out after her. 'And don't forget that the cathedral is closed to visitors in two hours.'

'Thanks, thank you, I'll be as quick as I can,' Joni replied softly across her shoulder, trying to disguise the relief she felt that they had treated her quite normally.

An idea for escape began to formulate in her mind. Perhaps if she mingled with the other visitors instead of trying to hide she might be able to slip out of one of the gateways unnoticed amongst them when the cathedral closed. But as Joni turned into the nave her hopes evaporated before she had taken another step. The huge, gloomy building seemed almost completely deserted, empty apart from the occasional black-robed cleric or workman moving through the echoing interior.

'Damn!' Joni muttered under her breath. If she was the only visitor she would stick out as clearly as a sore thumb when the police decided to search the place. Those two women sitting just inside the door couldn't fail to remember her. Another thought suddenly occurred to her – which, if any, of the other outer doors were left unlocked during the daytime? With the sinking feeling that she had walked into a trap, she crossed the nave and turned into the South Aisle. She stopped when she reached the monks' door that led out into the cloisters and pressed her nose against the glass panel, faintly misting the pane as she watched through the low archways and saw the rain drifting in an unending cold, grey curtain across the lawns.

'Well, at least I'm in out of the rain.' She sighed, turning away from the long, stone corridors of the cloisters as the atmosphere of the cathedral overwhelmed her.

It seemed so quiet and empty, as if it was brooding, almost listening, waiting for the slightest whisper so that it could make it echo in the silence forever. Joni shivered and hurried along the South Aisle, the feeling of being trapped making her edgy. She wanted to find a way out as quickly as she could.

Passing the choir she caught sight of a group of choirboys setting out song-sheets and she was almost glad they were there. They were laughing and joking in hushed whispers and their voices almost dispelled the heavy atmosphere. She moved silently past without revealing her presence and then turned into the South Transept.

Here she stopped. It was darker and much colder in the transept and there was a strange, musty smell, a scent of corruption and decay that seemed to cling to the ageless particles of dust that swirled in the gloomy light. But it wasn't the smell or the chill atmosphere that had made her hesitate. Directly ahead of her, close to the right-hand wall, she saw the life-sized figure of an angel upon a marble plinth. It was similar to the one outside only this one was carved in a dark, almost black, stone. It was crouching down, its right hand clenched into a fist and its wings rising in a feathery arch high above its head. There was something sinister, almost menacing, about the sculpture that made her reluctant to go past it, especially if the outer door of the transept at the far end was locked.

'You're imagining trouble, you fool!' she whispered to herself.

The sound of footsteps and the scrape of chairs on the stone floor made her look round quickly. A priest had begun to arrange the seats in a different order around the central altar. He was humming to himself and didn't seem to notice her, then he glanced up and looked in her direction. Joni felt her heart sink into her sodden shoes. Now she would have to stay where she was or, better still, move into the shadows of the dark, stone angel to avoid being seen. She would wait until he had finished arranging the chairs before she could try one of the outer doors.

She edged herself closer to the angel's plinth until she was standing almost beneath its outstretched hand and prepared to wait. The thick, stone columns and spreading arches that rose to support the vaulted roof gave her the impression that she was standing on the edge of a shadowy forest glade. She felt that at any moment she would hear the sharp snap and crack of twigs breaking beneath the cleric's foot as he moved backward and forward amongst the chairs. She could almost feel the wild animals lurking, waiting behind the ancient tombs that lined the walls. She felt as if the recumbent effigies of long-dead knights that lay upon them would stir and come to life.

Joni blinked, she was beginning to daydream. She tried to focus her attention on the two large wooden chests that stood half-hidden in the deep, shadowy alcoves further down the far side of the transept but her mind drifted and she began wondering how many thousand busy hands it must have taken to polish the grainy wood until it was as smooth and hard as blackened glass. She tried to imagine what treasures and jewelled vestments had once been lain within them.

The sound of the heavy outer door at the far end of the transept creaking open on rusty hinges made Joni jump. She leaned curiously forward and peered around the marble plinth as she watched a squat, untidy female figure, swathed rather than dressed in an odd assortment of clothes tied together with yards of string, shuffle and push her way through the doorway. There were bundles of newspapers under her arms and at least four bulging, sagging, carrier bags clutched in each dirty hand. The oak door ground back on its hinges and slammed shut behind her making the woman totter and almost drop some of her precious bundles in the outer porch. Joni heard her shout a string of curses and saw her wave a full fist of ragged, torn, plastic bags that threatened to burst open and scatter their contents across the porch. Slowly, she moved forward through the open inner doors and into the transept. Her shouts gradually subsided into a low, continuous, incoherent mumbling as she shuffled across toward the entrance of St Catherine's Chapel.

Joni recognised the woman as Mad Mary, a real vagrant who wandered the countryside for miles, sleeping in barns or under hedges. She appeared to hate everybody and kept herself to herself whenever she was in the city. Joni had heard a dozen stories of Mad Mary's past; some thought she had been an heiress, others that she was a convict on the run, yet others insisted she had escaped from an asylum but Joni thought they were probably all lies. She felt that beneath those filthy clothes, the wild, demented eyes and the shouts of abuse dwelt a frightened, lonely old woman who had shrunk into a madness beyond anyone's reach.

'Mary, Mary, we have told you a hundred times that you're not to come into the cathedral to sleep.'

The exasperated voice of the priest and the scrape and clatter of a falling chair made Joni press herself back into the shadows behind the angel as the cleric skirted the rows of chairs and hurried through the transept.

She expected Mary to scream and shout at the priest, and even, perhaps, to hurl some of her possessions at him. She had done it to the policeman who had tried to move her along in the marketplace. But to Joni's surprise she merely shrugged her shoulders and, without a pause in her mutterings, shuffled back into the porch and began to deposit her carrier bags and bundles on one of the stone benches.

The priest stopped when he reached the open doors of the transept and spoke softly in a low voice that Joni couldn't hear as he watched Mary begin to spread out her bed of newspapers. He glanced at his watch and then withdrew the restraining bolts that held the doors open, gently swinging them shut.

'We'll be shutting the cathedral soon. There'll be food left outside the clerics' kitchen for you. Now you remember that, Mary,' he instructed her through the closing gap before throwing the bolt to lock the doors on the inside. 'And don't forget to be gone by morning.'

The priest listened to the old vagrant as she settled down and then retraced his steps to re-arrange the last of the chairs around the central altar for the early morning service. Then he disappeared into the choir, calling out to the choirboys as he did so.

Joni waited in the shadow of the angel, undecided about what to do next. If the police were waiting anywhere it would be at the West Door to check on the visitors as they left. But if she drew the bolt on the door that the priest had just locked she could slip out that way. But she couldn't lock it again after her. A fine shower of stonedust sprinkled her forehead. She would have barely noticed, except that it went into her eyes and made her look up instinctively.

She blinked and gasped: she could have sworn that the outstretched hand of the angel had moved. The outer skin and muscles seemed to be trembling, almost flexing.

'Oh Jesus Christ!' she hissed in alarm as she backed away from the statue.

She didn't know whether it was a trick of the light or her imagination playing her up but, two magical statues in one day was too much. She had to get out of there fast. Turning, she ran the length of the transept and grabbed at the bolt. She threw it back and scrambled out without a glance back into the transept before heaving the door shut behind her. Mad Mary barely glanced up from where she lay on the stone bench to watch her flight. Slamming the outer door firmly shut behind her Joni leaned against it for a moment to recover her breath. It had been one hell of an afternoon.

Claustrophobia was beginning to tighten around Jarvin's throat like an ill-fitting neck-tie. He had to get out of that attic for a while. He had to have space to breathe if he was going to shake off the feeling of dread and apprehension that had been closing in on him as the evening shadows lengthened across the cathedral grounds and the lights of the city had begun to come on one by one. He couldn't get rid of the images of that dark angel; they kept crowding his mind no matter how many times he paced the creaky floorboards of his tiny room.

He licked his dry lips and swallowed. What he really needed was a drink and the sweet, heady oblivion that would follow. Screwing up the courage to face Mrs Sibson, he descended the stairs to ask for a key.

'A breath of fresh air, Mrs Sibson. No, I haven't any idea how long I'll be out. My regular evening walk normally takes about an hour but I'm not familiar with the layout of this city yet. I promise I won't be too long.' He hesitated, watching her face, expecting the frost around her lips to crackle as he asked, 'If you let me have a key it would save me disturbing everyone when I get back.'

To Jarvin's complete surprise, Mrs Sibson, after a moment's hesitation, reluctantly handed over a key to the front door, but she insisted he leave it on the hall table on his return.

He closed the front door softly behind him and descended the steps onto the wet pavement. He felt better already and, throwing his head back, he sucked in deep lungfuls of the damp evening air as he listened to the swish of the evening traffic driving through the puddles.

Overhead the night sky was streaked with rain clouds, their heavy underbellies reflecting the glow of the city, but between their black void eternity was strewn with sparkling stars.

'Now for that drink!' He ran his tongue around his lips as he turned toward the Erpingham Gate.

He remembered that he had passed a straggle of public houses and wine bars earlier on his way from the railway station.

Jarvin quickly retraced the route he had taken earlier and made his way back toward the centre of the city. As he turned into King Street he noticed the evening hum of the traffic grow suddenly louder, moving crowds thronged the pavements and paused to browse at the windows or examine menus before vanishing in noisy knots through open restaurant doorways. There was a smell of exotic food that made his mouth begin to water. Laughter, the sound of diesel taxi-cabs, voices and music in the warm night air filled Jarvin's head and he smiled. The anonymous rub of the crowds, disjointed snatches of conversation, the lurid, hot flicker of fluorescent light reflecting their shifting sea of liquid colours in the flooded gutters was exactly what he needed to silence the tormenting voices and banish the images that echoed inside his mind. Here in the crowded streets he could let the tide carry him along. Here he could escape for a while and forget the nightmares that haunted him.

He let the slow-moving crowd carry him along while he surveyed the frosted, opaque, engraved windows and doors and read the illuminated signs for somewhere to drown his memory. Above the procession of cars and taxis that filled the road a lit gallows sign caught his eye. It was a faded painting of three antiquated, lifting cranes beside a river. Their pulleys and derricks were hauling huge slabs of stone out of flat-bottomed sailing barges. In the background he could just make out the silhouette of the cathedral spire. Above the picture in bold gilt and black letters he read 'The Three Cranes'. The sign looked old, far older than the building it was hanging from, but it intrigued him and the lighted, leaded windows below it looked welcoming enough.

'"The Three Cranes" it is then,' he muttered to himself as he waited for a gap in the traffic before running across the road and up onto the pavement in front of the saloon door.

Somebody came up behind him as he reached for the door

latch, pushed briskly past him, threw open the door and vanished through it. Jarvin made to follow but hesitated and let his outstretched hand fall to his side. The heavy wooden door with its lighted panes of engraved glass swung back and clicked shut. The wave of conversation that had wafted out through the closing gap, the clink of glasses and the dim, shadowy figures that he had glimpsed momentarily in the smoky interior of the bar made him reluctant, almost afraid, to enter. It was as if, by lifting the latch, he would be trespassing into their private, secret domain.

'All you'll get is cobwebs growing on your tongue if you stand out here thinking about it!'

The soft, almost jocular voice at Jarvin's elbow made him turn, his eyebrows raised in surprise. He found, standing beside him, a short, middle-aged, stocky figure dressed in a rumpled tweed jacket and an open-necked check shirt. He was wearing baggy brown corduroys and battered brogues that had seen many better days. He smiled and the action involved the whole of his open round face from the tip of his receding widow's peak, outwards across his forehead and down to wrinkle the corners of his eyes. It stretched to the long, curling sideburns that reached almost to his chin and his full, moist lips which completed an almost perfect half-moon. But it was his eyes that Jarvin found most disarming: their direct gaze seemed to penetrate and reach right down inside him, to finger their way through to the secrets of his soul.

'Burr. Martyn Burr.'

The stranger introduced himself as if giving his name was an everyday occurrence. Sweeping the lapels of his jacket aside he pushed well-practised thumbs into the pockets of his waistcoat and nodded toward the closed door. 'You seemed to be at a loss, young man,' he continued without pause to draw breath. 'At a loss as to whether you should risk entering my local watering-hole or not. Well, I can assure you we haven't had a serious outbreak of typhus in the Cranes since 1720 or at least the day before yesterday.'

Martyn's voice exploded into a short, guttural exclamation of laughter as he stepped forward and reached out with his left hand to flip up the door latch before pushing the door invitingly open.

'After you, dear boy,' he beamed, the sideburns and his lips once again forming that almost perfect curve.

'Why thank you.'

Jarvin tried to return the smile as he found he didn't have any other choice but to enter the smoky interior of the pub. To refuse such a friendly gesture would have been unnecessarily rude.

Threading his way through the crowded room he found a space at the bar and dug into his back pocket to withdraw a crumpled five pound note. He held it up and began to wave it slightly from side to side as he tried to catch the attention of one of the busy barmen.

'I'll have a Scotch!' he called out as one of them came quite close to him and swept his eyes across the crowd. 'Teacher's will do . . .' he added, but the barman's eyes had drifted blindly over him as if he wasn't there and then he moved away and began to serve somebody to Jarvin's right.

Another server, his closed fist swathed in a cotton dish-cloth with which he was diligently polishing the inside of a pint glass, was approaching. Jarvin tried again. He leaned forward across the bar, almost waving the note under the barman's nose. 'I'd like a whisky. Teacher's.'

Almost directly behind him Martyn Burr's voice boomed out, 'Two whiskies, Brian, and a pint of the barge water you call stout to wash it down with, please.'

Brian's eyes briefly registered on Jarvin's fluttering five pound note before they blinked and moved past him.

79

'Coming right up, Doc!' he called, setting the pint glass underneath the pump and giving it a purposeful pull before he reached up to take down two small tumblers.

Jarvin felt the touch of a hand at his elbow and heard Martyn's voice insisting that he take one of the glasses. 'It's for you, dear boy, to help flush out the cobwebs while the staff of this establishment realise that the sole purpose of your visit here is to sample their refreshments.'

'But . . . but . . .' Jarvin stuttered, a hot flush of confusion rising through the stubble that shadowed his cheeks. He wasn't used to total strangers buying him drinks.

'Take it. Take it and consider it makes amends for my insisting that you drink in my local.'

Martyn beamed, purposefully pushing the small tumbler of amber liquid to stop directly in front of him and waving aside his embarrassment.

'There's nothing more frustrating than feeling that you have become invisible in a crowded room, is there? I had forgotten what bedlam it can become in here and how it's almost impossible to get served if you're not a regular. I have a theory, you know, for everyone who has managed to get a drink in their hand tonight a whole village will have been born, lived out their lives and died. Yes, a whole village.'

Martyn gave his deep laugh and lifted his own tumbler carefully between forefinger and thumb to examine the liquid. 'Well, here's to living and dying, my young friend,' he smiled, creating that almost perfect curve with his lips, before pressing them against the rim of the glass.

The crowd along the bar surged and swayed as the people at the back squeezed and pushed for any narrow opening that appeared. Jarvin staggered backward slightly as a burly figure pushed in between them before Martyn reappeared through the crush of elbows and glasses.

'I think it would be wiser to move to somewhere a little quieter before we're trodden into the floorboards. Follow me, there's bound to be an empty alcove in the snug. The second round's yours, I believe.'

He chuckled as he snatched the note from Jarvin's hand and reached across the bar to thrust it into the barman's top pocket. 'The same again, only this time make it doubles and send them through to the snug, there's a good chap.'

'Right you are, Doc. Someone will be right with you!' he shouted back without looking up as he pushed two more glasses beneath the pumps.

'I'm right behind you!' Jarvin called out as the doctor disappeared into the crowd.

He had little choice if he wanted to taste that second drink, the one he had already paid for. Somehow he managed to keep Martyn's rapidly vanishing head and shoulders in sight, muttering apologies to those he barged against or pushed as he followed him through a maze of rooms and passageways. There was another reason he didn't want to lose sight of him, there was something strangely compelling about Martyn Burr, something about him that made Jarvin want to unburden all his secret nightmare fears. Strangely he felt that he'd known him all his life.

Ducking through a low doorway they came to a shambling halt and he realised that they must have reached the snug bar. It was a small, dimly lit, low-beamed room somewhere toward the back of the rambling premises, divided into booths rather than alcoves by high-backed, old-fashioned, leather seats. Young couples seemed to have occupied most of the booths, their conversations a hum of intimate whispers. Martyn slowly scanned the room.

'Ah! Over there, in the corner by the window!' He ushered Jarvin toward two empty seats that he had spotted.

'I'm Jarvin, Jarvin Mandrake,' he offered as Martyn put

both his glasses on the brass table top and settled in opposite him.

Martyn nodded in a disarming way as if he had already discovered his name, and perhaps a dozen other things, when their eyes had first met on the pavement outside. He was thoughtfully stroking one of his sideburns and allowing the silence between them to lengthen as if he was waiting for Jarvin to unfold and confirm secrets that he had already glimpsed. Jarvin recoiled from the penetrating gaze and tried to think of something that would start the conversation. A young lad suddenly appeared through the doorway bearing a tray.

'Your drinks, Doc!' he called out, setting the tray down with a noisy clatter of metal on metal.

Before they had even had a chance to unload the tray Martyn had ordered another round and deposited a note in a puddle of beer.

'But I could never drink . . .' Jarvin began to protest.

'Doctor's orders!' the young boy cheekily interrupted as he gathered up the empty tray with the money and vanished through the doorway before Jarvin could finish his sentence.

'Come on, the night is young, Jarvin. Let us overflow our cups and celebrate. God knows, tomorrow will have enough tragedies of its own to grieve over. Drink up, drink up.'

Martyn rubbed his hands together so enthusiastically that Jarvin wouldn't have been surprised to see sparks crackle between his fingertips.

'A toast! Give us a toast.' The doctor laughed, lifting one of the brimming glasses of black, frothing stout to his lips and swallowing a long, uninterrupted draught.

Jarvin hesitated, his forehead crinkling into a frown. He raked his fingers through his untidy hair. Beads of sweat were forming on his temples, he had never intended to have more than one drink, he knew his weakness. He recognised the spectre that hovered at his elbow. Already the whisky fumes, the smoky atmosphere, the hum of conversation had combined to make him feel light-headed. He began to reach his trembling fingers toward the glass and then forced himself to stop. The muscles and sinews were knotting along his forearm, other voices and images began to crowd his mind; he saw the dark angel crouching and staring at him.

'I promise I'll do it slowly and savour each drop. I'll only drink one. Just enough, no more.' He spoke silently to himself as his fist closed purposefully around the glass and his resolve melted. He lifted it to his lips and swallowed it in one gulp. Blinking, he let the hot fire consume him and the devils that haunted him retreated into the shadows. He laughed and slapped the empty glass back onto the brass table top. Now his tongue felt looser and his mind more relaxed.

'Tell me, Martyn,' he asked, leaning forward and reaching for the other whisky glass. 'Why does that barman call you "Doc"? Are you a doctor? Is that why you invited me here, because I looked ill?'

Martyn straightened his pint glass and looked thoughtfully across the tide lines of beery foam that clung to the rim and stared at Jarvin.

'Yes,' he said softly. 'I'm the doctor of Magdalene Hill, nurse, midwife and confessor for lost souls. You looked haunted standing out there, Jarvin Mandrake, you looked like a lost soul alone on the pavement hovering by the door. That's why I encouraged you in. But . . .' Martyn stopped abruptly and then slapped the table with his hand. 'But the main reason I invited you in was because you looked so darned thirsty and I can get such excellent service in here. You see, I delivered the landlord's two children, safely in spite of a few complications.' And he burst into a gale of laughter.

He pushed the untouched pint glass beneath Jarvin's nose. 'Wash it down. Be quick or we'll not be ready for the next round.'

Jarvin didn't laugh with him. Martyn's acute observation had touched a raw nerve. 'Haunted? How could you know anything about the accident? How could you know about . . . ?' His voice trailed off in confusion, images crowded his spinning head. 'I haven't met you before, have I? I would remember if I had, wouldn't I?'

'No,' Martyn answered quickly, leaning forward across the table, his eyes sharpening into focus.

He sensed that the shadow he had glimpsed in the young man's eyes was more than indecision or fear of entering a strange place alone. He realised quickly that it was something more terrifying that haunted him, something that he probably needed help with.

'We all have our demons, Jarvin. We all have nightmares that stalk our sanity and they must be exorcised, dragged out screaming into the daylight to be banished. Do you want to talk about your accident and about everything that brought you to the door of the "Cranes" tonight?'

Jarvin opened his mouth to answer and then hesitated. He reached for the pint glass and closed his fingers around it. His head was spinning, demonic voices whispered and echoed and in the background were images of the dark, crouching angel and the girl vanishing as she touched the statue. All these began to combine with the other horrors that haunted him. He had to talk to someone now that he was away from Beckonsthorpe: he would go mad if he didn't. Somewhere in the blur of the alcohol fumes he remembered that Martyn Burr had said he was a doctor. He could talk to doctors: he would talk to him.

'Yes, I'd really like that,' he answered, slowly lifting the glass and burying his lips into the creamy head of froth before swallowing a quenching gulp of beer.

CHAPTER FOUR

Ritual Murder in the Dark

'JESUS CHRIST, I've got to get some fresh air before I suffocate,' Joni muttered irritably, wiping at the beads of perspiration that were breaking out on her forehead as she elbowed and pushed her way through the press and sprawl of bodies that crowded the squalid room. She forced herself towards the tall, sash window that overlooked the dark cathedral grounds.

Earlier she had been as eager to repossess the old Dean's Hall as all the others who had evaded capture. The crumbling building was like a rabbit warren and the church bailiffs had never managed to discover all the entrances they used and so could not keep them out. The atmosphere, as they drifted back together in the shadow of the guild hall at the bottom of Goal Hill, had been heady and charged with defiance and they had slipped back into the building through a disused cellar entrance, slamming and bolting it only moments before the bailiffs realised that they had broken in again.

But for Joni the euphoria quickly evaporated. The night seemed airless. The upstairs room chosen for the victory party was overcrowded and stifling and the loud rock music blaring out of the radio on the floor in the centre of the room throbbed painfully inside her head. Images of that leprous angel that she had momentarily clung to in the rain and memories of her abandoned earlier life kept recurring. They seemed to heighten her awareness of the squalor and make the acid, dirty smell of sweat more pungent. She could almost taste the fungal damp and decay in the hot, crowded room. It made her throat dry and burnt her nostrils. Her friends of yesterday seemed like strangers in the distorted, lurid, yellow glow that blinked from the flashing light of the road lamps that they had stolen on their way back through the city.

For Joni everything seemed different as she squeezed through the crowd and reached the window. After a moment of struggling with the rusty catch she managed to release it and forced the bottom window up enough for her to lean out and breathe in the still, humid night air. Somebody shouted her name from the noisy crowd behind her. It was a voice she didn't immediately recognise, it didn't seem to belong to anyone she knew in the squat and she tried to ignore it, to pretend she hadn't heard. As she breathed in deeply she smelt the dark scent of wet grass and wild flowers, but the voice grew louder and more persistent and a hand began to prod and sharply nudge her in the small of her back. It demanded that she give it her attention. Reluctantly Joni ducked back into the room and turned around.

'No, thank you . . .' she began, shaking her head at the offered bottle and barely glancing at the figure in the over-sized, shabby trenchcoat as she began to turn back towards the window. She didn't want to become part of the celebrations tonight. She didn't want to escape reality in an alcoholic haze, but the swaying figure in the coat wasn't so easy to put off. He took a staggering step closer to her, his wet mouth splitting open into a loose grin full of blackened teeth.

'Hey, Joni, aren't you going to drink and pop some of these fliers with me?' He slurred his words carelessly, but it didn't disguise the demand for her attention and the painful thrust of the bottle in her ribs with the open handful of multicoloured capsules pushed under her nose merely emphasised it.

Joni felt a surge of cold panic as she recognised the dishevelled, angular face with its dark, predatory eyes above hollow cheeks and the mouth full of rotten teeth. He was a friend of Greg's, their self-elected leader. Greg had brought him into the squat a couple of nights ago under the cover of darkness; she remembered that he had introduced himself as 'Voodoo' and had given them some story or another about needing somewhere to hide up until he could get out of the country. Joni had sensed a brutality, a ruthlessness, behind his cold eyes. He wasn't like any of the other members of the group and she had tried to keep well out of his way.

'What's the fucking problem? Isn't my speed good enough for you?' he snarled, sensing her reluctance. His alcoholic grin was collapsing into a menacing scowl and his voice had become an angry, bewildered shout. 'Perhaps there's a whole lot of other things you don't share with us. Greg's told me that he has his suspicions about where you come from. He said you're too secretive.'

A ripple of quiet passed through the crowded room. Only the radio continued to pound out its relentless rhythm and the flickering, yellow lights still danced across the ceiling. Startled, curious eyes were turning towards her. Joni heard the accusing threat in his voice and she realised how odd her behaviour must seem tonight. It was unlikely that anyone else in the squat would refuse to share with Voodoo. Sharing was the first, the most basic rule, that bound them together and fuelled their survival. People who stopped sharing were quick to drop out and vanish from their group. She was afraid of being exiled from the squat but she couldn't explain why she didn't want to get high or drunk tonight. The memories after touching that statue were too profound, too private to share. She didn't feel as if she had anything to celebrate but she had to do something to placate their suspicions. She had to do it quickly if she wanted to avoid the ugly scene that was developing. She had to get high whether she wanted to or not.

She laughed and pressed her hands to her temples. 'It's these headaches, they make me crazy sometimes. The thunder brings them on.'

Reaching out she took three of the brightly coloured capsules from his hand, mumbling her thanks as she crammed them into her mouth. She tipped up the bottle, took a long gulp and swallowed. The mixture of cheap sherry and methylated spirits tasted as harsh as smouldering sawdust as it hit the back of her throat. It made her retch and double up, her eyes clouding with tears. Waves of dizziness swept through her and she staggered and clutched at the windowsill to stop herself from falling. Perhaps after all it was better to blur those memories of the past and disguise them in an oblivion of meaningless shapes and colours.

Reality rapidly shrank, gurgling away all those painful memories through a tiny hole somewhere in the centre of Joni's consciousness. Her body felt as light as a feather: one puff of wind and she would float. She laughed and a stream of senseless words spilled through her lips; thin, faraway sounds that she didn't recognise, distorted noises that didn't matter any more. Vaguely she became aware of moving shapes pressing in all around her; hazy, swaying figures seen through a halo of brilliant, shifting colours. But the figures were moving closer, growing larger, covering her in shadows of deepest indigo. She heard fragmented sounds, words and snatches of shrieking laughter, which scratched at her eardrums. She was being smothered, absorbed into the shifting, amorphous mass of bodies, of grey plasticine faces with bulbous, grasshopper eyes and cavernous mouths that loomed in front of her. Hundreds of grave-white hands suddenly reached out of the mass and tried to touch her, to grab at her with their long, tentacle fingers.

Joni staggered away from them and fell back against the windowsill, screaming and beating her hands at their grasping hands. The cocktail of oblivion had turned into a nightmare. One by one the hands had metamorphosed into huge spiders that were spinning a cocoon of silence around her. She had to escape, she had to get away, to fly before they swallowed her in their stifling silence. She wriggled backwards across the windowsill and then half-turned before leaping, launching herself into the darkness. She spread her arms, clawing at the night with outspread fingers as she plummeted from the first floor. The lights of the city spun and she heard shrieks and a thin voice wailing as she twisted and turned. Then it stopped abruptly as she hit the wet grass. She rolled over onto her face as darkness enveloped her in its secret shrouds and mercifully blacked out the hallucinations. Heads and shoulders crowded the open window and peered down. There were questions, concerned at first, and then laughter before, one by one, the heads vanished from sight as they were drawn back into the party and she was forgotten.

Joni's void of unconsciousness became a deep, drug-induced sleep. Vivid dreams filled her mind, stark images of the world that she had turned her back on jostled for attention. She tried to run away from them only to become lost in a maze of windowless corridors and empty halls. There was a train – she could see it in the distance – it was waiting for her, waiting for her to escape. No matter how hard she tried to reach it she couldn't. Her feet seemed leaden. A shrill whistle sounded and all she could do was to watch helplessly as the engine vanished and became a silver dot of perspective upon a grey, windswept canvas of her despair. Now her past was whispering from the lengthening shadows, closing in, relentlessly pursuing her, ruffling her hair with the breath of regret, touching the back of her neck with its ice-cold fingers.

'No!' she screamed out in her dream, silently.

She reached out to tear the fingers away. Her body was twitching as a searing stab of pain shot up her right arm from where it had twisted beneath her in the fall. She cried out loud and started awake, blinking in confusion, not knowing where she was. She was shivering with cold as she sat up. It was pitch dark and pouring with rain. Nursing her right arm she climbed awkwardly to her feet. She realised she had a thundering headache as she straightened up. Her mind felt like soft putty as she tried to remember how she had come to be lying asleep out there on the wet grass. She looked across the dark lawns towards the bulk of the cathedral and then she glanced up at the half-open window above her head. She worked out that it must have been somewhere between midnight and dawn and slowly, piece by piece, she managed to put the evening back together.

'Damn you! Damn you all to hell!' she muttered angrily as she gathered her damp, denim jacket more tightly across her shoulders with her left hand. Her teeth were chattering with more than just the cold as she remembered Voodoo pressing the drugs onto her.

Looking up to the dark, half-open window she was about to call out, to try and attract someone's attention when she realised that the party must have finished hours ago. The house was wrapped in total silence and there wasn't a light on at any of the other upper windows. All the lower ground floor windows had been boarded up by the bailiffs months ago. She doubted if anybody would hear if she shouted and even if she did manage to wake anyone she wasn't sure that they would be able to help her get back into the house. She knew the cathedral gates were locked and she wouldn't be able to get out into Tombland until morning. The only way into the house was to scale the wall to the first floor window that she had fallen out of, but even if somebody did lower a rope or something she wouldn't be able to climb it with her right arm hurting so much.

The patter of raindrops suddenly grew heavier. Rumbles of distant thunder broke the silence. The storm was returning, sweeping back across the sleeping city with jagged fingers of lightning stroking the night, etching the huge bulk of the cathedral in stark outline against the sky. Joni had to find shelter and quickly before the rain soaked through her clothes and chilled her to the bone. But where? The thunder pealed loudly and a barrage of lightning flashed and crackled, momentarily illuminating the soaring spire and sending fleeing shadows from the startled gargoyles which were poised on every gutter spout. It highlighted the high arches of the flying buttresses and picked out the intricate stone tracery on the stained glass windows. The light flickered and faded into rumbling darkness behind the cathedral. She watched as the lightning died away and remembered that the outer doors of the south porch were probably still unlocked, the same ones that she had used to slip out of the cathedral late in the afternoon of the day before. As she ran through the worsening deluge she hoped that Mary hadn't bothered to get out of her bed of newspapers to throw the bolts before she fell asleep.

Joni reached the oak doors, grasped the large iron ring in her left hand and threw her weight against it as she turned. The latch lifted and the heavy door groaned and creaked open an inch. She breathed a sigh of relief and leaned her weight fully against it, peering into the gloomy interior of the porch as it slowly opened. The inside of the porch was dimly lit by the glow of a single lamp. The low wattage bulb was barely visible through the shroud of cobwebs and dust that clung to the glass but it cast enough light for Joni to see the two, broad stone benches that flanked either side of the tiny vestibule.

Opening the outer door obviously hadn't disturbed Mary – she could hear her snoring as loudly as a rusty chainsaw – but it took her a few moments to pick out the top of her woollen bonnet and the straggle of dirty, grey hair as she lay, or rather sprawled, along the left hand bench underneath the sea of crumpled newspapers and pieces of old, hessian sacking that served as her blanket. The carrier bags that contained all her possessions had fallen over and spilled their contents untidily across the flagstone floor.

Joni stepped in over the threshold and came out of the rain before reaching for the latch to push the door shut. But she hesitated, wrinkling her nose at the overpowering stench of decay that seemed to waft through the porch and decided to leave it slightly open. If it hadn't been pouring with rain she would have retraced her steps but she had to keep dry and reluctantly she began to pick her way towards the right hand bench through the grey, mouldy crusts of bread and battered food tins that had fallen out of the bulging carrier bags. Something moved in the shadows beneath Mary's bench and a baked bean can rolled sideways, its buckled open top catching the feeble light. A large rat, disturbed in its scavenging, gave a high-pitched squeal as it ran between Joni's feet and fled out over the threshold into the rainy darkness.

She jumped. A shudder of revulsion made her teeth rasp together but she fought to stifle the scream and forced it back down her throat. She was afraid to wake the filthy vagrant, afraid that she would drive her out into the rain.

Stepping quickly through the mess on the floor she reached the empty bench and sat down. Rumbles of thunder were breaking directly overhead and the lightning flashed in brilliant, illuminating sheets across the lawns. A chill wind had risen and it was blowing the rain in a soaking mist through the open door of the porch. It glistened on the stone bench in the cold light of the lamp and formed a fine film on her denim jacket. Joni shivered and moved further into the corner away from the door and into the shadows, her knees drawn up to her chin. She huddled tightly in cold misery, her back against the rough stone wall of the transept, as she watched the storm through the open door and listened to the rhythm of the rain drumming on the roof of the porch above her head.

Despite trembling with cold she soon began to feel drowsy and her eyelids felt heavy and began to close. Her head nodded forward and fell onto her knees. She was rapidly drifting, slipping into a light, fitful sleep, lulled by the sound of the rain drumming on the roof. It was beginning to blend in her mind into soft, swelling waves of music.

Suddenly another sound, a sharp metallic click, invaded her fading consciousness. It made her start awake and blink. She turned her head to stare at the doors that led into the transept: she could have sworn that the sound that had woken her was someone trying to lift the latch from inside the transept. The echo of the noise was still in her head and a cold shiver of fear travelled up her spine.

She listened intently, trying to calm her racing heart. There couldn't be anybody in the cathedral. The place had been cleared of visitors and locked up hours ago. Anyway it was pitch dark in there: nobody in their right mind would want to stay in there all night. She had almost convinced herself that the noise must have been the thunder or a severe crackle of lightning and she was settling back to watch the storm when the iron ring set in the door closest to her began to turn slowly. The latch lifted half-way and the heavy oak door groaned on its hinges and shook, but the latch held. A knot of panic tightened in Joni's stomach. The doors were not locked – she remembered unlocking them as the place was closing so that she could slip out of the cathedral unnoticed. Anybody could have got in that way.

The handle turned again and the door rattled violently against the latch as it began to creak open inch by inch. Mary turned fitfully in her sleep, disturbed by the noise. The overpowering stench of decay that Joni had smelt when she had first opened the outer door of the porch billowed through the widening gap, ruffling the newspapers that covered the tramp as it blew through the porch. Weird inhuman whispers and the rush of footsteps poured out of the darkened transept.

Joni knew she had to get out of there and she leapt to her feet. She was about to make a dash for the outer door when the draught from the opening doors behind her slammed it shut cutting off her escape. She dropped to her knees and scrambled under the stone bench in desperation and terror, pressing herself into the shadows. The inner doors creaked fully open and she watched in horror as a horde of demonic creatures with claws and hideously deformed bodies swarmed across the floor towards where Mary lay asleep.

Joni swallowed the scream of terror that was clawing its way up out of her lungs and bit hard on the knuckles of her right hand. She had to be hallucinating. This nightmare had to be caused by the residue of the drugs in her blood-stream: they were conjuring up monstrous creations from the pits of Hell.

She fought to overcome her panic knowing that it would only multiply and intensify the visions in her mind if she didn't do something to destroy the illusion before it got a real hold on her. But what could she do? Huddled beneath the bench she felt so helplessly alone, so trapped, then she remembered that sometimes, if you reached out and confronted the hallucination, touched whatever was terrifying you, you destroyed it. But she hesitated. They looked so terrifyingly real as they reached the other bench and began to claw at the loose ends of the newspapers that covered Mary. One of them jumped up, hooking its claws into her hair, its voice rising in an excited chatter.

Joni forced herself to remember they were only there in her imagination, that she only had to reach out to banish them. Then suddenly she froze. Beads of cold perspiration broke out on her forehead. She might be hallucinating these creatures but she hadn't opened the doors to the transept or imagined the overpowering stench of decay. Illusions, no matter how bizarre and frightening had to start with a thread of reality, no matter how tenuous. There had to be someone or something in the transept; something that was making that low-pitched whirring noise that was getting louder and louder and setting her teeth on edge.

Mary awoke with a cry and sat bolt upright, scattering her blanket of newspapers and shouting a string of obscene curses as she snatched at what she thought was a rat whose claws were tangled in her hair.

'Get off! Get off you fucking bastard!' she screamed, tearing the creature free and hurling it with all her strength against the far wall.

The creature hit the wall hard and let out a snarling shriek as it slithered down onto the bench at her feet. It lay quivering for a moment and leapt back at her, its claws outstretched and its eyes glowing red, its hideous mouth of razor-sharp teeth gaping open. Mary stared at it, blinking her bleary eyes in confusion and trying to scramble backwards along the bench, raising her hand to protect her face. She was trying to ward off its renewed attack when a chilling voice hissed out from the darkness of the transept.

'Ishtaz, be still, she is mine to sacrifice.'

The demon stopped, its mouth snarling and twitching, dribbling hot trails of saliva. It jumped onto her stomach and crouched, baring its fangs, pinning her onto the bench with its long talons. Mary screamed and struggled violently, trying desperately to break free, but her terrified eyes were now focused on something above and behind the head of the grotesque creature that was squatting heavily on her stomach.

'Mother of Jesus, Lord have mercy!' she cried out, repeating the words over and over again until they blurred into a jumble of incoherent gasps as she cowered and stared wildly up at something that was advancing towards her through the open doors, its huge shadow slowly engulfing her.

Joni watched the terror widen across the face of the old vagrant and edged forward as far as she dared in the cramped space beneath the bench. Twisting her head to one side she looked up and her blood froze in her veins. Towering above her, its outspread wings brushing against the walls of the porch, she saw the dark angel in the feeble glow of the lamp. Its skin looked as smooth and as black as death, its broken iron chains hung loosely from its wrists and ankles, but there was nothing angelic in its sinister face. Its eyes were narrow, glistening slits, its mouth a snarling line of hate as it paused above the cowering woman. It spoke in a hard, menacing voice.

'Ishtaz, Akkabal, Guardians of the Gates of Hell, hold the sacrifice still.'

The demons swarmed up from the floor onto the bench their voices rising in pitiless shrieks as they grasped hold of Mary's flailing arms and legs, their sharp talons tearing through her ragged clothing, puncturing her skin, as they stretched and restrained her.

'Take care!' the angel hissed angrily. 'Do not let her bleed wantonly. Her blood must be used to anoint the bloodstone.'

The beats of its wings began to lessen as it descended to straddle the old woman, its muscular legs and feet planted firmly on either side of her narrow chest.

Joni watched, paralysed with horror. The gigantic, sinister figure now astride the old vagrant looked like the dark statue of the kneeling angel that she had hidden behind in the transept the day before, but that wasn't possible: statues couldn't come to life.

Yet something told her this wasn't an hallucination, or a nightmare, whatever was happening was terrifyingly real. The angel folded its wings across its back, its feathers grating softly together and it bent forwards, a cold, pitiless smile curving its lips, and it reached down with an outstretched hand to caress the old woman's terrified face, tracing its contours with gentle fingertips as it whispered.

'Sammeal, the moon is in the seventh house. It is time to awaken.'

Suddenly the soft whispers turned into a shriek of cruel laughter. The angel threw back its head and shouted out Sammeal's name and the caressing hand quivered and grasped Mary's scrawny throat. She screamed, twisting her head violently from side to side as she tried to escape from the strangling grip. Her eyes bulged, her face blackened and her tongue protruded from between her teeth in a choking gasp as the angel's fingers tightened, grinding and crushing her larynx with one brutal squeeze. Mary's body convulsed, her back arched and her hands and feet twitched against the claws that held them. Suddenly her mouth snapped shut, her few remaining, blackened teeth cutting through her tongue.

Trickles of blood darkened her swollen lips and ran down her chin, hissing and bubbling as they spread across the knuckles of the angel's strangling hand.

It shook its victim violently, hurling her up into the air, dislodging the demons and scattering them across the stone bench as it cried out, 'It is time to awaken, Sammeal! I, Abaddon, the angel of darkness, summon you to arise!'

Joni was trembling uncontrollably from head to foot in the darkness beneath the bench. There was a knot of revulsion in her stomach at what she had just witnessed and it was beginning to travel up towards the back of her throat. She was going to be sick but the terror of being discovered made her fight to swallow the bile. Her eyes were watering in an effort not to cough or gasp too loudly for air and give herself away.

The small, demonic creatures began to dance in a howling, leaping, shadowy circle around the angel's feet chanting its name over and over again. Round and round, faster and faster their scrabbling claws moved.

'Awaken, Sammeal!' Abaddon cried, stabbing its right hand brutally at Mary's chest.

Joni heard the sternum crack and saw its ridged fingers tear right through Mary's coat of rags, her filthy undergarments, skin, flesh and bone as he smashed a gaping hole in her rib cage. Then it tore out her heart and lifted the pulsating, bleeding organ high above its head.

'Sammeal, Sammeal, I now anoint the bloodstone!'

Abaddon squeezed the ruptured heart with all its strength, anointing its head with rivulets of blood that trickled and spread in a darkening stain down through its tousled curls and across its forehead, cheeks, neck and shoulders, hissing and bubbling as it soaked into its skin, tinging the feathers of its wings a darker, wetter shade of red. It squeezed and rubbed the bloody heart all over its head and shoulders before holding up its hand to still the leaping, dancing circle of demons who suddenly stopped, their heads turned expectantly toward the open doors that led into the transept. It was as if they were listening, waiting for some long-awaited footfall before they performed their much-practised rite. The silence lengthened broken only by the distant rumble of thunder and the rattle of rain on the roof overhead.

The angel fell to its knees and offered up the limp body of the old woman, holding her toward the open doors. 'Sammeal!' it called out in a desolate, despairing voice. 'Have I not sacrificed enough? Have I not wet the blood-stone enough times to resurrect you from eternal darkness?'

The silence seemed to deepen, muffling even the patter of raindrops on the roof. Wearily Abaddon rose and let Mary's body slip from his outstretched fingers into the waiting claws of the monstrous little creatures that crowded at his feet.

'Take her, devour the husk of the sacrifice and bury her bones. Remove all trace of the body,' the angel hissed.

It strode into the cathedral without a backward glance at the swarm of demons as they shrieked and chattered and clambered all over the old vagrant's body, greedily gnawing at her fingers and toes, tearing off strips of her skin and hungrily devouring her as they slowly pulled and dragged the carcass after the angel into the darkened transept.

Joni shuddered with revulsion. Watching the demons devouring Mary's body was more than she could bear. Her sight blurred, her head swam dizzily and she blacked out, her head striking the cold, stone floor. The vile picture of them stripping the old woman to the bone followed her into merciful oblivion.

CHAPTER FIVE

A Vanishing Death

J ARVIN WOKE up with a throbbing headache and a dry, parched mouth. He hurried down to the dining room but as he entered he felt as though he could have dissected the atmosphere at the breakfast table with a blunt butter knife. His fellow lodgers, five black-frocked novices, sat at the far end of the table and they barely acknowledged his mumbled greetings, carefully avoiding his eyes as they ate. He shrugged it off as he sat down and smiled up at Mrs Sibson as she bustled in from the kitchen with a plate of bacon and eggs. He had words ready to apologise for being late down but the puckered frown of disapproval around her thin mouth and the severe tone of her voice wiped the smile from his face and silenced him in an instant. She left him in no doubt that he was the root cause of the stifling atmosphere.

'We don't hold with drinking in this house, Mr Mandrake. Or with coming in at all hours and making enough noise to wake the dead. You're lucky, considering the circumstances, that I've saved you any breakfast at all.'

'I . . . I . . . I'm sorry,' he stuttered, feeling his face flush with embarrassment, but she turned away from him abruptly and began to clear the plates noisily at the end of the table, muttering loudly to the flock of novices as she declaimed the evil of drink.

Jarvin looked down at the two watery fried eggs and the wrinkled scrap of bacon staring up at him through a puddle of tepid, congealing grease and felt his stomach heave with nausea. He knew it didn't matter how much Mrs Sibson berated him: he wasn't able to swallow a mouthful and be sure of keeping it down. He pushed the plate away and picked up the luke-warm cup of coffee, nursing it with both hands as he sipped it slowly. He tried to remember how he had got back the previous night after he had left the 'Three Cranes' following his chance meeting with Martyn Burr. He clearly remembered the doctor's infectious smile and his raucous laugh, and the procession of empty glasses that had crowded the brass-topped table, but after that he only had the vaguest recollection of snatches of conversation, laughter and singing. Somewhere in the memories he could recall telling Martyn about the accident and how he had acquired the job as ecclesiastical archaeologist. Jarvin frowned and thoughtfully put his coffee cup back into the saucer. A shadow of anxiety darkened his eyes and he wondered exactly what he had said in that haze of tobacco smoke and alcohol.

'You're letting your breakfast get cold!' Mrs Sibson's brittle accusation cut through his thoughts, her tone sawing at his headache and demanding his attention.

He blinked painfully and looked up to find that the clerics had evacuated, completing their escape while he had been ruminating, and Mrs Sibson was standing over him, holding his untouched plate between thumb and forefinger.

'I am sorry. I'm afraid I don't feel at all well this morning. I think I had better get a breath of air before . . .' he stammered, pushing his chair back hastily.

He stood up and made good his escape before she could draw enough breath to berate him for wasting her good cooking. He could imagine the lecture on famine and hunger that she was about to deliver.

Breathing a sigh of relief he pulled the front door of the

Gatehouse firmly shut behind him and glanced at his watch as he descended the front steps to the pavement. Despite being late down to breakfast it was still very early to be up and about by his standards, especially as something was trying to excavate a hole in the centre of his forehead. He wasn't sure where to go, or how to fill the couple of hours before he had to present himself to the Dean and collect the keys to his own office, if he had one, and to the library and the archives, and then begin his first proper day working in the cathedral.

The morning rush hour hadn't quite got into its noisy, carbon-fumed stride yet and in the early silence he could hear skylarks and blackbirds, sparrows squabbling for territory in the yew trees. He breathed in deeply, there was a faint scent of wild jasmine and honeysuckle in the cold, clear air. It was going to be a beautiful morning with small, candyfloss clouds speckling an empty rain-washed sky. He wouldn't have appreciated it more if he had had ten more hours of blissful oblivion with his head buried beneath the blankets, though the glare, possibly, wouldn't have hurt his eyes so much.

'Now where?' he muttered to himself, thrusting his hands deep into his pockets. He considered walking into the city centre and finding a cafe, one with the blinds still down, where he could sit in a dark corner and slowly drown the pain inside his head in a bottomless cup of black coffee, but the thought of smelling all that greasy food and having it eaten all around him made his stomach churn.

The front door of the Gatehouse slammed shut behind him and one of the young novices, a bundle of books clutched beneath his arm, ran down the steps brushing past him and almost knocking him over. He mumbled brief apologies as he hurried along the pavement, long robes flapping around his legs, and turned into the Erpingham

Gate. Jarvin noticed other priests hurrying along Tombland and turning into other entrances and realised that the cathedral would already be open. The clergy had a tradition of getting up at the most unfriendly hours. He could spend his time in there, curled up in a nice, dark pew, even resting his eyes if he could find a quiet corner. He turned towards the Erpingham Gate, a smile widening across his stubbly cheeks. In an abstract way he would even be early for work.

He followed the hurrying priest into the Erpingham Gate. His footsteps echoed as he passed beneath the gloomy archway and for a moment it sounded as if there were crowds all around him, accompanying him. He glanced back to find he was alone and shrugged his shoulders: it must have been a trick of the acoustics. Walking out into the sunlight he blinked and shaded his eyes. The cathedral and its needle-fine spire looked so crisp and symmetrical in the bright morning light, so permanent, a part of the landscape that nature itself might have sculpted in sugar frost above the gnarled, olive-dark avenue of yew trees. He wished he had brought a pair of sunglasses with him to dull the morning. Quickening his stride he covered the short distance between the gate arch and the avenue glad to be in amongst their welcoming shadows.

Ahead he could see that a small knot of people, clerics from different denominations, were beginning to gather outside the West Door of the cathedral. As he drew closer he saw the young priest who had been sent out to meet him the day before emerge from the Dean's office, his face looked equally officious and sour and his manner towards the shifting group was abrupt and organising as he consulted a clipboard and began calling out names. Jarvin hesitated and then turned off the gravel path and walked between the yew trees leaving clear footprints in the dew-wet grass as he skirted the cloisters to look for another, quieter, entrance. He would rather not have to meet that priest again so soon. Following the outer wall of the cloisters he turned left and found another, narrower, gravelled path that led to the door of a porch. Glancing at the long morning shadows cast across the lawn he realised that it must be the porch that led into the South Transept.

The large oak door was shut and, Jarvin thought, probably still locked at this early hour. He almost turned away to continue his slow, exploratory preamble around the outside of the building without bothering to try the latch when he noticed the corner of a newspaper protruding from beneath the bottom of the door. It looked so incongruous, so completely out of place, spoiling the neatly-raked paths and tidy mown lawns that he thought he had better dispose of it. It would only take a moment. Stooping and gripping hold of the iron latch ring on the door with his left hand to keep his balance he grasped the edge of the newspaper with his other hand and tried to pull it free. It moved easily toward him and he almost had it all when it snagged on the inside of the door and began to tear through his fingers.

'Damn!' Jarvin muttered under his breath as a wedge of the flimsy newsprint came away in his hand and flew into the air.

All he had managed to achieve was to scatter the doorway with fluttering scraps of paper and bending down had prompted his hangover to start hammering away at the inside of his skull. Leaning heavily on the latch ring he straightened up, twisting the ring as he did so. To his surprise the latch lifted and the door creaked open half an inch. Jarvin pushed his hand against it and it swung open, dragging the mess of crumpled paper back into the porch.

He stepped in over the threshold and tried to free the newspaper from behind the door but he paused and wrinkled his nose. A faint, stale odour had wafted past him, reminding him of a smell from his past, which he called the 'fragrance of time'. It was an odour he had often encountered when excavating ancient tombs and opening up new burial sites.

It made him glance anxiously around the porch, but there wasn't anything to account for it, just two, plain, stone benches that lined the outer walls and the closed iron-bound doors that led to the transept. A couple of old newspapers and a battered baked bean tin littered the floor and that was all. He shrugged, perhaps he would always catch the scent of the past in old buildings, even when the smell was so faint that other people may not notice. He bent down to pull out the crumpled paper from behind the door, balling it in his hands and dropping it beside the open doorway, before crouching down to gather up the rest of the loose newspapers.

He glanced idly under the bench directly in front of him and froze, his hand poised and trembling just above the floor. His mouth fell soundlessly open. There was something half-hidden in the shadows and from the vague contours he could just make out the shape of an arm, a pale hand and the outline of a woman's face pressing against the cold, stone floor. Beads of perspiration broke out on his forehead and ran down his spine as he realised that he was staring at a body that had been wedged into the corner beneath the bench. He was looking at the victim of some hideous murder. He wanted to look away, to get up and run out of there, but he couldn't. Waves of nausea, far worse than those he had experienced at the breakfast table, were knotting up his stomach and beginning to bubble and rush up into the back of his throat. Nothing in all his archaeological excavations, none of the mouldering, dusty bones and crumbling flesh, had prepared him for the sudden shock of this moment.

He didn't know how long he would have squatted there staring at the body if it hadn't suddenly twitched and the arm and hand closest to him moved slightly. He heard a low, whispering groan and the two eyes opened in the shadows beneath the bench. They blinked and focused, widening with terror as they stared directly at him. Jarvin gasped in surprise and recoiled, overbalancing and falling against the other bench, catching the hard edge of the seat squarely across both shoulder blades as he sat down heavily on the stone floor. The pain across his back broke his trance. He scrambled forward on his knees and called out, 'You're alive, alive! Give me your hand.' And he reached his own hand toward her.

Joni screamed. At the moment of resurfacing to consciousness she had imagined that the figure, the voice trying to reach into her hiding place and pull her out, was the dark angel. She could see its murderous hand only inches from her face. The hideous howling voices of the demons were still so vivid, so real to her, they were crawling all over her. She could feel their hot, burning claws on her arms and legs, trying to force her out from beneath the bench. 'No! Get off, get off you're not going to get me. Help me, help!' she screamed, kicking and scratching at her attacker as she desperately tried to ward the angel off.

Jarvin hastily backed away from her but not before she had scratched the backs of his hands. He could hear the panic and terror in her voice and wondered if she had hidden in the porch to escape from someone who was attacking her. Perhaps she thought that he was that attacker.

'I'm not going to hurt you. I'm just trying to help you,' he called out softly as he knelt by the other bench. 'My name's Jarvin, Jarvin Mandrake. I work here in the cathedral. I'll go and get the police if you would rather they help you.'

The sound of Jarvin's voice made Joni stop lashing out and she fell silent and huddled against the far wall. Her mind was a blur of confusion. The figure crouching opposite her was nothing like the dark angel, it didn't even have wings, and the demons had vanished. There were no claw marks on her hands or legs, just the hot tingle of cramp or pins and needles. Looking across to the other bench she saw that it was completely empty. Mary's body, her bed of newspapers, everything had disappeared.

'I'll call the police if you want.' Jarvin's voice cut through her confusion.

'No. Wait!' She wriggled sideways to get a better look at him. 'You're that priest, aren't you? The one who didn't want us evicted from the Erpingham Gate?'

Jarvin smiled as he tried to put her at ease, then he shook his head. 'No, I'm sorry, no, I'm not a priest, I'm . . .'

He hesitated. What he did or was didn't matter right now, getting her out from beneath the bench was more important. She had edged forward a little and he recognised her face and the tangle of blonde hair.

'I watched you running away from the police yester- day afternoon. You ran across the grass toward the cathedral.'

He paused. Seeing her face made him remember her colli- sion with the statue and the way she had mysteriously van- ished. He had watched while the policeman had searched in bewildered circles around the white angel. He opened his mouth to ask her about it but stopped: it wasn't the right moment. Instead he offered her his hands again and asked, 'Have you been hiding here all night? You must be numb with cramp. Here, take hold of my hands and I'll help you out.'

Joni drew back away from him, the fear still shadowing her eyes. 'You won't call the police will you?' she asked, and after another moment, 'You won't tell anybody else I've been here?'

'No, not if you don't want me to,' Jarvin answered softly, trying to reassure her.

Joni began to work her way out awkwardly from beneath the bench. Her head and shoulder came out first and she pushed hard against the wall with her feet, wriggling her lower back across the stone floor. Jarvin took hold of her right arm and she climbed onto her knees before he pulled her up to her feet. She gave a cry of pain and jerked her arm away from him, swearing under her breath. She swayed unsteadily and collapsed onto the bench. Her legs felt rubbery and her feet were so numb that it felt as if she were standing on her ankle bones. Both arms were being tortured with red hot pins and needles and the right one really throbbed with pain; she was filthy dirty and her head ached. She looked at the stone bench opposite her and thought of what she had seen. The thought of poor Mary made her bow her head forward into her hands and weep, her shoulders shaking and trembling with emotion.

'What you need now is something hot to drink. Then you should get some rest and try to forget . . .' Jarvin had barely begun to talk when her head snapped up showing her grimy face streaked with tears, her red, ruined eyes glaring angrily up at him.

'What the hell do you know about it? How could I ever, ever forget . . .'

Her anger trailed off: it wasn't really directed at him, and her gaze shifted past him to the empty stone bench. New tears welled up and trickled unnoticed down her cheeks. She didn't even understand it herself. Last night had been too real to be a dream, but if it wasn't a dream what had happened to Mary's body What had happened to the blood, the newspapers? How could it all have disappeared, even her carrier bags bulging with her meagre possessions?

Joni glanced down at the floor and saw the couple of newspapers and the battered tin can and gave a cry as she reached down to snatch it up and clutch it to her chest. 'It was real, it really did happen! I didn't hallucinate and it wasn't a nightmare. But where have they hidden the body?' she whispered to herself, ignoring Jarvin's presence and bending forward to look underneath the other bench.

She searched the empty shadows and looked for spots of blood on the stone floor, or anything to show that the old woman had spent the night sleeping in the porch, but there was nothing. Frowning, she picked up one of the scattered newspapers, crumpling it together with the buckled can against her chest. They were all she had, the slenderest of threads, and they didn't amount to much.

'But she can't have just vanished into thin air. They must have put her body somewhere,' she muttered to herself. Vivid glimpses of her last moments of consciousness came flooding back and she shuddered, her breaths quickening, her knuckles whitening as her fingers tightened, tearing through the crumpled newspaper and gripping the tin can as she lifted her eyes to stare at the huge oak doors that led into the transept.

'Body? Whose body?' Jarvin's voice cut the silence and made her start. She had momentarily forgotten about him.

She shivered and turned to face him, glad that he was there, and she opened her mouth to tell him what had happened, but she hesitated. Nobody would believe her. Nobody would believe about the dark angel and his swarm of demons and how they murdered an old vagrant. They would think she had been hallucinating, high on drugs. And even if they did believe her it would mean getting involved with the police and then her parents would find out where she was.

'It was nothing,' she answered flatly. 'I must have fallen asleep and had a bad nightmare. They sometimes seem so real in the few moments after you wake up. Thanks anyway for helping me out from under that bench.'

Joni tried to smile as she stood up and began to edge toward the open doorway, but she couldn't help glancing back toward the closed doors that led into the transept, fearing that at any moment they would burst open and those creatures would come pouring out.

'Wait!' Jarvin called, putting his hand on her arm. He had seen that look of fear reflected in her eyes and he recognised it. The same look stared back at him out of every mirror, haunting him in every unguarded moment. 'I think something did happen in here last night. Something that really terrified you. It might just help if you talked about it.'

Joni shook her head fiercely and tried to pull free from his grip. 'No! I don't want to talk about it. Even if I did you wouldn't believe me. Anyway, why should I trust you? Now, let me go, you're hurting my arm.'

Jarvin released his grip but he spoke quickly as she hurried away from him toward the open door. 'Yesterday when you were running from the police you collided with the statue of a white angel and you vanished. That policeman was almost on top of you but he couldn't see you. I don't know what made that happen but it certainly was no trick of the light. I didn't tell anybody though. Perhaps I am the one you can trust.'

Joni stopped in the doorway and turned. She looked so worn out, so thin and dishevelled in her torn jeans and denim jacket and there were tears in her eyes, helpless tears of confusion. She raised a quivering hand and pointed at the empty stone bench beside him and whispered, her voice trembling with fear.

'First, promise you won't think I'm mad.'

Jarvin nodded.

'There's an old woman, a tramp, called Mary. The priests let her sleep in here sometimes. She was asleep on that bench last night, beneath a blanket of old newspapers. All her things were scattered across the floor around her, then . . .'

Faint voices and footsteps beyond the heavy doors made Joni cry out in terror and scramble out of the porch. Jarvin recognised the dry, monotonous voice of the young cleric. 'It's all right,' he called out, running after her. 'It's only the priest, the one who wanted your friends moved on. He's showing a group of visitors around.'

Joni slowed and then stopped and turned towards him, watching his eyes as she spoke. 'Mary was murdered last night while she slept on that bench. Murdered by that dark angel, the one that kneels on a plinth inside the cathedral. I watched it happen, then I must have blacked out. But there's nothing there this morning, no body, no blood, nothing except a few newspapers and an old baked bean tin to prove she was ever there at all. There's nothing to show that it happened.' She fell silent and stood there shivering and waiting for Jarvin's reaction. Suppose he laughed or tried to tell her she had been dreaming?

He took off his coat and carefully put it around her shoulders. 'I want you to tell me exactly what happened. Everything from the moment you collided with that statue. But first let us find a cafe somewhere and get you something hot to eat and drink.'

Dean Woodhouse didn't seem very amused at the interruption as Jarvin hurried into the office muttering his apologies for being late. The Dean said something to his clerk, who was standing beside him gathering up a sheaf of signed documents, and he hurried away leaving them alone together.

'It's Mr Mandrake isn't it? Bishop Mandrake's nephew? I've been expecting you.'

His smile seemed a little frosty as he glanced pointedly at his watch and then looked up over the pile of books and papers that were spread across his desk to confirm his fears with the wall clock.

'Bartram informed me that you arrived yesterday afternoon and that he had shown you around the cathedral and then escorted you to your lodgings. Mrs Sibson is a very fine woman, she's been looking after our novices for years. I hope you'll enjoy your stay there.'

Jarvin nodded and tried to smile as he felt the colour rising in his cheeks. He hoped that word of his late night session in 'The Cranes' and his abortive attempt to eat breakfast had not reached the Dean's ears. 'Yes, yes, it's very nice,' he mumbled, fishing in his pocket and offering the letter of introduction that his uncle had given him.

The Dean didn't offer him a seat as he took the letter and smoothed it out. Slowly he read it and then shuffled through the papers on his desk until he uncovered the buff folder that he was looking for. It had Jarvin's name neatly written across the front in large black letters. He flicked the folder open and deposited the letter inside it. Jarvin had a moment's glimpse of another letter, also with his uncle's crest at the top but this time addressed to the Bishop of Norwich. Obviously another request to find him some useful employment using his talents as an archaeologist. He noticed a small note had been written at the bottom in red ink. He would have loved to have read it but the Dean closed the folder with a sigh and sat back in his chair.

Dean Woodhouse pressed his fingertips together and brought them thoughtfully to his lips as he studied Jarvin's face. 'Having our own ecclesiastical archaeologist in the cathedral is quite a rarity. I'm not quite sure . . .' He paused, his face softening a little. 'I don't know how long you'll be with us, Jarvin, or if you have any particular line of enquiry you would like to pursue while you're here. Obviously the library and the archives are at your disposal and I'm having a small office – well, a large cupboard, I'm afraid – cleared out for you to use. It's not very big but it's the best I can offer, it is next to the library however.

'So, what will it be, Jarvin? A little digging on the site of the Chapter House? I'm sure something out in the open like that won't get in the way too much, or perhaps you would like to excavate the stone mason's yard. Of course I'm afraid we haven't got the resources to offer you much in the way of assistance but then I expect you will have brought all your own equipment.'

The Dean rose from his chair and indicated that the interview was over. Jarvin tried to force a smile. The veiled references to his post had not been lost on him and he was becoming acutely aware of the transient nature of his position. The Dean was making little attempt to hide his discomfort behind a thin, lukewarm smile. The post of ecclesiastical archaeologist was, as he had already suspected, a favour to his uncle, a way of distancing him from the stigma of being a patient at the Beckonsthorpe Institute.

'No, no digging: I thought I might catalogue your medieval carvings,' Jarvin stammered as the Dean led him to the door. 'I would like to start inside the cathedral and make a list, setting out their historical importance. I noticed so many beautiful examples yesterday afternoon and I wouldn't get in anybody's way. You could present my findings to the local university.'

Joni's account of what had happened to her the night before was still ringing in his ears. He didn't know how much of it was the effect of the drugs that she admitted having taken, or the concussion from her fall. Fatigue and shock could play the strangest tricks on the mind. But from the look of terror in her eyes as she related the story he was sure that something had really frightened her as she had lain huddled under the stone bench. A lot of what she had said made no sense but there was something strange, even sinister, about that kneeling statue of the angel. He had sensed it himself and he wanted to take a closer look, devote some of the time he was going to spend at the cathedral trying to uncover the truth.

Dean Woodhouse paused, his hand on the door handle, his face pinched into a frown of irritation. He would have preferred the young man to have been well out of the way. 'Well, I'm not sure. The cathedral is so busy,' he murmured, shaking his head.

'Most of my research would be carried out in the library and the archives and if I do need to study any of the carvings or sculptures for any length of time I can do it after everyone's left.'

'Oh, very well then,' the Dean sighed, opening the door and ushering him out. He had a string of appointments that were going to take up most of the morning and he needed to get on. 'But make sure that you're at your studies, research, or whatever you call it, by eight-thirty each morning. We have a strict rule about punctuality. Ask my secretary to organise an official name tag for you to wear.'

Jarvin smiled and nodded as he left the office. 'Oh, I almost forgot.' He paused and turned back. 'I noticed an old tramp going into the porch of the South Transept late yesterday evening after the cathedral had closed. I could see her from my lodgings. I wasn't sure if I should have called the police or informed somebody here after the trouble earlier with those squatters in the Erpingham Gate.'

The Dean thought for a moment and then shook his head. 'That was probably only old Mary. She's one of the local vagrants, we let her shelter in the south porch from time to time if the weather is bad. She's never been any trouble, I'm glad you didn't contact the police. Wait there a moment and I'll check to see if the duty verger recorded anything. We find it useful to keep a record in case the Social Services need to contact her.'

The Dean hurried past Jarvin into one of the other offices and spoke to someone that Jarvin couldn't see. He was back a minute later carrying a clipboard. He glanced down at the board and ran his finger down the list of names and smiled. 'Yes, here it is. The duty verger recorded Mary's name against the South Porch at five-thirty yesterday afternoon, so there's nothing for you to worry about. Now, if you'll excuse me, I have a mountain of work.'

'Do you keep a record of when they leave?' Jarvin persisted as the Dean began to close his office door.

His eyebrows rose in neat, fluffy arches of surprise. 'Goodness no! If we had lists for everything the cathedral would be buried beneath a sea of paper. Good day, Mr Mandrake.' And he firmly closed the door.

Jarvin quickly dealt with the administrative details with the Dean's secretary – the identity badge would enable him to work in the cathedral whenever he chose – and then he made his way thoughtfully across the gravel drive and in through the West Door to take a closer, more penetrating look at the statue of the dark angel. He now knew for sure that Mary had been in the South Porch the night before, that part of Joni's story, at least, was true. But what had happened to her? Statues couldn't come to life and then commit a murder, there had to be some rational explanation, something that had terrified Joni.

*

It had been a long and very tiring day and Jarvin had little to show for it. He yawned and drew meaningless, idle pictures in the shallow puddles of beer that stained the small, brass table top as he glanced from his watch to the noisy crowd at the bar. He shifted his weight on the hard, uncomfortable chair and continued his solitary vigil of watching the door, wondering if somehow he had missed her in the dim, tobacco light and shifting crowds. Joni had promised to meet him here in the 'Three Cranes' at nine o'clock. That morning she had seemed so intent to find out what had happened to the old tramp that he hadn't for one moment thought that she wouldn't turn up. He glanced at his watch again. He had waited for over an hour already. He decided to give her another ten minutes and he sipped unenthusiastically at his glass of beer and then pushed it away, the glass chinking against the one he had bought for her when he had arrived.

The dirty shreds of the previous night's hangover still clung to the inside of his skull and he didn't want a repeat performance so soon. Anyway the Dean had made it abundantly clear that he was only there on a very temporary basis and he assumed that it also applied to his lodgings and upsetting his landlady might accelerate his departure. Mrs Sibson hadn't seemed at all pleased when she caught him slipping out after supper even though he had assured her that it was only for a short evening stroll, but as his absence lengthened he imagined her setting an ambush with her flock of whispering novices nodding their approval as she prepared her own personal breathalyser test.

The watched door opened at last and he half-rose from his chair, a smile broadening across his face as she entered. Figures at the bar turned and the hum of conversation faltered momentarily as they scrutinised her ragged appearance and untidy mane of blonde hair. Joni soon spotted him at the corner table and waved as she hurried through the crowd.

'Well?' she asked abruptly, pushing the tangle of hair out of her eyes and sitting down opposite him with no word of excuse or apology. 'Did you go and look at that statue? What did you find out?'

Jarvin pushed the untouched drink towards her. 'Not much, I'm afraid, except that Mary was in the porch last night, that is certain. The duty verger noted down that she was there at five-thirty.'

'But I told you she was there, it was the one thing I was certain of!' Joni frowned, her thin face darkening with anger as she stood up. 'You must have thought I was making it all up this morning. You must have thought that I was some crazy druggy who needed humouring.'

She paused, her lip trembling, and backed away from the table. She had been so frightened in that porch early in the morning that she would probably have taken comfort from anyone, but it hurt to think that he had only been stringing her along. She wanted to ask him what he had got out of it but what the hell did it matter, she barely knew his name and when she walked out of there she would never see him again. She was even beginning to doubt if it had really happened herself. The idea of a murdering angel and a swarm of demons was crazy, and she had nothing with which to substantiate the reality except a few scraps of newspaper and a buckled, old tin can.

'No, please wait, Joni.' Jarvin half-rose as he spoke, almost upsetting the glass on the table in his haste to stop her. 'Please! I never said I didn't believe you.'

There was something in his manner and a direct look in his eyes that made her hesitate. Slowly she sat down. He sat back down with relief and lifted his glass to take a swallow of beer before he leaned forward across the table toward her, inhaling a shallow breath before he spoke. 'I'm an archaeologist by profession, a historical detective if you like. About six months ago I had a terrible accident while we were excavating a temple in the Middle East. The floor beneath me gave way without warning and I plunged down into a place called the "Labyrinth of Secrets". There were things, unimaginable creatures that guarded that black darkness – they clawed at me and tore my clothes – they broke my leg as easily as if it were made of straw. Monstrous phantoms reared up to howl and curse me for daring to violate their innermost sanctum. It took my rescuers twelve hours to get me out – they said I was lucky to get away with my life. Sometimes I'm not so sure. I've carried hideous echoes of that time with me ever since. The demons are always here, haunting me, living with me at all times.

'I knew something had happened to you last night, I saw the shadow of it in your eyes. The terror was in your voice. But, you see, proving that these things exist, that they're real enough to shatter bones or rip out hearts, is so difficult. When the lower chambers of that burial site were cleared of rubble there was nothing there, nothing that could have done those terrible things to me. They had melted into the darkness. The doctors said I had suffered acute claustrophobia. No one would believe me and I have no way of ever proving they were real. That is why it is so important to establish that Mary was actually there last night: it gives us somewhere to start.'

Jarvin paused for breath and took a long swallow from his glass before putting it down thoughtfully. 'I spent all afternoon, until the cathedral closed, nosing around in the transepts, examining that statue of the angel and searching for clues.'

He shifted on his chair and pulled out a small, dog-eared notebook from his jacket pocket and quickly thumbed through it, stopping when he reached a couple of pages covered in minute, almost illegible notes and a spidery list of measurements that marched erratically across both of the pages. He looked up from the book and shrugged his shoulders before he spoke. 'Nothing! I couldn't find any trace of the old woman's body. I'm not very familiar with the layout of the cathedral yet so I searched in the archives and found some of the old plans of the building and made my own measurements of both the South and the North Transepts, I also measured the tower area and the choir and compared them with these plans. I couldn't find any obvious hiding places, like double wall cavities, concealed doorways or dead spaces that I couldn't account for. There wasn't anything else, except . . .'

He stopped and smoothed out the creased page before carefully folding the notebook and pushing it back into his pocket.

'Except what?' Joni asked eagerly, leaning closer.

'That smell, the one you told me about, the one you smelled so strongly that night. I caught a whiff of it when I first opened the porch door yesterday morning. Well, there was the faintest trace of it still lingering in the South Transept all afternoon. I couldn't find the source or any-where that it was particularly strong, but it was definitely there.' He looked about to go on but then shook his head and fell silent.

'Go on. There's something else isn't there? I know you're not telling me everything.'

Jarvin shrugged. 'I don't know, it's difficult to put into words. I spent a long time looking at that statue of the angel today. It seemed different, more sinister and menacing, but I wonder how I would have felt about it if I hadn't heard your story. It's so easy to let your emotions cloud the facts, but there's something about it, something about the statue that's wrong. I sensed it yesterday when I first set my eyes on it – I'm pretty sure it's not medieval, although that's what the guidebook says. I'd say it's much older, more classical, and there's nothing on it, no markings or anything to help me date it. Its origins are a mystery.'

Jarvin frowned and traced his finger through the drying puddle of beer. 'But it's not the age or the origins that really bother me, I've got a lot of ground to cover in the archives before I draw a blank in that department, no, it's the figure itself that gave me the creeps today. It seemed to be kneeling in exactly the same position as when I first saw it, and I could almost swear that the mass of broken chains and shackles it has gripped in its left hand were exactly in place, not a crease smoothed out or a rusty link turned the wrong way, but the feathery arch of its wings really caught my eye. They seemed more elongated, higher above its head, they threw an entirely different shadow, as if they had frozen at a different moment as they beat in the air. And its colour, the blood dark texture of its skin, it seemed slightly deeper and its lips looked almost wet as they glistened in the shadows. I felt I wanted to touch it, to prove to myself that it wasn't stone, but every time I tried to go close I was filled with this overpowering sense of dread that dragged at my footsteps and stopped me. The worst of it was that each time I tried I had the distinct feeling that the angel became more aware of my presence.'

Jarvin was so engrossed in his description of the angel that he jumped as a bell rang noisily from behind the bar. He glanced quickly at his watch. 'My God! Mrs Sibson's going to kill me!' he cried, rising to his feet and pushing his chair back. 'I'm sorry, I really have to get back to my lodgings or the old dragon will have my throat cut.' He managed a smile. 'Which way are you going? Can I walk you anywhere?'

Joni smiled, it had been a long time since anyone had offered to escort her anywhere. She had been back at the squat for most of the day trying to sleep and get herself together. She had been too frightened to share her experience with anyone there and her silence had created an atmosphere of suspicion. She felt she didn't fit in with the group any more but she didn't have any other place to go to, she would have to stay there at least for a couple of nights until she found somewhere else. 'Yes, I'm going in your direction, but we'd better separate before we get into Tombland, it probably wouldn't look good if you're seen out with one of the squatters,' Joni laughed.

The crowds were quickly thinning and the hum of the city diminishing into the background as they crossed Pottergate into Madder Street. The street lights were causing their shadows to condense and then stretch out into elongated giants as their footsteps echoed on the cobbles.

'I felt as if the angel's eyes followed me wherever I went. It was as if it was alive.' Jarvin spoke softly, trying to pick up the thread of what he had been talking about when the landlord had called 'time'.

'No, not now.' Joni shivered. 'Don't talk about it out here in the dark. Somehow it makes it more frightening, it's as though it's listening.'

Jarvin wanted to laugh and set her mind at ease. He hadn't meant to frighten her or awaken the spectres of her nightmares. He didn't know what had really happened the night before but there was something odd about that statue, though it didn't amount to much, certainly it didn't hint at murder. But his laughter and reproach died on his lips as they rounded the corner of St Andrews and he saw ahead of them the buttressed shoulders and the needle spire of the cathedral rising between the steep, weatherbeaten roofs and crowded rows of chimney pots. It seemed to stand alone, separated from the hum of the city, wrapped and brooding in its own secret, sinister silence. A cold, hostile fortress of medieval stone.

'Yes, perhaps we should be careful. Perhaps . . .' He fell silent and began to glance cautiously into the doorways and alleys as they passed, even looking back over his shoulder. With nothing but the distant rumble of the night traffic and the soft echo of their own footsteps to keep them company his imagination began to open the door to spectres that haunted him and he quickened his stride.

A sense of foreboding stirred within the dark angel. It shivered slightly and awoke, but not a muscle or a feather moved. Its pitiless eyes blinked wide open and began to search the inky darkness beneath each hidden arch and choir stall. It swept its gaze along the clerestories and galleries, listening for the whisper of an inhaled breath, the tell-tale scrape of a foot or the mumbling rhythm of a beating heart that would reveal the hapless choirboy or priest who had witnessed the sacrifice. But there was nothing to see or hear. The cathedral was empty of life.

Abaddon frowned. The sense of foreboding deepened. The blood of the sacrifice was still wet on its lips but Sammeal had not risen, the bloodstone was not saturated enough. Deep down, in the blackest depth of the angel's being, there was the echo of Sammeal's voice warning it that the ritual had been violated. Telling Abaddon that it could not sleep undisturbed until the Midwinter Solstice, it could not rest until the watcher had been destroyed. But there were two voices inside its head, two images had awoken it. This time two people must have observed the ritual and the watchers were close by now. It could sense their presence strongly and it knew what it had to do.

With the harsh and brittle whisper of stone feathers rubbing against each other Abaddon stretched and beat its wings. Link by link the iron chains that had once held him prisoner to the plinth rattled through his open fingers and fell away in clattering, rusty loops. The angel rose in a widening arch, pausing and hovering at each of the stained glass windows, watching and listening, staring out across the darkened lawns. Faintly, no more than a murmur mingled with the night sounds of the city. He heard their voices.

'Ishtaz, Zahrim, Guardians of the crypt, awake!' Abaddon hissed, landing in a shower of fine stonedust beside the secret entrance of the crypt. Bending forward and clawing at the edges of the heavy slab of stone it expertly levered it up and dragged it aside. A foul draught of corrupt and decaying air wafted up. The angel fell to its knees, its head thrust down into the darkness, its voice echoing as it called out, waking the demons.

The floor of the transept trembled as a hot wind billowed out through the entrance. The flames on the altar candles danced madly on their wicks and trickles of molten wax spilled down their sides and spread out across the altar cloth. The tremor travelled up through the huge slabs of stone that formed the lantern of the tower and forced them to grind against each other, puffs of stonedust and flakes of mortar erupted from the crumbling joints. There was a rush of scrabbling, clawed feet and howling shrieks came from the bowels of the earth. A flickering, phosphorous glow illuminated the entrance to the crypt as the small, hideous creatures began to swarm out in a black, shadowy tide.

'There were two violators who spied on our sacrifice. We must hunt them down and silence them,' Abaddon hissed urgently. 'They are close by. Go, climb up onto the roofs, spires and buttresses. Disguise yourselves as gargoyles and watch and listen. They must not escape!'

Shrieking and chattering the demons spread out through the cathedral, climbing over pews, swarming up the walls and running along the galleries, squeezing through the tiniest gaps and openings, breaking holes in the top of the stained glass windows to scuttle out onto the roofs where they draped themselves on the gutter spouts and corner stones, moulding themselves into the shapes of fantastical creatures. They watched, they listened, their grotesque heads turning and following Jarvin and Joni's voices as they drew steadily closer.

CHAPTER SIX

Pieces of the Jigsaw

J ARVIN LOOKED down with a dissatisfied frown at the scant scrawl of notes that covered the two open pages of his notebook and the handful of jottings and calculations that lay beside it on the crumpled scraps of paper that littered the top of the rickety table that served as his desk. It wasn't much to show after his first attempt at combing through the cathedral archives and his optimism for finding the answers was evaporating into bewilderment. He had been convinced, after questioning Joni more closely the following evening, that she had witnessed some sort of ritual sacrifice and that the old woman's murder had been committed to evoke or resurrect something evil, and whatever it was dwelt within the cathedral itself, but now he was beginning to have doubts. It had seemed logical to scour the archives for any mention of the Devil or of devil-worship, witchcraft or pagan festivals. If anything like it had ever happened before, and if there had ever been witnesses, there would be records. Good and evil were invariably bound together, especially on religious sites, and monks and priests were the most particularly thorough and painstaking scribes. He discovered that the cathedral's turbulent past had indeed been well-documented. It had been besieged as a fortress when it became a sanctuary for embattled knights in the centre of violent riots and it had ridden out the ravages of plagues and famines. But to his surprise he had drawn a blank when he had tried to find any reference to witchcraft or devil-worship.

The only reference he could find to anything that hinted at an evil presence within the cathedral had been on a fragment of ancient, twelfth century, illuminated manuscript during Bishop Elmphric's reign. From a rough translation of the Latin he discovered that an apprentice stonemason had his eyes gouged out and his tongue severed at its root by an unknown evil that had clawed his face to ribbons while he was seeking sanctuary beneath the high altar. There had been more, something about a miraculous carving of an angel, but the manuscript had been so scorched that it would take weeks to decipher the whole story.

The mention of the miraculous carving of the angel had made him wonder, although it was difficult to be sure which angel it was referring to. The dark angel itself was an even greater mystery. There was no definite reference to its origins: but it always seemed to have been there and to have had a strange gift for surviving natural disasters and catastrophes. In fact, its survival was well-documented. It had been discovered untouched by the scorching heat of the fires that damaged the cathedral in 1170 and again in 1272. It had been found unharmed amongst the ruins of the spire in 1362 when a freak gale had blown it down and again when lightning struck the new spire in 1463 it had been dug out of the smoking ruins completely undamaged. The history of its ability to survive seemed endless: even the Luftwaffe's bombs hadn't harmed a single feather of its arched wings, even when they destroyed the roof of the transept. Its survival seemed to be nothing short of a miracle and that word 'miraculous' stuck in his mind. He remembered the early fragment of manuscript which described the unknown evil assailant's attack on the mason and the way the young man's face had been clawed 'as if by demons'; and then there was mention of the carving of the 'miraculous' angel, which he connected with the sinister figure that now crouched in the South Transept. He realised that the link was vague but it was about all he had.

Jarvin scratched thoughtfully at the thickening line of stubble on his chin and made a mental note to remember to shave, and then instantly dismissed it. There had to be some clue that he had completely overlooked, or perhaps he should look at everything from a totally different angle, or take a different approach, but how? Wearily he ran his fingers through his hair, pushing it out of his eyes. He had been sleeping badly, plagued by bad dreams and startled awake by noises in the dark that had left him trembling beneath the blankets, straining his ears to catch the shrinking echoes, not daring to imagine what kind of creatures could be trespassing in the night. His flesh had been left crawling in anticipation of the blind touch that he felt was coming and thinking about it had begun to open the door to his own phantoms. He could even now feel the cold sweat begin to bead his forehead and he shivered as he forced his mind to focus on the dark angel and wondered where to continue the search.

He yawned and stretched out his arms, forgetting the cramped confines of his tiny office, and cursed loudly when he knocked his knuckles on the rough, unplastered walls. The sunlight that streamed in through the open doorway at his back was suddenly blocked out as a shadow fell across his desk. He heard a dry, shallow cough immediately behind him. Jarvin scraped back his chair and tried to rise to his feet as he found the Dean looming in the doorway. His face was set in a mask of disapproval and an outstretched hand forbade Jarvin from rising. Jarvin had a sinking feeling as he realised that this was not to be a social call.

'I have received a complaint from Mrs Sibson.' The Dean

paused to allow the severity of his words sink in and frowned as he scrutinised Jarvin's untidy appearance. He had intended that this visit be a warning, a reprimand, but now he wondered if they had not been a little foolish to accommodate Bishop Mandrake's nephew at all. Perhaps he had been released from Beckonsthorpe prematurely. He coughed again and softened his tone. 'This is an ecclesiastical establishment, Jarvin: we have certain standards and ethics to maintain otherwise how could we give a lead to our parishioners? I know you are only with us for a short while but it would be helpful to us all if you could conform to Mrs Sibson's simple house-rules and abstain from alcohol.'

The Dean paused again as he considered the possibility that Jarvin might have an addiction. He smiled icily and rubbed his hands together so enthusiastically that, for a moment, Jarvin imagined that his long, thin fingers were going to ignite. 'You never know, young man,' he concluded, generously. 'Mrs Sibson is very understanding, she might be able to help you to rehabilitate and overcome your illness.'

The words stung Jarvin to the quick. What the hell had his uncle written in that letter? No wonder that first priest had been so cold and offhand when he had met him: he must have thought he was a drunk. They must all think he was an alcoholic! It would explain why almost everybody he had come into contact with in the cathedral had treated him so distantly.

'No, no, no, I . . . I . . .' he stuttered in protest as he tried, once again, to stand up. But the Dean shook his head and pressed his hand down firmly on Jarvin's shoulder.

'Of course we'll help you, I promised your uncle, but you must help yourself first. Take more interest in your appearance, shave and get your hair cut.' He hesitated and looked down over Jarvin's shoulder to the scattered notes and the open notebook before a shadow of a smile returned. 'Well at least you have made a start on cataloguing the medieval carvings. Immersing yourself in a good, honest task is a positive step. Let me see which carvings you have started with.' He bent closer and reached down to pick up the notepad.

Jarvin's indignation at being thought an alcoholic turned to sheer panic. If the Dean read through his notes, or even glanced at his list of rudimentary headings of pagan rituals, devil-worship and witchcraft, he would have a shock. And he would certainly demand some sort of explanation if he went on to read Jarvin's description of the sacrifice, especially if he realised that the witness had been one of the squatters from the old Dean's Hall. He would think that Jarvin was stark, staring mad as well as alcoholic, and would probably have him locked up in the nearest mental institution before the lunch tables in the refectory had been laid out. Jarvin made a desperate grab at his notebook, snapping it shut a moment before the Dean's fingers touched it, then twisted around in his chair.

'They are only meaningless scribbles at the moment.' He tried to laugh off his panic as he snatched at the book and slipped it into his pocket, simultaneously gathering up the loosely scattered notes and hiding them beneath a large textbook. 'It . . . it's just a few measurements, notes and calculations. I'm trying to establish where all the carvings from that period have stood throughout the long history of the cathedral. It's amazing how they get moved about. But if you would like me to write up the results of these notes I'll . . .' His voice trailed away as he realised that the Dean's face had hardened into a scowl. He wasn't prepared to wait. At any moment Jarvin expected him to demand to see the notebook, to insist that he handed it over at once, but as he opened his mouth to speak something beneath the desk caught his attention. He looked down and Jarvin followed his gaze to a crumpled, old carrier bag that he had pushed into a corner under the desk for safe keeping.

'What have we got here?' The Dean's voice made it clear that he expected to find a bottle, Jarvin's secret supply that he had hidden under the desk. Crouching down he pulled the bag out, feeling the contour of something cylindrical. He held Jarvin's eye as he fished inside the bag, wincing as he cut himself on something sharp. A flicker of doubt crossed his eyes as he first pulled out an old, battered and rusty baked bean tin and then a bundle of yellowing newspapers that he deposited on Jarvin's desk.

'They belonged to a friend of mine,' Jarvin offered lamely. 'I brought them in with me the other morning, only I forgot to throw them away. I'm sorry, is your finger badly cut?'

'No, no, it's nothing,' the Dean snapped back, dabbing at the swelling globule of blood on his index finger with a crisp, white handkerchief. 'Things like that should be put into the rubbish bin in the first place and not be left lying around here where anybody could accidentally stumble over them.' Muttering more to himself than to Jarvin, he retreated out through the doorway, binding the handkerchief around the spreading stain of blood on his fingertip.

Expelling a sigh of relief Jarvin got up from the chair and rubbed away the cold beads of sweat that had formed on his forehead. He carefully put the tin and the newspapers back into the carrier bag and this time pushed it even further out of sight beneath his desk. He had no intention of throwing them away, since they were the only pieces of evidence they had to prove that Mary had ever been in the porch the night she was murdered. He had to get out of the cramped office for a while, it felt as though the walls were closing in on him and he needed to breathe some fresh air and walk about in the sunshine. Anyway, he was afraid that the Dean might come storming back in. He paused in the doorway, checking that he hadn't left anything incriminating behind him and then he laughed. If they really did think he was an alcoholic they probably wouldn't pay much attention to what he did anyway. As long as he kept busy and appeared to be sober they would leave him alone. But he had better gather together some ordinary research notes just in case the Dean, or anyone else, came snooping around: it would save a lot of unwanted questions.

It was a beautiful morning and there was one other carved angel he wanted to take a look at. It stood in the centre of the graves and he needed to examine it closely before being certain that all his investigations had drawn a complete blank. He didn't really believe that there was any connection but Joni's vanishing trick when she had collided with the figure had made him curious. She had called the statue 'magical' and the word had stuck in his mind: there had to be a link, no matter how tenuous. He slowed down as he crossed the neatly mown lawns and shaded his eyes from the glare of the sun as he looked up at the white stone angel. The wind and rain had leprously scoured out the features of the stone figure as it stood alone upon its plinth of grey-veined marble. It was a forlorn, solitary figure robed in pleats of folded stone and yet there was immense power in it. Its wings were outstretched, every feather tensed as if they were ready to lift the angel and carry it to soar in the air. There was a deep sense of sadness in its blind featureless face and its head was turned towards the cathedral, slightly tilted to one side as though it were listening for some silent prayer; at the same time, its hands were lifted high and it looked as though it were warding off some imaginary foe.

Jarvin circled the figure twice to examine it from every angle before drawing close enough to reach out and touch the angel. He scanned the names and dates that had been chiselled onto every face of the plinth. The oldest belonged to a Thomas Joseph, cloth merchant of Bishopsgate, who had died in 1509, aged sixty-eight years. Below that first inscription death marched in an expanding ribbon of capitals claiming his wife, his sons and his daughters, and then, with the passing years, their children and their children's children until the last three members of the Joseph's ancient line who died together in 1942 beneath the howling shriek of the German bombs. 10th June 1942 was the last mark that the stonemason's chisel had made in the plinth.

Jarvin straightened his back and followed Joseph's line back to its founder and found himself wondering what kind of man he was when he noticed that below his name, almost completely obliterated by the spongy growths of lichen that clung to the stone, there was an inscription. Taking out his pocket knife he picked at the moss, easing it away from the stone, and by rubbing gently with his fingertips he uncovered the words: 'I have raised thee, fallen angel, out of the ruins to stand once more in glory so that you may herald my procession into Heaven. 1480.'

Jarvin read the inscription twice and then copied it and the date, 1480, and then the date when Joseph died, 1509, into his notebook. There were a couple of things about the monument that struck him as odd. Why had Thomas Joseph built his tomb almost thirty years before he died? It might have belonged to an earlier member of his family but the names had been erased from the stone, but in that case they should be in the cathedral records. And why had Joseph called the statue a 'fallen angel'? That must have caused a considerable stir in the religious climate of the fifteenth century. The statue was of a different type of stone from the plinth and, by the look of it, far older, perhaps twelfth century. Jarvin shrugged: it was a riddle he would probably never unravel. He pushed the notebook back into his pocket. It was time he reached up to touch the angel to see if he could experience the sensations that Joni had tried to describe to him.

To his surprise the crumbling surface of the statue felt as smooth as silk. He explored the lower folds of its robes where they draped over the plinth and traced the outline of its legs from knee to ankle where they abruptly vanished into a solid lump of mortar. Then he withdrew his hand and looked around. The colours of the world hadn't changed, he hadn't heard anything strange above the distant sounds of the city, or seen any visions of his yesterdays. Even the squabbling of the blackbirds in the yew trees close by had gone on unaltered. But the sensation of touching the angel did linger on his fingertips: they tingled and felt cold. He rubbed his hands together and that stopped the weird sensation. Looking down at his hands he saw traces of fine stonedust on his fingertips which was exactly what he would have expected after touching a crumbling piece of stone.

'That's very odd,' he muttered to himself, rubbing his hand firmly along one of the folds in the angel's robes; then almost cried out as he snatched his hand away and stared down at the ugly red graze on his skin which the rough surface of the stone had caused. Stepping back and nursing his grazed hand he looked up in surprise at the statue. Nothing around the cathedral was ever exactly what it was supposed to be. He shouted out in frustration: 'What's happening around here? I never seem to get any closer to finding out what it's all about. I don't even know where to start looking!'

Then he fell silent and looked quickly behind him, with a strong feeling that he was being watched. He blushed scarlet, but there was no one there. The only onlookers were the gargoyles that crowded the gutter-spouts on the cathedral roof.

'I'm not losing my mind,' he muttered defiantly, glaring down at his watch and seeing that it was almost midday.

He began to retrace his footsteps towards the refectory but as he drew closer he hesitated. Suddenly he couldn't face sitting in there, surrounded by the pious, after what the Dean had said to him earlier. He was close to the South Porch but hurried past it and entered the cathedral by the West Door instead.

The interior of the cathedral felt cool after the heat of the sun outside and the vast building seemed to be filled with a whispering, eerie silence that brought Jarvin to a halt. It wasn't the sounds of the small groups of visitors, the monotonous chant of their guides or the scrape of solitary footsteps as figures slowly moved through the bright shafts of sunlight that were streaming down into the nave. Those everyday sounds and the soft strains of music coming from the organ loft were only a background noise. It was the sensation that he had caught a whisper of the past that had stopped him. There was a timeless echo, perhaps all that remained of the endeavour and the effort that it had taken to raise the great monument of stone. He frowned. Perhaps touching the statue of the white angel had affected him after all – perhaps it had triggered his senses so that he could now hear ancient sounds . . . Images from the walls of the building filled his mind.

Sunlight and the shadows from a forest of wooden scaffold poles touched his face, the endless 'tap tap tap' of masons' chisels filled his ears and his mouth seemed to be dry and full of stonedust but before the images had faded the shadow of a winged figure slid silently across his vision. He blinked, the images dissolved into one another and fell back into the whispering silence, but the memory of that winged shape lingered, causing a shiver of fear to touch his spine. Jarvin frowned and drank in the silent atmosphere as he let his gaze slowly travel along the nave through the patterns of light and shadow that lay across the pews. Brick by brick his eyes climbed the soaring columns and now he saw it all very differently. There was a spectre of evil hiding there, that was the message in the images, he was sure of it. Joni had witnessed some form of ritual evil that dwelt within the fabric of the building, something that was as old as time itself, something so devious, so elusive, that it was almost invisible. But where was he to start? The first thing he had done was to examine the transept and the porch and he had drawn a blank. He still wasn't even sure what he was looking for, apart from the remains of the old woman's body.

The incarnadine angel knelt there, mocking him with its sinister silence as he walked slowly along the North Aisle avoiding the groups of visitors and turned into the central area beneath the tower. It seemed the most logical place for him to start, the very heart of the cathedral. Sections of the area were roped off and tiers of scaffolding had been erected along the inner walls. It reached high up, almost to the roof of the lantern of the tower. A gang of workmen dressed in white overalls were climbing down and gathering near the bronze lectern to stow their tools in preparation for their lunch break. Jarvin was curious and wondered what they were doing when he felt a slight tremor in the floor beneath his feet. Panic bells rang inside his head as dark memories of the collapsing temple floor flooded his mind, but he fought the terror down and watched the workmen, expecting them to scatter and run for safety. But they seemed unperturbed, as if they hadn't noticed the tremor, and they continued to stow away their tools in a leisurely fashion, laughing and talking quietly amongst themselves.

He had to warn them to get out before it was too late!

Ducking underneath the rope he ran toward them, waving his arms, gesticulating wildly as he shouted, 'Get out of here! This floor could collapse at any moment!'

Jarvin's shouts made the foreman glance around anxiously.

'Get your men out of here. Didn't you feel that tremor?' Jarvin shouted breathlessly, clutching at the foreman's arm. 'If this floor collapses it will bring the whole tower and the spire crashing down on top of you!'

'Now just a minute,' the foreman answered crossly, pulling away from Jarvin's grip while taking a moment to read the official badge pinned to his lapel. He couldn't understand what all the commotion was about but he smiled as he read Jarvin's name: he had heard the gossip in the refectory about this newly-appointed archaeologist.

'The floor! Didn't you feel the tremor?' Jarvin urged.

The foreman just laughed. 'Well, yes, of course we did, but after you've worked here for a while you'll get used to it and hardly take any notice of them.'

He was about to turn away when he saw the panic in Jarvin's eyes. 'Look, mate, there's nothing wrong with the floor or the tower for that matter. We're standing on a solid foundation of rocks and rubble and the tower is as safe as the Rock of Gibraltar. But you don't have to believe me: go on, take a look at the last engineer's report up in the Dean's office – it said that the tower was structurally sound and it should stand for at least another six hundred years.'

'But the tremors? What causes the tremors?' Jarvin frowned.

The foreman shrugged. 'Nobody really seems to know. The borough engineers, the Clerk of Works, they'll all give you a different answer. It's a natural or an unnatural phenomenon, a geological fault or something, beneath the cathedral. The experts all have at least a dozen theories but I've always thought it has something to do with the underground spring, or whatever it is that continually fills the Font of Tears over there near the pulpit. The odd thing is, you can watch the droplets form on the rim of the font and then trickle down into it, but it never overflows. They say the water is blessed, that it's a miracle, but I say it's a real mystery. It doesn't matter whether it's holy water or not nobody's ever been able to explain why it happens.'

'Come on, George, before they shut the refectory. You've already told him this place is as safe as houses, leave it at that,' one of the workmen muttered irritably.

'Yeah, hurry up, guvnor, or we'll have to eat our sandwiches outside!' another called out impatiently as the group of workmen began to move across the tower, ducking under the rope one by one. The foreman nodded to Jarvin and followed them.

'But what are you doing up there if you're not checking the safety of the tower?' he called after them.

The foreman paused, his hand on the rope, and pointed up to the stained-glass windows at the top of the lantern. 'We've just finished replacing the glass that was broken in that storm the other night. We'll be dismantling and removing our scaffolding this afternoon then we'll clean up the floor, so be careful where you tread, there's a lot of fragments of glass lying about.'

The foreman ducked under the rope and, with a wave of his hand, hurried after the others, leaving Jarvin standing alone beside the lectern. He felt his eyes drawn across into the South Transept, where he picked out the dark shape of the angel crouching, wrapped in silence upon its plinth. The feathery spread of its wings cast long, distorted shadows across the floor. Staring at the statue was beginning to mesmerise him and awaken the phantoms that lay hidden beneath the blanket of his consciousness. The floor trembled slightly under his feet and the smell of the tomb began to fill his nostrils.

'No!' he hissed, balling his hands into fists and clenching them until his nails cut painfully into the palms. 'The answers are here in the fabric of the building. I've got to start looking for them. I've got to stop my imagination running away with me.'

He tore his gaze away from the angel and stumbled dizzily across the tower toward the font. Broken pieces of glass crunched beneath his shoes, sparkling as brightly as new-cut diamonds in the sunlight. He reached the font, grasping the smooth, polished outer lip of stone with both hands, stared at his reflection in the crystal clear water. The claustrophobia was tightening its grip again, sending flashes of panic through him. Suddenly the floor trembled, his ears began to buzz with noise and minute ripples spread across the surface of the water breaking up his reflection and spreading a thousand shimmering particles of light dancing across his face. His throat felt as though it were filling with choking dust, he couldn't breathe and his field of vision was shrinking into a black tunnel of terror. Without knowing what he was doing he plunged his hands into the water, sending icy droplets across the floor as he scooped up a brimming handful and drank deeply. He gasped at the shock of the coldness and the horror of what he had done. His eyes were tightly shut and he shivered violently as the water ran over his chin and down his neck.

After a moment he blinked and opened his eyes. The phantoms had vanished, the claustrophobia had shrunk back and for a second he stared foolishly down at the water dripping off his hands and the mess he had made on the floor. Then he glanced round quickly to see if anyone had been watching the near-blasphemy: he could only begin to imagine the Dean's wrath if he was caught drinking the holy water. Luckily, the area beyond the ropes was empty. Looking down at the font he watched as the tears from around the rim trickled down, refilling the water he had spilled. The floor trembled again, more violently than before, and he gripped the stone and instinctively looked up into the lantern of the tower. He could have sworn that the walls shimmered and fine puffs of stonedust billowed out in the cracks between the massive blocks of stone.

Jarvin took a step back and rubbed his hand thoughtfully across his wet forehead, pushing the hair back out of his eyes. If he was right and the vibrations in the tower *were* destroying the mortar between the blocks of stone, loosening the joints, eventually a savage storm would bring the whole lot crashing down, but how could he get anybody to take any notice of him. He moved further back, splinters of glass ground beneath his shoes. Suddenly he laughed. Of course, he could do the simplest test in the world and nobody need ever know until he had the result! Bending down he quickly searched across the floor beneath the scaffolding and gathered up ten pieces of glass, all about two inches long. Some were more than an inch wide but some were barely more than splinters. All he needed now was a strong, quick-drying cement. He crossed to the workmen's tool boxes and luck was with him: two of them were unlocked. Throwing back the lids he rifled through their tools, delving amongst the strips of lead, dummy hammers, pliers, coils of soft solder, knives and chisels. At last he found what he was after amidst bottles of turpentine, rags and stopping fluid – a battered, grey gunmetal tin labelled 'jointing cement'. Prising open the lid, he pushed his finger into the soft, white, pliable substance. Exactly what he was looking for. He slipped the tin into his pocket and wrapped the pieces of glass in a strip of rag.

Carefully and slowly, Jarvin scaled the nearest ladder. Moving along the topmost scaffold board he chose ten different places and applied a liberal blob of the cement to each end of each piece of glass before firmly pressing them into place across the joints where the huge blocks of stone met. He glanced at his watch after positioning the last one and then scrambled down the ladder. It had taken him almost forty minutes to position the ten tell-tales. All he had to do now was to hope that the cement dried quickly enough and held the pieces of glass in place. If the tower was moving the tell- tales would break and then he would have his proof. He could hear the workmen returning along the South Aisle, so he stuffed the rag into his pocket on top of the tin of cement and ducked beneath the rope before hurrying away along the North Aisle towards the West Door. At last he had done something positive, even if it didn't have anything to do with the dark angel and its ritual sacrifices.

Jarvin needed somewhere to sit down quietly and think. He had to try to rationalise the abstractions of absurdity that were filling his head. Stone statues could not perform ritual sacrifices, nor could they change their shape or do vanishing tricks. The scientist inside him was beginning to cast a shadow of doubt over what Joni had said that she'd seen, the images of the winged creatures and the whispers of history that he had experienced. He needed some hard evidence: visions and flashes of inspiration were not enough to enable him to get to the bottom of this affair. Hunches, blind luck and gut feelings often played a part in any archaeological investigation but he was all too well aware that painstaking research following up every clue was the real, the professional, method of laying bare the bones of what was going on in the cathedral, if anything was. But what were the elusive clues? What had he missed?

Pausing in the shadows beneath the Erpingham Gate he stepped aside to allow a noisy group of foreign visitors past. He was undecided about where to spend the afternoon: it was already after two-thirty and he knew that the cafes and restaurants close to the cathedral would be closing. He fiddled absently with the front door key to his lodgings and listened to it jangling against the loose change in his pocket. The West Gatehouse was only a footstep away and the solitude of his eyrie in the attic the perfect place, but after a moment's thought he shook his head. He didn't want to see Mrs Sibson so soon after her complaint to the Dean. He couldn't be sure that he would be able to control his anger.

'Rules of the house!' he muttered thickly. 'You ought to see me when I've really had a skinful.' Briefly, he toyed with the idea of trying to slip into the house unnoticed and then creep up to his room but his landlady had the hunting instincts and the hearing of a wolf. She would know the moment he inserted his key into the lock.

He hadn't spent much time familiarising himself with the pubs in the city since his arrival: the only one he had been into was the 'Three Cranes', but then he remembered that Martyn Burr had said something about it being the most excellent of hostelries because it stayed open throughout the afternoons during the summer months and that its sandwiches were a legend, a monumental feast. Jarvin ducked through the low doorway at the rear of the 'Cranes' and surveyed what the landlord had grandly called the 'beer garden'. To call it a garden at all was stretching the truth rather thin: it was a bare dusty oblong of paving slabs with lush ranks of yellow-headed chickweed growing through the cracks. Four rickety wooden tables and benches that had seen better days stood beneath the ragged shadows of a handful of hawthorn trees and cordwoods that had run to seed and bolted for the light. The narrow garden lay in almost perpetual shadow as snugly as a stranded sardine between the high brick walls of the two adjoining buildings. A broken wattle fence bordered the far end and barely masked the piles of beer crates and overflowing rubbish bins that had been left there. Beyond the fence Jarvin could see a warren of neglected alleyways and the bare, featureless backs of an anonymous row of terraced houses.

It might not have been paradise, but it was quiet and deserted, a perfect place to mull over the muddle inside his head. Jarvin chose a table beneath the largest of the trees to sit down, swallowed a long, refreshing draught from his glass and hungrily attacked the thick, doorstep cheese sandwich that he had bought from the bar before he pushed the plate away and took out his notebook to leaf through it.

He read slowly through his notes trying to glean some sense from them. Instinct was nagging at the edges of his consciousness, looking for the elusive clues that must have been in there somewhere. They must be right in front of him, staring up out of the open pages, only he wasn't seeing or translating them into language he could understand. It didn't seem to matter how many times he went over what had happened in the porch he couldn't find anything to prove it had ever really happened at all. He couldn't be absolutely certain that Joni hadn't fantasised it all in some complicated dreamscape. So far there wasn't a single shred of evidence to substantiate the cold-blooded murder that she said she had witnessed. The only positive action that he could think of was to organise a search for the old vagrant: if the police or the social workers found her alive then it would prove that Joni had dreamt or hallucinated the whole thing. But he couldn't think of a plausible reason why the police should instigate a search; and if he told them about the sacrifice, they'd lock him up forever. Anyway finding old Mary alive wouldn't explain away the feeling of dread that he had experienced near the statue of the dark angel, the slight distortion of its wings and the hundred and one other disquieting phenomena that he had encountered since arriving at the cathedral, unless the trauma from his accident had set his imagination on fire.

He frowned and dropped his notebook onto the table and pushed it away. Whatever it was that haunted the cathedral had burrowed its way beneath his skin and become a painful, persistent itch that would drive him mad before he scratched himself to death. He had to get to the bottom of it. What he needed was to get the few pieces of the puzzle that he did have into perspective, physically to lay out the pieces of the jigsaw. He knew from previous work that he had done on hieroglyphic writing in the tomb of Mereruka that if he set out all the pieces of information that he had he would be able to look at the whole and this might reveal a shape to the puzzle and show him where the missing parts fitted in the overall picture. Thoughtfully, he picked up his notebook. Perhaps if he made a crude storyboard and laid it all out on the table.

He tore out three empty pages from the back of the book and folded them into four equal squares before carefully tearing them apart. Then he gathered them into a pile of twelve and, finding his pen, wrote upon one of them THE SACRIFICE in large, bold capital letters and put it on the left-hand side of the table. Around it he positioned another four squares of paper, one with Joni's name on it, one for Mary, the dark angel in larger letters and one for the demons. On another he wrote, again in large capitals, THE CATHEDRAL and surrounded it with four blank squares of

153

paper. After a moment's reflection he wrote out another one for the white angel and put a question mark beside it before laying it separately upon the table to the right. Working directly from his notes he transcribed every detail that appeared to have any relevance, carefully writing them under a particular heading. Thus for 'Mary' it read, 'old vagrant, sometimes slept in South Porch. Arrived (date and time as shown in verger's log). Only surviving possessions, baked bean can and newspapers, in plastic carrier bag beneath desk. Believed to have been murdered some time after midnight.'

When Jarvin had finished he sat back, took a long swallow from his glass and scratched contemplatively at the stubble on his chin as he surveyed the storyboard. Two things were immediately apparent. First, he had gathered a lot more information on the dark angel than he had imagined, that piece of paper was so crammed full of dates that it would need extra space if he needed to add anything else. There were a couple of other very curious things. People had been disappearing from the cathedral for hundreds of years, just vanishing without collecting their clothes or wages, leaving their possessions where they slept and there wasn't a single plausible explanation. The other puzzling thing was that the building seemed to have suffered from an extraordinary number of disasters during its long history. After a moment's cross-reference it appeared that the dark angel must have been very mobile to have been miraculously salvaged from the centre of each one of them. The picture was already expanding. He couldn't see what, if any, connection there was between the disappearances and the dark angel or if it was the only medieval sculpture to survive everything. He made a note to tell himself to investigate the Prior's accounts, to see if they threw any light on what had happened to the vanishing masons and clerics, and also he intended to take another look at the structures of the building more thoroughly, especially the transepts and the central tower area. He had to see if there were any records of why the statue of the angel had been moved and how recently it had happened before each disaster. As an afterthought he made a note to see if the trembling in the floor followed a pattern or a cycle of any kind and if it affected the Font of Tears.

A shout of raucous laughter from the doorway behind him made him turn his head and look across his shoulder. 'Jarvin, my dear boy. How excellent it is to see you again. Mine host informed me that you were out here sampling the delights of his Garden of Eden!'

Jarvin felt a smile spread across his face as he recognised Martyn Burr emerging through the darkened doorway armed with two brimming pints of beer, his Gladstone bag grasped precariously beneath one arm. From the clues of the stethoscope and other instruments that bulged and sagged in the pockets of his old tweed jacket and the leather bag beneath his arm Jarvin realised that Martyn must have been on a house-call somewhere close by.

'No, no, don't get up!' Martyn laughed as he threaded his way to where Jarvin sat. 'Refreshments!' He smiled as he deposited the two glasses safely onto the table. 'You needn't worry that I may be after canvassing you for custom, dear boy: I've been across to a house close by, tinkering with a troublesome pneumonia.' He waved a vague, dismissive hand towards an anonymous row of terraced houses beyond the broken wattle fence.

Martyn tossed his medical bag onto one of the seats and withdrew a large, spotted handkerchief from his trouser pocket and mopped his forehead. 'Damned hot, isn't it, even here out of the sun. Hello, what have we got here, a sacrifice?'

He bent forward to read the rest of what Jarvin had written on the small squares of paper. 'I thought you were here to dig up a load of old bones. I didn't realise you were so upset at being sent here you are planning to sacrifice the Bishop to the Gods of the Nile!' At this he leaned back and burst out laughing.

'Oh no, it's not like that, it's nothing at all, just a silly game,' Jarvin retorted quickly as he tried to gather up the scattered pieces of paper before Martyn could read too much. But he wasn't quick enough to hide the shadow of fear that clouded his eyes or to stop the doctor from picking up the one he had written out for Mary.

Martyn read slowly, the laughter dying from his face. He looked up and held Jarvin's gaze and his voice was little more than a whisper when he said, 'Murder isn't a game, Jarvin, it's a deadly serious business. What do you know about old Mary? Why did you write down her name? You couldn't have known anything about her, you haven't been here for a week yet.'

Jarvin shrugged and pulled his arm away before replying defensively, 'She was just an old woman. Mary's a common name, anyway what does it matter to you whose name I write down for a victim? I told you it's only a game.'

Martyn mopped at the stray beads of perspiration on his forehead and read through the information again. 'Did the baked bean tin still have any label wrapped around it?'

Jarvin nodded. 'Well, part of it was still stuck to the can, but why does that matter?'

'The label was Asda's own brand; the newspapers were all the *Guardian* and there was a large "B" scrawled in pencil on the top of each front page.'

'How do you know that?' Any pretence of it still being a game had been forgotten.

'Because I always give her my old newspapers and a couple of tins of food. Mary's my patient – I've been treating her for diabetes. She comes to the back door of my house before I open surgery. If you check the verger's records you'll find her visits to the cathedral coincide with her cycle of treatment. She may have the outward appearance of being irrational and aggressive but she has never missed collecting her injections – she knows her life depends upon them. She was due six days ago!'

Jarvin felt his spine tingle and the colour bleach out of his cheeks. He had gradually been coming around to the idea that the old woman might have left the porch while Joni slept but now he realised that she would have been unlikely to have left without her medicine. His head spun. Joni might not have hallucinated the murder.

'Could . . . could the old woman just have forgotten, just wandered off? Couldn't she just be at one of her other haunts?' Jarvin stammered. He had to know, to be sure.

Martyn shook his head. 'No, it's very unlikely that she would have lasted out in the open for more than a day or two without her insulin. Living rough and existing on an erratic diet would have compounded the body's breakdown. She would probably have fallen into a coma quite quickly. I alerted the police when she failed to collect her medication three days ago but so far they haven't been able to find her. Nobody's seen her in any of her usual haunts and I've checked with all the hospitals in the areas that she frequents. There's nothing – she's just vanished from the face of the earth, so perhaps you had better enlighten me about your little game. Who are Joni and the dark angel?' Martyn picked up the two pieces of paper with those headings and quickly glanced at them.

Jarvin didn't make any attempt to try to stop him. A part of him wanted, no desperately needed, to share the burden of what he had unwittingly stumbled into, but still, through fear of ridicule, he threw up his hands and cried out, 'You're never going to believe a word of all this. It's so incredibly bizarre, so ridiculous, that you're going to think I've gone barking mad, that they should never have let me out of Beckonsthorpe!'

Martyn lifted his eyes from the two small squares of paper and there wasn't a flicker of humour in them. 'Murder is horrifying and grotesque and often the ultimate act of a madness that possesses the murderer's soul, not that of the unfortunate witness. I don't think you're mad, Jarvin, but what you have written down here is, I agree, difficult to believe.'

'There! I told you that you'd think I'd gone mad!'

Martyn shook his head and put his hand on Jarvin's arm to quieten him. 'No, I didn't say that, only that it's . . .' he paused and smiled. 'Now why don't you start at the beginning and tell me everything that has happened and then I'll be able to make a proper assessment. Perhaps I'll even be able to throw some light on it.'

There was something about Martyn that made Jarvin want to confide in him, he felt he could trust him to be told everything. He took a deep breath and ploughed straight into it, pointing to each of the small squares of paper and the notes in his pad. 'I don't think Mary is the first person to vanish without trace in the vicinity of the cathedral . . .' He left nothing out. 'Well, do you believe me now?' he asked after he had finished relating the story, then, in a rush, he blurted out his inner thoughts. 'Or has that accident driven me completely insane? Has it distorted my imagination so much that I feel as if I'm being sucked further and further into a world of black fantasy? I can't sleep any more because I imagine I'm hearing the creatures scrabbling all over the roof of my lodgings at night. I'll swear they're trying to move the slates and they're scratching at the glass to try to get in. I have the feeling I'm being watched whenever I'm in the cathedral, that there are eyes everywhere following me. Am I losing my grip on reality, Martyn, or did that nightmare sacrifice really happen in the porch? You see I'm so confused, so lost for answers . . .'

'Wait! Hold on, not so fast! Give me a moment to try and grasp what you're saying. I can't even begin to understand: the implications are horrendous if what you say is true. It's almost too fantastic to believe and I wouldn't have believed you but for Mary's disappearance and you knowing her name, it's too much of a coincidence, and . . .' Martyn frowned and put his finger on the piece of paper labelled *The Dark Angel*. 'This has brought old memories to the surface. Mary talked about that statue once or twice, or one very like it – she used to tell me that she saw some ghosts or the shadow of a dark angel in the moonlight in the cathedral grounds. I remember she said that she had once seen it down near the banks of the River Wensum when she had been sleeping in some bus shelter or doorway in Fishergate. I didn't take that much notice of her ramblings – I just let her talk – she was always insisting that she had seen fairies: her head was full of weird stories – she even thought the fish in the river talked to her, and her tales got even wilder if she ever managed to get hold of a drink. So you see I never took her angel stories any more seriously than all the rest, but it used to frighten her. I remember quite distinctly how once she told me how she had hidden behind another statue and watched the dark angel and a swarm of demons go by.'

Martyn fell silent and shifted in his seat, the movement making the instruments crammed into his pockets rattle against one another noisily.

'But don't you see, I can't prove anything I've just told

you?' Jarvin's voice was tight and agitated with frustration. 'There's nothing to say the sacrifice ever happened, no blood, no body, no physical evidence at all, nothing to support what Joni told me. I can't go to the police – they'll have me locked away in some asylum within the hour, that's why I laid out this crude storyboard. The most frustrating thing is I can't just shrug my shoulders and walk away, I must find another angle. There must be something I've missed.'

They both looked down at the table, wrapped silently in their own thoughts.

'Of course!' Jarvin exclaimed suddenly. 'The story is so absurd nobody is going to believe me, they didn't listen to Mary's ramblings or anybody else who might have seen the angel or witnessed the ritual. Think of it, Martyn: the fear of being burned for witchcraft, stoned or driven out, or being excommunicated for heresy would have put a stop on your tongue at any time over the last thousand years. Imagine what the Dean's reaction would be now, and we live in a liberal age. Of course there wouldn't be any records in the archives. I've been looking in completely the wrong place. I've been so stupid!'

Martyn Burr stared at him in bewilderment.

'Well it's obvious to me now. Mary was a vagrant, she lived rough, I don't know if she was literate but it probably never occurred to her to write down what she had seen, but she did pass the information on in story form, at least to you. Look, talking about Mary and her sudden disappearance has made me think of something else. I'll bet if anybody ever did witness the ritual or see the angel moving about they would have passed the story on somehow: it's too weird, too fantastic a tale to resist, but they would have to be careful, the threat of accusations of heresy or witchcraft would have always been at their elbow.' Jarvin paused and took a sip from his glass. 'You see, Mary's the link, or rather her being in the cathedral grounds at all sorts of odd hours. She would have been more likely to see the angel than anybody else wouldn't she? Everybody else would have been in bed. Well, think back two, three hundred years or earlier, and look at that piece of paper that I wrote out for the cathedral. People have been continually disappearing. I was wondering why there wasn't more written in the archives, proper investigations, but it's easy for us to forget that the place was full, crowded out with workmen coming and going all the time, moving from job to job.'

Martyn nodded silently, although he still hadn't caught onto Jarvin's drift.

'Well, the disappearances might be important, even connected to the angel, I don't know, but it tells us that the building must have had an almost continuous occupation of masons, carpenters, joiners. There must have been hundreds of ordinary craftsmen, most of them illiterate apart from the clergy, and they must have all lived and worked inside the cathedral. I'll bet if they saw the angel then they recorded it secretly in their work.'

'You mean in the stonework, the gargoyles, the stained-glass windows?' Martyn exclaimed suddenly picking up the thread that Jarvin was unravelling.

Jarvin nodded and drained the remainder of his first glass, smacking his lips triumphantly together in a broad, wet, foamy grin.

'Yes, you're right! Those workers were certainly in the right place, or as in poor Mary's case the wrong place, to have accidentally witnessed or become the victim of the sacrifice,' Martyn murmured before sweeping his gaze across Jarvin's notes again. 'But there's a lot about this gruesome business that doesn't make any sense. Where are the bodies for instance? If we assume that this sacrificial murder has been going on, even if only intermittently, for hundreds of years, then a lot of flesh and bones would have to be disposed of, and blood sacrifices would be pretty gory. Come to think of it, the porch must have looked like an abattoir after that angel had smashed open Mary's sternum and torn out her heart. The fountain of blood would have hit the ceiling and sprayed the walls. It would have been everywhere.'

'No, there wasn't anything there except the old baked bean tin and those newspapers, nothing at all. If Joni hadn't seen it you wouldn't have thought anything had happened. That's the weirdest thing about this, the lack of any evidence. The last thing that Joni remembered before she passed out was seeing the demons devouring Mary's body as they dragged it into the transept, but there wasn't a trace of blood anywhere on the stone floor either. And no sign of it having been scrubbed,' Jarvin said, gathering his notes together.

'I think I'll take a look myself.' Martyn frowned. 'But I still can't understand how a gruesome sacrificial ritual like this could have gone on for so long right underneath the clergy's noses without anyone finding out about it. Surely people working in the cathedral would have reported it when their friends or members of their families went missing. You can't just ignore something like that. There must be records.'

'Yes, that's something else I'm following up. I'm going to the archives this afternoon, but I won't be surprised if I draw a blank. It would have been a lot easier to have vanished here in medieval England than it would be today. The constant stream of pilgrims visiting the cathedral and the itinerant workmen would have supplied an endless source of victims. Communications were at their most rudimentary and each community was isolated from its neighbours. If a traveller disappeared the people would have probably just assumed that he had packed up his possessions and moved on. Even if they did think the circumstances of the disappearance were suspicious they didn't have our sophisticated means of detection. Oh, and don't forget, medieval literature is full of visions and miracles, of angels and demons all fighting it out to possess your soul. Heaven and Hell were much more a real part of their everyday lives than they are in ours, that's why I found it so strange that the archives were so empty of such occurrences. Unless . . .' Jarvin paused, suddenly thoughtful. 'Unless the angel somehow senses when the ritual has been observed and then murders the witness or witnesses, removing all trace of what they have seen. Perhaps it had been stalking Mary, waiting for her next visit. And now it will go after Joni if it sensed her presence in the porch.'

'Murderers are usually very cunning creatures,' Martyn observed with a shiver as he buried his lips in the thin rim of froth that still covered the top of his glass and drank slowly.

'Those noises I keep hearing at night, do you think they're the demons scrambling over the roof looking for her? Jesus Christ, Martyn, if that's what's happening then we've got to find a way to stop it before it's too late!' Jarvin cried, leaping to his feet. 'I'll make a start right now – my camera's at my digs and I've got a couple of unused rolls of film. I'll get them on my way back and then I'll start photographing everything inside that cathedral, all the carvings – everything!'

'Wait!' Martyn called out, clutching at Jarvin's untouched glass and steadying it as the table rocked. 'It's almost six o'clock. You've been sitting here all afternoon – the cathedral closed an hour ago. I don't think it would be sensible to go wandering around in there on your own even if you could get in. It will be getting dark in a couple of hours.'

Jarvin looked around at the lengthening shadows across the garden and noticed that two other couples had come out and were sitting at a table near the door. He slowly resumed his seat and tossed his notebook and the scraps of paper back onto the table. 'No, perhaps you're right, I'll . . .' He caught a movement in the doorway and spun around. 'Joni!' he called out recognising the hesitant figure who was about to retreat back inside. 'Joni, over here! I've got someone with me I'd like you to meet.'

Joni moved reluctantly across the garden, threading her way in between the tables.

'Joni, this is Martyn, Martyn Burr, he's . . .'

'What the fucking hell have you been telling him?' Her thin face was wild, her eyes blazing with fury as she caught sight of the open notebook on the table. 'I thought I could trust you, Jarvin, but you're no better than the rest!' Her mouth trembled with anger and her fists clenched as she turned and began to run towards the door.

Martyn called after her, stopping her before she had taken three paces from them. 'Joan Fuller, or Joni Frost, it doesn't matter what you call yourself – you can't very well run away from this.'

She turned back and stared at him. 'You don't remember me do you?' Martyn asked her quietly.

Joni shook her head.

'A friend of yours from that squat in the old Dean's Hall brought you into my surgery a couple of weeks after Christmas. You had a raging fever and a chest infection and I prescribed a course of antibiotics for you. I told your friend to bring you back but . . .'

'Yes, yes, I remember now, vaguely.' The anger left her

164

face, softening it, and a haunted, weary tiredness took its place as she sat down.

'Jarvin's been telling me about poor Mary and what you saw. It must have been a terrible shock seeing that.'

'I don't know what you're talking about!' Joni snapped back defensively. She averted her eyes, hugging and folding her arms tightly across her chest. 'It was just a vivid nightmare – I dreamed an old woman was there. For all I know Mary was miles away, asleep in an old barn. Anyway, what's it got to do with you? Why are you so interested?'

'Martyn happened to see my notebook,' Jarvin explained. 'Anyway, he's my friend: I didn't think it would do any harm telling him about it. Mary was his patient – he was expecting her to turn up at his surgery early that morning and when she didn't show up he asked the police to start looking for her. I really didn't think you'd mind him knowing.' Bewildered by her reaction, Jarvin tried desperately to placate her.

'Police?' Joni muttered under her breath. Before she could disguise it Martyn saw a shadow of panic momentarily darken her eyes. It made him wonder what she was really trying to hide.

'I told you it was all a bad dream, a nightmare, and I really don't want to think about it any more.'

'But . . . but you can't deny that something happened. You were terrified when I found you – it's all in my book, I wrote it down.' By now Jarvin's voice had risen in agitation and the drinkers at the other table began to be disturbed by his rising voice and turned round to listen as he fumbled to pick up his notebook.

'Dreams, hallucinations, they can sometimes be so real. I'm sorry, Joni, I really didn't intend to pry.' Martyn apologised, laughing in an attempt to diffuse the tension. He looked at his watch and quickly rose to his feet. 'My God,

I should have opened the surgery ten minutes ago. I must fly! I'll be in here tomorrow night.' He smiled at Jarvin as he swallowed the dregs of his beer, gathered up his bag, said goodbye to Joni and headed towards the door.

Joni didn't bother to acknowledge his departing gesture and turned to hiss at Jarvin the minute the doctor's back was turned, and long before he was out of earshot. 'Have you gone raving mad? How much did you tell him? Don't you realise we'll have the police following me, as if I don't have enough problems?'

Martyn frowned. Obviously there was more to this than he had first imagined.

'What's the matter? Has something happened? You seem so frantic tonight.' Jarvin asked in a loud whisper.

Joni shuddered and drew closer to him. 'Something got into the squat last night. I don't know what it was but it bit Jules on the face – it almost tore his cheek off – and it attacked some new girl, I don't know her name. Anyway everybody's moving out, splitting up, they think it's over-run with a plague of . . .'

The door to the beer garden burst open and a noisy, laughing crowd emerged. One of them recognised Martyn and shouted out his name, drowning out the last part of what Joni was saying. As he reached the door he glanced back to where he had been sitting. Joni was gesticulating angrily and seemed to be on the verge of tears, while Jarvin looked lost, bewildered, his notebook clutched tightly in his right hand.

'Damn!' Martyn muttered to himself: he would have liked to eavesdrop longer and find out exactly what it was that was making her so angry.

Martyn drove his big car erratically along St Andrews, straddling the centre line. He had to swerve and stamp hard on the brake to avoid a collision as he reached the junction with Princes Street and he grinned apologetically, waving his hand, at the car he had so narrowly missed. He turned slowly down into Elm Hill and felt the vibration of the cobbles slightly trembling the steering wheel of his old Silver Shadow but his mind shut out the rumbling of the tyres and the narrowness of the lane. There was obviously a lot more to this angel story than Jarvin had told him. Joni, Joan, or whoever she was, had certainly over-reacted when he had mentioned Mary's name, but why? What was she trying to hide? What did she really know about the old woman's disappearance?

He managed to switch his mind back to his driving just in time to stop at the junction with Wensum Street and wait for a gap in the traffic before he turned across. His years of training in psychology and his consultant work in the Anderson Clinic had developed in him a sort of second sight, or rather a fine nose for the odour of insanity. It was this that had first made him aware of Jarvin when he was hovering in the doorway of the 'Cranes', his footsteps strangled with doubt. He had never lost his enthusiasm for the complexities of the mind, or ceased to be thrilled at the chance to unravel the mechanics of insanity. Each individual held such a fascination for him that to befriend Jarvin had been second nature. It had been easy getting him to talk that first time, to get him to unburden the nightmares that haunted him, but he was still very disturbed. It bothered Martyn enough to have made a note in his diary after that meeting and now he felt he had to have a word with the Bishop. He could have a quiet talk with him and make him aware how much help Jarvin still needed. Perhaps he could suggest that he should attend his clinic a couple of times a week. It should just be a matter of some gentle persuasion. That had been his intention before Jarvin had become involved with this young girl from the squat. He couldn't quite understand how he had been drawn into Mary's disappearance, or how the squatters were involved, but he feared that the angel story was rapidly threatening to tip the balance of Jarvin's mind. But what, if any, purpose would that serve them, unless. . . .

The harsh blare of a car horn made Martyn jump and look up at his rear view mirror to see a reflecting, angry face and a raised fist of the driver of the car immediately behind him. 'All right, all right!' he muttered irritably, nosing the bonnet of his big car out of Elm Hill and into the traffic of Wensum Street. Then he turned sharply to his left and, with a squeal of tyres on the warm tarmac, he was in Palace Street. Everyone was in such a darned hurry these days, it didn't give him a chance to think. Martyn slowed his car as he drove through St Martins and he wondered if he should give the Bishop a ring and drop round to see him after evening surgery. His residence was only a two minute walk away and he wanted to share his concern over Mary's vanishing act, to establish whether she really did spend that last night sheltering from the storm in the South Porch. He turned into Bishopsgate and saw the familiar straggle of disgruntled patients that always seemed to gather, morning and evening, as regularly as a flock of hungry starlings, outside his surgery door. He pulled up at the kerb.

'I'm so sorry I'm late,' he beamed as he grabbed his bag out of the car and locked the door before running up the surgery steps. 'It really couldn't be helped, there was an emergency.'

He winked at a small, tearful child who was clinging tightly to her mother's hand before throwing open the waiting-room door. 'Make yourselves comfortable.' He smiled, putting Mary's disappearance aside as the first of the patients followed him into the surgery.

CHAPTER SEVEN

A Lucky Arrest

J ARVIN WAS in no hurry to return to his lodgings to face the recriminations he knew were due to him for failing to appear at supper. He had already had enough of Joni's accusations: she hadn't given him a moment to explain before she had stormed off without saying good-bye or even thanking him for at least trying to find out what had been going on. He tried to shrug off the feeling that he had failed her and forgave her for her outburst because he knew she was running scared. He was reluctant to move and swallowed the last dregs of beer slowly as he sat there watching the twilight soften the last of the bleak, dusty, daylight outline of the beer garden. The gloom hid the dingy air of neglect, covering it in deep indigo shadows. Above his head strings of previously unnoticed coloured lamps were woven through the branches of the trees and one by one they blinked on, casting shifting pools of light across the table tops. The atmosphere in the garden was changing as the evening crowds began to slowly fill the tables. It wasn't the place to sit and think any more and he listened for a moment to the hum of conversation and the chink of glasses, feeling more and more isolated and utterly alone. He rose to his feet, slipped unobserved out of the 'Cranes' and began to walk, not caring where, letting the rhythm of his stride and the echo of his footsteps find their own way. If only he had thought to examine the carvings and sculptures earlier he might have had some answers by now and could have stopped Joni from running away.

He was so deep in thought, wrapped up in his own misery and sense of failure, that he forgot the time. He stopped to look at his watch and was shocked to find that it was after twelve-thirty. He looked up in a panic and didn't recognise any of the street signs. He was lost! A moment of panic seized him as he imagined Mrs Sibson's wrath and he hurriedly tried to retrace his steps. More by luck than judgement he found himself in Magdalen Street and remembered that it crossed the Wensum and would eventually lead him into Tombland. The streets were almost completely deserted, disturbed only by the occasional prowling police car by the time he had reached his lodgings. He began to fumble amongst the loose change in his pocket, finding his key only when he reached the door. The key turned round and round without releasing the lock.

'Damn! Damn! Damn!' he muttered under his breath. Mrs Sibson had locked him out.

The noise of an approaching car made Jarvin glance quickly along Tombland toward the bridge he had just crossed. A thin, wet mist was rising from the River Wensum. It clung to the road in swirling shrouds and boiled up across the pavements, ghosting the doorways and seeping into the dark alleyways on either side of the street, distorting the oncoming headlamps into ochre orbs of light as the car drew closer. Jarvin shivered in the damp; he had to get into the house, he couldn't think of anywhere else to go and he was cold and tired. He returned his attentions to the door, cursing Mrs Sibson for locking him out and then his uncle for making him come to this god-forsaken city. Tears of frustration welled in the corners of his eyes as he fiercely rattled his key in the lock.

'Open, damn you, open!' He hammered on the heavy oak door with his other hand.

Jarvin was so intent on venting his anger on the door that he didn't notice that a car had drawn into the kerb and stopped directly behind him. Somewhere, on the edge of his anger, he was aware of car doors opening and footsteps closing in on him but he didn't connect the sound with his predicament until a voice cautioned him to step back away from the doorway and told him to keep his hands in sight. He just had time to turn around before a strong hand gripped his arm forcefully and someone shone a torch in his eyes.

'What the hell is happening?' Jarvin cried out in confusion, struggling as he automatically raised his arm to shield his eyes from the glaring light.

'Stand still,' the officer holding the torch ordered as the man holding his arm twisted it painfully. 'What are you doing trying to break in to the Gatehouse?'

Jarvin still struggled against the light, not realising what was happening.

'If you don't keep still I'll handcuff you.'

The other policeman reached for his other arm and pulled it down and away from his face.

Jarvin blinked and twisted his head from side to side, screwing up his eyes to try to see. He caught sight of the glint of the buttons on their uniform and understood. 'I live here, officer. I'm trying to get in, but my landlady's locked me out!'

The torch beam steadied as the officers scrutinised him and then slowly travelled from his face, dishevelled hair and stubbly chin down across his old, tweed jacket and shabby corduroy trousers.

'Oh, no you don't!' one of them replied coldly. 'The only people who lodge here are priests. I don't know where you got that key but *you* are definitely not a priest – you were trying to break in.'

'He reeks of beer. I think we had better take him down to the station, we can sort it out there,' the other policeman interrupted.

'But . . . I told you, I lodge here. If you don't believe me wake up Mrs Sibson and ask her!' Jarvin shouted, struggling violently as the policemen manhandled him into the car and drove him through the empty streets towards the police station.

Jarvin was beside himself with anger by the time they arrived at the station. His temper and composure had snapped completely and he was struggling violently. It took three police officers to secure him in an interview room. He refused to empty his pockets or give them any form of identification and accused them of wrongful arrest at the top of his voice. He demanded that they telephone the Beckensthorpe Institute or Dr Martyn Burr, or better still, wake up Mrs Sibson. They could wake up the whole city for all he cared!

Eventually, after a struggle, two officers succeeded in emptying his pockets and removing his shoe-laces. The duty sergeant sifted through his meagre collection of personal effects, pausing to read the label on the small bottle of tablets and leafing through his notebook. He put the bottle to one side and tossed the notebook into the property box before glaring stonily at Jarvin.

'Are you a patient of Dr Burr?' he asked as he began to fill out his report.

'Phone him and ask him yourself,' Jarvin answered crossly.

The duty sergeant shrugged as he first filled out the name he had learned from the bottle and wrote below it 'address unknown'. He had learned that the man had recently been a patient at the Beckonsthorpe Institute from the label and he could see that he had obviously been drinking heavily throughout the evening. He looked at his watch and carefully wrote the time down on the report before putting his pen back into his top pocket.

'I will contact the Institute in the morning, Mr Mandrake. They'll tell me where you're supposed to be staying. In the meantime you can spend the rest of the night in one of our cells.'

'But this is ridiculous! You're treating me like some sort of common thief. I've told you, I'm living in the Gatehouse. Why don't you telephone someone?' Jarvin shouted, banging his fist on the table in helpless frustration.

'No, I will not telephone anybody!' the sergeant snapped back as he rose from his chair. 'What we will do is keep you out of harm's way and give you a chance to sober up. It's half past two in the morning and we will not telephone anybody at this time of night – it can wait until the morning. Think yourself lucky I'm not charging you with resisting arrest.'

'Damn you all to hell!' Jarvin shouted as the cell door slammed shut. 'You can't do this to me. I'm innocent! I wasn't trying to break in, you've got to believe me!!'

Jarvin beat his fists on the cell door until his knuckles bled. He shouted and cursed with frustration until his throat was sore but nobody answered him. He had been locked up until he was sober for his own protection, left to the stifling silence and the muffled echo of his own voice. He was utterly alone, worn out and wretched with despair, at a loss to understand why or where his nightmare had begun. He sank down onto the narrow, iron-framed bed, curling himself into a tight, foetal position, his head buried between his hands and his knees drawn up against his stomach. He wept and tried to let sleep claim him but forgotten voices, whispers from his past, images and memories of all his inadequacies welled up to fill his head, tormenting him, only to be pushed aside as the phantoms from the tomb shrieked and echoed as they flooded through the labyrinth of his mind. Their hideous shrieks faded and were replaced by the sweat and odour of death and decay which burned at his nostrils, making him gasp for air and he sat up on the bed clutching at the cold, metal frame.

The cell seemed smaller now, pressing in on him until he could barely breathe. He was wide awake and his heart thudded in his chest as he waited for the claustrophobia to strike. He hadn't had a serious attack since the day of his arrival. He listened to the silence and felt in his pocket for his bottle of tablets, tearing at the lining when he couldn't find them. A knot of panic tightened as he remembered that the police hadn't returned them to him when they had locked him up. Jarvin clenched his right hand into a trembling fist and bit hard on his knuckles. He was helplessly lost without their help: he would go mad with terror. He caught a shallow breath as the glare of the light bulb behind its reinforced glass panel went out. The cell was momentarily plunged into total darkness. He would have screamed if his throat had not been paralysed but mercifully a smaller night-light came on and cast a weaker glow into his cell. Jarvin concentrated his whole attention onto the soft light. It was enough to give him the courage to fight. Beads of perspiration broke out on his forehead as he forced the phantoms back into the darkness. Their voices howled and whined, their hideous shapes crowded forward to block out the light. Inside his head he whispered over and over, 'You're not real. You're in my imagination. This is a sickness. There is nothing to fear in the dark, nothing. There's nothing there.'

One by one the nightmares that had haunted him since that terrible accident reached out to smother him and then they began to melt and shrivel as they receded to the edges of his subconscious. Jarvin gradually became aware of the taste of blood on his knuckles and the silence in his cell. He blinked at the sweat that had trickled into his eyes and a smile formed on his lips. Despite everything that had happened tonight he had beaten the claustrophobia. Beaten it without the aid of those tranquillisers. He sighed and lay down, curling himself back into a ball, and then fell into a deep, exhausted sleep.

The scrape of a heavy key turning in the lock of the cell door followed by a creak of hinges as it swung open jolted Jarvin awake. He sat up, confused and disorientated, blinking his eyes and wondering where the hell he was. He found himself staring at the spidery scrawls of obscenity and the graffitied messages that were written everywhere across the unfamiliar walls of the narrow, dimly-lit room. He rubbed his head and pushed the untidy mess of hair out of his eyes. The meaningless messages on the walls swam into focus and he remembered the ordeal of being locked up, accused of being a common thief. He also remembered the terror of that attack of claustrophobia and the fact that he had beaten it, on his own, without drugs.

A movement in the open doorway caught his attention and he turned his head. The thickset police sergeant that he had met the previous night was hovering in the doorway. His mouth twitched as if he was trying to accomplish a smile but his eyes were hard and cold as he spoke. 'It seems as if there was a mistake, Mr Mandrake. We owe you an apology for detaining you last night.' He stepped back and turned abruptly on his heel, throwing the last of his words back across his shoulder as he strode towards the shallow flight of steps that led toward the duty room. 'If you would be good enough to follow me I'll return your possessions. There's a police car waiting to take you to the Gatehouse.'

'There! I told you I was innocent last night! You should

have telephoned Mrs Sibson earlier!' Jarvin shouted as he reached the foot of the stairs.

The sergeant paused and looked down at him, his face a mask of disdain. 'We haven't phoned anybody yet. Your innocence is still a matter of conjecture. Mrs Sibson has just telephoned us to report a break-in during the night. She confirmed that you are, at the moment, lodging temporarily in the Gatehouse.'

'Break-in?' Jarvin frowned. He wanted to ask about it but he was hustled so quickly through the duty room that he barely had time to gather up his possessions and was still stuffing them into his pocket as he followed the sergeant out to the waiting car.

'I want you to get a full report,' the sergeant demanded as the car pulled away.

Two other police cars were already parked outside the Gatehouse when they arrived and the front door stood wide open. Jarvin ran up the front steps to find Mrs Sibson standing in the hall surrounded by four more policemen, who seemed to be waiting for him. Her face was so drawn it was skeletal and her lips trembled as she said, 'Go up to your room, Mr Mandrake.' She pointed a quivering finger toward the stairs.

'My room? What's wrong with my room?' Jarvin cried, dashing across the hall and taking the stairs two at a time.

One of the policemen was on his heels when he reached the top landing and turned in through the open doorway. 'Holy Jesus!' The words were uttered in a strangled gasp as Jarvin choked, gagging at the foul stench that filled the room.

He staggered backwards, clutching at the inner handle of the door for support but snatching his hand away as it came into contact with a cold, sticky mucous substance that made his flesh crawl. The slime was everywhere, smeared on the brass handle and across the lower areas of the walls and the windowsill. He moved back another step into the doorway and stared speechlessly in at the reeking, shredded remains of his room. Whoever – or whatever – had got in had come through the roof. Sunlight and the faint sound of birds singing from the yew trees in the cathedral grounds were filtering down through a jagged opening of broken roof slates. Wooden lathes and crumbling pieces of horse-hair plaster edged the hole. But it was the sight of the iron-framed bed, where Jarvin should have been sleeping, that made his blood run cold. The frame had been tortuously twisted inside out. The rusty springs were unravelled and smashed into a thousand razor-sharp shards that had been stabbed and thrust through the tangle of mattress. They would have sliced straight through him if he had been sleeping. The floorboards had been gouged and disfigured and the floor was littered with the shredded remains of his suit-case of clothes and the other few possessions that he had brought with him from Beckonsthorpe. Over everything there was a trail of shimmering, glistening, stinking slime.

He shuddered. The knot of revulsion tightened in his stomach and he realised that he was going to be sick. He turned and stumbled past the policeman as he fled down the stairs, bursting through the nearest bathroom door just in time to reach the toilet bowl. He was grey-faced and sweating as he straightened up and the shock made his legs tremble. His mouth tasted foul and he moved to the basin to gargle but the bitter, burning taste remained. Mrs Sibson's voice, urgent and demanding, floated up to him. He caught sight of his wild, untidy appearance in the mirror and pulled a hand towel from the rail to dry his face, throwing it down into the basin as he walked away. His head ached and spun dizzily as he shakily made his way down into the hall, gripping the banister rail for support. The policeman who had followed him up the stairs was a pace behind him.

'No!' he cried at the barrage of questions that greeted him when he reached the hall, then he sat down abruptly on the bottom step as a wave of nausea swept over him. 'No, I haven't the faintest idea who could have destroyed my room, or why. I haven't been in here since breakfast yesterday morning. The front door was locked when I returned here late last night and, as you already know, I spent the night in the police station.'

'They wouldn't have arrested you if you hadn't been wandering around in a drunken stupor.' Mrs Sibson couldn't contain her anger, or the conviction that Jarvin, or some of his disreputable friends, must have smashed up his room. She took a pace toward him, stabbing an accusing, bony finger at his chest. 'You have been nothing but trouble.'

'Perhaps you could give us some precise details, ma'am,' one of the policemen interrupted in an effort to divert her accusations. 'Could you tell me exactly what time did you lock your house last night? And do you know if the damage could have been done before then?'

'What?' She looked up at the policeman, reluctant to allow her finger to drop.

'Have you any idea when the break-in occurred?' he pressed, flicking open his notebook.

Mrs Sibson thought for a moment and let her hand fall back to her side. 'I locked the front door quite early yesterday evening, Officer. You see I'd had quite enough of Mr Mandrake's funny ways. Archaeologist indeed!' She paused a moment to glare at him. 'When he didn't bother to come in for his supper it was the last straw. I locked the door so that he had to knock for me to let him in. You see I was going to make him mend his ways or have him thrown out on his ear, he was setting such a bad example to the others – staying out to all hours and coming back so drunk that he wasn't capable of bolting the door. We could have been burgled, murdered in our beds even.' She stopped quite suddenly and frowned at the policemen before renewing her attack on Jarvin.

'It's him you should be questioning, officer, him not me. You should find out how he got up onto the roof and tore that gaping hole in the slates. I'll tell you only a drunken mob could have made such a disgusting mess of that room. I want him sued for every penny it'll cost to put it right. Yes, and I want him out of my house now, right now! In fact I'm going to get the Dean this instant.' She stormed out of the front door, slamming it shut behind her.

'But I didn't do it!' Jarvin protested to the policeman as he rose to his feet. 'I'd be completely out of my head to destroy everything I brought with me, and I couldn't have got in to do it anyway, she'd locked me out. Do you really think I'm crazy enough to climb up onto that roof?'

'No, we're not accusing you of the break-in, Mr Mandrake,' the interviewing officer quickly interrupted, glancing darkly past Jarvin and up the winding flight of stairs toward the attic. 'No, it would have taken somebody with the agility of an acrobat to scale the steep pitch of that roof. It was fairly obvious from Mrs Sibson's original call this morning that it was your room that had been broken into. Now could you tell us if anything is missing, or perhaps throw any light on who might have done it. Do you have any enemies in the area?'

'Enemies?' Jarvin laughed, but the sound was bitter. 'What kind of enemies would I need to have? Everything I brought here with me has been destroyed, shredded. It looks as though all my possessions have been torn to ribbons, as though hundreds of claws . . .' He stopped, a cold finger of fear touching his spine. Claws, hundreds of claws, the words echoed in his head. His mind began to race. Joni had described the demons that had swarmed all over Mary's body as having clawed hands and feet and the smell in his room was the same vile smell of death that he had smelt in the porch. He had also been kept awake for the past few nights by noises that sounded like claws scrabbling across the slates. And now Joni had said that the squat had been abandoned and she was getting out of the city because something had got in there, something that had clawed and bitten at one of their faces and it had spent hours scratching and gnawing at the door of the room she had been hiding in. The stark reality struck home. The demons were hunting for her: they had gone to the squat, but why had they broken into his attic room? Why were they hunting him as well? He felt dizzy and sick again and would have fallen but one of the policemen gripped his arm.

'Are you all right? You look awful.'

'Yes, yes, I'm OK, but I need some fresh air. Everything I have has been ruined and I'm pretty sure I'll have to find somewhere to stay tonight. I'd better be making a start if that's all right.' Jarvin staggered toward the front door, mopping his grey, perspiring forehead with his sleeve. He couldn't tell the police about the demons or the dark angel: they'd never believe him. They'd probably lock him up and get him certified and then he would be completely unable to stop this nightmare. He couldn't tell anybody, except perhaps Martyn. He had already told him the rest of the story, but he wasn't completely sure that he had really believed him.

'You'll ring the station and let us know where you are staying?'

Jarvin stopped as he pulled open the front door and glanced back. 'Yes, yes, of course I will.'

A sense of urgency filled his mind, shutting out the sounds of the city and the dappled strands of sunlight that lay across the pavements. He reached the bottom step and turned sharply toward the Erpingham Gate, oblivious to the slam of a car door that had pulled up behind one of the police cars and not noticing the figure of Martyn Burr hurrying across the pavement to intercept him.

Dread gnawed at his stomach. Time was running out: he had to examine those carvings in the cathedral and hope to God that they could give him some answers before it was too late. Somewhere, somehow, there had to be a way of stopping those demonic creatures from hunting them down. Clothes, possessions, nothing else mattered now.

'Jarvin! What the hell's going on? Jarvin!' Martyn grabbed hold of Jarvin's arm to prevent him hurrying straight past and roughly spun him around. 'Jarvin, Jarvin, it's me, Martyn.' He grasped his other arm and shook him, making him blink. Jarvin's eyes sharpened into focus. 'Jarvin, talk to me. What the devil's going on? I was on my way back from an early call and I saw the police cars. Has there been an accident? Is anyone hurt?'

'Accident?' Jarvin repeated slowly. 'No, I don't think it was an accident. They broke in quite deliberately, but I'm not sure why.'

Martyn looked up and down the street at the line of police cars and listened to the crackle of their shortwave radios before he looked towards the open front door of the Gatehouse where a policeman was standing. 'Has somebody burgled your lodgings? What did they take?'

Jarvin shrugged and answered without emotion. 'I'm not sure. You won't believe me if I tell you.' He paused and then continued in the same monotone, 'It was those demons, the ones Joni said were swarming all over Mary's body in the porch. They broke into my room. Go and take a look for yourself, they've destroyed everything. I'm in a hurry to examine those carvings so I won't come back with you.'

He waited long enough to see a flicker of disbelief cross Martyn's eyes before pulling his arms free and walking away, turning underneath the Erpingham Gate only to come face to face with the Dean and Mrs Sibson.

'Mr Mandrake, I want to see you in my office the moment I get back from inspecting the damage.' The Dean's tone and manner were aggressive and abrupt. Mrs Sibson glared at him through her tears as they swept past.

'If you want to see me I'll be in the cathedral examining the medieval carvings,' Jarvin answered. His voice was surprisingly calm. He didn't give a damn about the Dean or Mrs Sibson any more and he hurried past them and down the gravel path before he veered off towards the South Porch. It was only when he reached the shadows that he hesitated for a moment, his hand upon the heavy iron latch ring. The strength that he had found inside himself in the police cell wavered and the resolve to face and destroy the demons crumbled away. The sound of a footstep on the path behind made him spin round to find Martyn hurrying toward him.

'Wait, Jarvin, wait!' he called out as he hurried along the gravel path breathlessly. He reached the door, his cheeks puffing in and out as he hunted for air. 'Awful mess,' he gasped, dragging loose the knot of his tie and popping open the top button of his shirt. 'I told Mrs Sibson and the Dean that I'd never seen anything like it – and that ghastly smell, it's worse than anything I've ever been unfortunate enough to smell in the mortuary.' He paused and then pulled a heavy, black leather bag off his shoulder and thrust it into Jarvin's hand. 'I remembered you saying that you were going to photograph those carvings.' He grinned. 'Well, you had better borrow my camera – it was in the boot of my car. I don't think there'll be anything worth salvaging from your room, do you?'

'Why, thanks.' Jarvin smiled in surprise. 'I think the shock of seeing what those creatures had done drove the idea of photographing the carvings right out of my mind, but . . .' He paused, unbuckling the two leather straps of the bag and opening the lid to see an old-fashioned Chinon CG5, single reflex camera along with both a wide-angled and a telephoto lens and at least four rolls of fast film crammed in beside it. 'But do you believe me now? Do you really believe that what Joni told me really happened to that woman now that you have seen what those demons are capable of doing?' As he waited for Martyn's answer he shouldered the bag and lifted the latch of the porch door and pushed it open.

'The mess in your room was awful, absolutely awful,' Martyn agreed, trying to hedge around a discreet answer. He had never seen anything like it in his life and he couldn't imagine what had created that disgusting odour or the gouge marks on the floors and walls. The way everything had been torn to ribbons certainly lent credence to Jarvin's wild story but it wasn't enough, not on its own. He didn't doubt for one moment that what he had just seen in that tiny attic room would reinforce Jarvin's belief in the supernatural and anything out of the ordinary that happened now would only go to confirm everything in his mind. What he feared most was that the type of madness that affected him was strengthening its grip on the last shreds of his sanity and it had the power to create its own unique reality. Soon he would be seeing those demons and they would appear so real in every terrifying detail. He needed help and he needed it fast.

'You haven't answered me. You still think we're making

it all up don't you?' Jarvin's face was becoming a mask of distrust.

'No, no: I do believe you. I brought you the camera didn't I?' Martyn answered quickly. Keeping his trust was critical. 'I'm sorry, I was thinking about which room to put you in. Oh, I forgot to tell you, I told Mrs Sibson that you couldn't possibly sleep in that room tonight even if she manages to get it cleaned up, there's still a hole in the roof and the broken plaster. So you're coming to stay with me, I've got plenty of spare rooms, it's just a matter of choosing one. We have to choose the most secure in case those creatures come back, and I'm sure some of my clothes will fit you, well at least where they touch.' He paused and breathed a silent sigh of relief as Jarvin's face relaxed and he craned his neck to see past Jarvin's shoulder into the gloomy interior of the porch. 'Is this where it happened? Is this where the angel murdered Mary?'

'Yes, and Joni saw it all from where she was hiding beneath that stone bench, the one on the right,' Jarvin answered grimly.

Martyn followed him over the threshold and crouched down to look under both of the benches, brushing his fingers slowly over the cold, stone floor between them. 'You're quite right, Jarvin, they have removed all trace of the murder.' He rose to his feet and rubbed his fingertips together to remove the feeling that there was something sticky clinging to them.

'I'm worried about Joni,' Jarvin whispered as he lifted the latch of the tall, iron-bound door that opened into the transept. 'She told me last night that something, perhaps one of the demons, had got into the squat where she lived. It had bitten someone's face and clawed at the door of her room all night. It was trying to get at her that's why she was so agitated last night when you met her. She was scared.

After you left me she told me that everyone was abandoning the squat, moving out, I only hope she didn't go back there on her own.'

'Perhaps we had better get the police to take a look,' Martyn murmured as they stepped into the South Transept, privately wondering what the hell the girl and her friends were playing at. Why did they need to reinforce this angel/demon fantasy in Jarvin's mind if they were quitting the squat and vanishing into the obscurity of the world they lived in? Why go to all the trouble of destroying his room?

'No!' Jarvin hissed, shaking his head. 'Joni was afraid of the police, really afraid.'

Martyn shrugged noncommittally and let his gaze travel slowly along the forest of stone columns and intricate archways as they moved toward the central tower. She was afraid all right: who wouldn't be with the body of an old vagrant to hide and a murder to cover up?

Shafts of sunlight poured down through the high windows of the lantern of the tower filling the central area with misty light and throwing the transept in gloomy shadows. Their footsteps echoed eerily in the early morning silence. 'Is that the dark angel, the one kneeling in that alcove ahead of us to the left?' Martyn whispered softly, touching Jarvin's arm as he moved toward it.

'Yes, yes it is,' Jarvin answered, reluctant to follow him across the transept. 'Martyn, what are you doing for God's sake? Come away!' he hissed in alarm, but Martyn ignored him and whistled softly to himself as he walked directly up to the figure and looked up. 'Martyn, please come away, please, now,' Jarvin implored, hurrying past the figure to the other side of the transept and only stopping when he had reached the presbytery steps.

Martyn took a moment to examine the angel. It was very lifelike in every detail and had been sculpted with a brutal reality. It was easy to see why Jarvin had fixated on the figure given his fragile mental state. 'I'll be back,' he promised the petrified statue, before turning on his heel and hurrying across to where Jarvin was anxiously waiting.

A method of treatment was beginning to form in Martyn's head, one he had successfully used before. He had to gradually reduce the menace this statue held over Jarvin, make it appear so mundane that he could reach out and touch it. But he knew from experience that he must only move forward one step at a time.

'Yes, there is certainly something unusual about that angel. The colour and surface texture is so dark, what did you say it was made of?'

Jarvin shrugged. 'I didn't. I don't know, the guidebook says it is a rare pink marble that has darkened with age, but I've never come across a stone like that, and I'm sure it isn't wood.'

'Why don't you take a couple of photographs of it now, while I'm here? Then I can sort out anything you're not familiar with about the camera.'

Jarvin readily agreed and rummaged in the camera bag, glancing up at the figure of the angel as he fitted the telephoto lens. He wasn't going any closer. He took a light reading, set the shutter speed and stepped down the aperture before adjusting the focus. Suddenly he gasped and staggered backward, letting the camera slip through his fingers to swing and dangle from the strap that he'd slung around his neck.

'I can't! The angel's watching me. I swear it opened its eyes, it knows I'm here. If you don't believe me look for yourself.' With a fumbling, jerky movement he pulled the camera strap over his head and thrust the camera into Martyn's hands. 'Go on, look!' he muttered wretchedly, retreating into the presbytery.

'We'll need this as evidence,' Martyn answered, keeping a serious tone to his voice as he dropped the strap over his head and walked a couple of paces toward the statue. This was exactly what he needed, a chance to prove to Jarvin that there wasn't anything abnormal about the figure. Photographic evidence, a couple of ordinary photographs, would be the first step in breaking the cycle of madness. Martyn adjusted the focus and caught his breath as the huge, winged figure leapt into view. The dull sheen of its skin seemed to absorb the shadows, creating the illusion that it was crouching in darkness, waiting to spring out toward him. For an instant he felt afraid, as if he wanted to jump backward and out of its reach. He pressed the shutter, the mechanism whirred and clicked. 'You don't frighten me,' Martyn whispered, moving to the left and right and shooting off another six frames of the angel while he regained his composure. With a broad, half-moon grin he handed the camera back to Jarvin and then glanced at his watch.

'My God, look at the time! I've got to dash or I'll have a queue of patients from the surgery door to the north coast. Why don't you start photographing the choirstalls – take as many pictures as you like. You'll find my house in Bishopsgate – you can't miss it, the name's engraved in brass beside the surgery door. Come round to the back – I'll leave the door unlocked for you. Try and get there before five and a friend of mine who has a photographic studio in King Street will get the films developed and printed immediately – he owes me a favour. I'll ring him this morning and arrange it.'

Jarvin was only too pleased to get away from the sinister, crouching figure. He took back the camera and slung the case over his shoulder as he hurried through the central area beneath the tower into the choir.

Martyn retraced his footsteps slowly and left the presbytery and walked back through the central area into the South Transept. He paused in front of the statue of the dark angel: his patients could wait another five minutes. He absently stroked at his sideburns and muttered to himself as he thought out loud. 'Now, how can I begin to convince Jarvin that you're only a statue, only an angel made of stone . . .' Martyn paused and looked up into the enveloping shadows cast by the feathery arc of its wings and suddenly laughed. 'Of course! How obvious, how brilliantly simple. If I take a sample and have it analysed at the museum it would tell us exactly what sort of stone you're made of!'

Martyn rummaged in his pockets, found his penknife in one and took some rather creased and grubby envelopes from an inner pocket and sorted out two of them to use, stuffing the rest of the contents back into his jacket. Glancing nervously around him to check that he wasn't being observed he opened the small blade of the knife and held the envelope beneath it as he scratched at the angel's leg. The blade skidded down the hard surface of the statue emitting the same high-pitched screech that fingernails would make being dragged across a blackboard. The sound made Martyn's teeth ache and he flinched and snatched the blade away. His hand was trembling with anxiety. He looked into the bottom of the envelope and was relieved when he saw that he had managed to catch a sprinkling of fine, dark particles of stonedust. He examined the statue's leg and saw to his surprise that the blade of the knife had left a small, pink scar in the dark surface of the stone. It made him wonder if the guidebook was right after all and it was merely age that had darkened the pink marble and given it that dull sheen. Carefully, he folded the tongue of the envelope back over the top to trap the particles of dust and wrote 'Angel's leg' upon the outside before purposefully putting it into his jacket pocket.

He drew a deep breath and opened the other envelope, holding it beneath the angel's clenched hand before taking another scraping from the fist where the stone was almost black. 'That should tell us what you're made of,' he growled while writing 'Angel's hand' on the front. He put it carefully into his jacket pocket with the other one. He was curious when he noticed that the blade hadn't revealed a lighter mark on the surface of the knuckle as it had on the leg but he didn't have the time to speculate – he was already late for morning surgery. He hurried through the outer door of the transept and then paused for a moment in the porch. Another opportunity to prove whether the murder had taken place there occurred to him. The stone was porous, even if the floor had been meticulously and repeatedly scrubbed there would still be traces of blood that would have soaked into the floor. Taking out his knife again and a third envelope he scraped at the floor gathering a small pile of stonedust on the blade that he deposited in the envelope before he left.

CHAPTER EIGHT

A Night of Terror

THE EVIDENCE of evil that Jarvin was looking for was hidden everywhere. Vivid images of the terror that had stalked the cathedral for the last thousand years were scratched and carved into the wood and stone. Hundreds of terrified craftsmen had hastily recorded stories of the sacrifice or the part of it they had accidentally witnessed. They had not dared to speak of it for fear of accusation of heresy or devil-worship but they had told of it secretly in their work. They had carved it in wood and chiselled it in stone, they had woven their message of the winged terror in the tapestries and painted it in secret brush-strokes between the leads of the stained-glass windows. Wherever Jarvin looked he discovered signs that warned against evil, symbolic pictures of the dark angel anointing itself with the blood of its victims. There were also hideous scratchings depicting the demons dragging away the corpses of the sacrifices through a doorway framed with flames. Joni hadn't exaggerated. Everything she had described and more was all there, hidden in plain sight, waiting to be understood. The truth was waiting to be unravelled.

Jarvin's hands were slippery with the cold sweat of excitement as he worked the shutter, shooting off frame after frame, adjusting the speed and the aperture as he worked in the dark, gloomy corners. There was so much to see, so many symbols at every turn. There were figures, perhaps some sort of hieroglyphics or magic symbols, scribbled haphazardly throughout the fabric of the cathedral. They had been cleverly hidden and individually their message could easily have been missed or misinterpreted, but collectively they made a chilling story which told of hundreds of ritual murders. If he had seen just one on its own he would never have understood it, never have been able to piece the story together.

He photographed the miseries in the ancient monastic stalls, the canopies and the choir screen, the carvings in the capitals and the spandrels above them. In the nave he changed to the telephoto lens and progressed slowly between the rows of pews, filming the intricately carved and painted ceiling bosses that locked together the stone ribs that supported the vaulted roof high above his head. But craning his neck so far back and trying to keep the camera still made him dizzy and he had to sit for a moment or ruin the next sequence of frames with camera shake. He perched on the edge of a pew near the altar and waited to regain his balance. He watched the clerics and listened to the soft echo of their footsteps as they went about their morning chores, oblivious to the nightmare that hid in the shadows. Somewhere in one of the smaller chapels he could hear the murmur and chant of a service, and closer behind the choir screen the low melodic hum of air rising in the organ pipes. He sighed, wondering what they would have done if they discovered the ritual sacrifices that were going on underneath their noses undetected.

'Refuse to believe it until a formal Committee of Investigation had endorsed it, I suppose,' he muttered to himself, stifling a yawn. He jumped quickly to his feet when he spotted the Dean entering the nave through the West Door.

Jarvin wasn't in the mood for another confrontation with authority. A night in the cells and Mrs Sibson's accusations were quite enough. He had too much to do and too little time to do it in to squander it pleading his innocence with the Dean. Stooping, he gathered up the strap of the camera bag, slung it across his shoulder and slipped unnoticed into the North Aisle. He kept to the shadows of the huge columns that rose to support the roof and hurried along the aisle towards the West Door, stopping only when he reached the narrow, spiral stone stairway that led up to the clerestory. He could hear the Dean's cold, precise voice asking about his whereabouts of the two morning volunteers who sat at the visitors' inquiry desk and demanded that they tell him to report to his office immediately. He didn't wait to listen to anything else but quickly climbed the winding steps and looked towards the tower, where visitors were not permitted.

The narrow, stone corridor had a timeless air of neglect. Corners of the small leaded panes of glass were cracked and broken and a dead pigeon lay upon a windowsill, its bedraggled feathers ruffled by the summer breeze. Fragments of masonry and crumbling drifts of mortar littered the dusty floor. The surface of the outer wall of the clerestory was scarred and pitted and there were countless thin, spidery, medieval scratchings, drawings of devils and fantastical beasts and horned monsters, six-pointed stars and hundreds of eyes and signs of the cross to ward off evil. Some of them were so faintly drawn that the slightest touch would have obliterated them forever. Jarvin quickly changed to the wide-angle lens, his new discoveries making him forget the Dean completely, and began to photograph the medieval graffiti.

He picked his way carefully along the corridor, glancing down at the dusty floor in front of him as he wound the film on. Suddenly he froze. A shiver of fear tightened his stomach. There were footprints in the dust, hundreds of small, clawed footprints, about the size of his hand. They were going in both directions. 'Oh Jesus Christ, they're everywhere!' he whispered, his voice tight with ill-controlled panic. He followed the trails of claw prints along the clerestory. Upon closer inspection of the walls he realised that there were gouge marks criss-crossing them. He spread the fingers on his right hand and made them into a claw. The middle three fingers roughly matched a recurring pattern of scrapes on the wall. If he followed them carefully they disappeared up into the shadows of the roof, high above his head. His spine tingled. He hunched his shoulders and looked up. These almost-forgotten corridors must be where the demons roosted, like hideous carnivorous bats, clinging in the shadows to the stone ribs of the roof.

Jarvin fought to stifle the impulse to turn and run. He had discovered the demons' lair. He couldn't duck out now: they had to be up there somewhere. He had to try to capture them on film. He had to have the evidence so that Martyn would help to destroy them. With trembling, fumbling fingers he fitted the flash gun and switched it on. It seemed to take an age for the red light to go out. He raised the camera and pointed it up at the shadows in the roof above his head. Holding his breath, he pressed the shutter.

The exploding flash of light blinded him as it whitened the gloom above. The whirr of the shutter and the sound of the battery recharging sounded like a roll of thunder in his ears. He tensed, his fingers clamped onto the body of the camera. In that brief second of searing light he had imagined that he had seen a thousand distorted, hideous bodies dropping onto him, their claws outstretched to rip and tear. But nothing happened. The silence lengthened. He moved the camera and pressed the shutter again and again, taking random pictures of the dusty floor and the mass of symbols scratched on the walls as he hurried toward the tower. He stopped when he reached the end of the clerestory where it turned sharply to the left and skirted the west side of the North Transept. Looking ahead through the narrow, Norman archway he could see the massive framework and the upper windows of the lantern of the tower, while below and to his right, but hidden by the bulk of the organ loft and the choir screen, lay the choir. Immediately to his left there was a small, wooden door that probably led out onto the cathedral roof.

Jarvin looked anxiously behind him along the gloomy corridor. It was empty. He let out a shallow sigh of relief and panned the camera across all the dark, inaccessible nooks and crannies that he hadn't been able to see from the ground and took another sequence of photographs. He cursed as the winder jammed and then he remembered to check the frame counter. He had finished the film.

'Damn!'

He had already used up three of the four rolls of film that were in the bag and there was still so much to photograph. He had barely started. Kneeling, he rewound the used film and sealed it carefully in its plastic container, dropping it into the camera bag before carefully loading the last film. As he stood up he noticed a myriad of tiny points of light on the four walls of the tower, but he was too far away to be able to see exactly what was causing them. He fished in the camera bag, brought out the telephoto lens and fitted it onto the camera, looking through the viewfinder to bring the walls of the tower leaping toward him. He adjusted the focus and let a whistle of surprise escape from between his lips. The pinpoints of light that he could see was sunlight reflecting from the broken glass tell-tales that he had cemented across the crumbling mortar joints in the tower walls only twenty-four hours before.

'And this tower is as safe as the Rock of Gibraltar,' he muttered thickly as he took pictures of them.

A faint noise, the scrape of something like wings flapping from the gloomy shadows of the vaulted roof made him leap to his feet and spin around. He pressed his back against the single, iron guard-rail that prevented him from plunging into the North Transept sixty feet below. The camera bag swung free from the strap around his neck and he clenched his hands into fists as he wished that he had something more substantial to ward off the demons. The sound was getting louder and grey, white-winged shapes were rapidly descending, flying all around his head. He shouted in terror and raised his arms, flailing them wildly and scattering the startled flock of pigeons that were flying past him and out of the clerestory. They circled and wheeled through the archways of the lantern of the tower to settle and strut, cooing noisily on the windowsills.

'Pigeons! Only pigeons,' Jarvin gasped, sagging weakly against the guard-rail as relief flooded through him. He watched the birds for a moment as they strutted through the patches of sunlight on the dusty windowsills. The sudden fright had made him feel claustrophobic and he knew he needed to get out of that gloomy, narrow corridor now. He needed to feel the hot sunlight on his face and the warm breeze against his skin. He remembered the small door that he thought must lead out onto the roof and reached out to try the handle. It swung open and he ducked through the doorway, blinking and shielding his eyes until they were accustomed to the bright sunlight. He inhaled a deep breath of air. Frowning and sniffing he stepped out onto the narrow, leaded walkway. There was a faint odour of corruption and decay similar to the one he had smelled that morning in his room and then again in the porch when he had found Joni hiding under the bench. He sniffed again, trying to trace the direction that it was coming from, but it was gone, carried away by the mid-morning breezes.

He looked cautiously along the walkway in both directions. The top of the main cathedral wall was peopled with gargoyles, crouching and sitting over dozens of gutter spouts, but nothing seemed out of place. He swept his gaze up across the steep rake of the leaded roof, but there was nothing that could have created that smell. Away to the right on the west side of the North Transept he spotted two workmen on top of some scaffolding cleaning the stonework. He wondered if the smell could have been a chemical they were using. He shouted and waved to catch their attention and they waved back.

Moving along the walkway toward the west end of the cathedral he paused beside one of the gargoyles that was perched on its own on top of the wall looking out across the city. The dark, verdant foliage of the tree tops contrasted with the softer, warmer colours of the roofs. Forests of blackened chimney stacks marched away in every direction in diminishing perspective, broken by the sharp, clear outline of church spires rising against the distant sweep of the hills beyond. Jarvin smiled. It was so beautiful, so enduring. The cathedral clock struck two o'clock – it was later than he thought – Martyn had told him to be at his place before five to have the films developed. He glanced at the frame counter and saw that he had twenty-five exposures left. If he photographed the gargoyles as he worked his way along the roof and the workmen let him climb down one of their ladders he could film the stonework they were cleaning. And then, if he had any exposures left, he could use them in the cloisters. Turning toward the gargoyle he was standing beside he rubbed his hand across its hideous, scaly head. It felt warm from the sun and soft, probably from layers of moss that had grown upon it.

'Picture time,' he murmured and took a detailed close-up. Then he moved on, filming them each in turn. It was only after he had reached the scaffolding that he looked back at the line of small, grotesque, petrified figures and realised that there was something about them, something odd that he couldn't quite put his finger on. He was about to retrace his footsteps when one of the workmen called out to ask him who he was and what he wanted. Jarvin pointed to his badge as he gave his name and asked if he could photograph their work for the archives.

'The Dean's been in a fine old temper. He's been looking everywhere for you,' the workman replied, moving closer for a better look at Jarvin's badge, but he grinned as he asked, 'What have you done, mate, stolen the silver?'

Jarvin grinned sheepishly back and shook his head. 'No, it's just a rather large difference of personal opinions.' And he descended the ladder.

Jarvin looked at his watch for the twentieth time. The second hand seemed to creep so slowly around the dial: there was still more than two hours to wait before the guy who promised to do the photographs as a favour to Martyn dropped into the 'Cranes' with them. He fidgeted uncomfortably in his chair. Martyn's help and generosity seemed to know no bounds, but the clothes he had lent to him certainly knew their limitations. The shirt was stretched as tightly as a trampoline across his back and the buttons were tugging at the buttonholes, the old corduroy jacket restricted his arms and shoulders and he found it difficult to move them, but the trousers were roomy enough around the waist even if the turn-ups were dangling three inches above his shoes. However the shoes and socks were a perfect fit and he was grateful for the loan of everything until he could replenish his ruined wardrobe.

He caught sight of Martyn negotiating his way through the noisy crush at the bar before returning with a brimming pint of beer in each hand. Jarvin half-rose to reach out and take his glass but thought better of it as the jacket tightened its stranglehold on his arms. 'Food's on the way.' Martyn grinned, depositing the glasses on the table and sitting down. He glanced back toward the bar as he picked up his glass. 'But by the look of the crowd in here tonight I think we'll have to wait a while for it. Drink up, we'll have plenty of time for another.'

'I'm sure I've found them, Martyn,' Jarvin hissed excitedly, checking his watch again and shaking it fiercely. 'I can't wait to see those photographs to show you where those demons roost. Has my watch stopped? What time do you make it?'

'There's nothing wrong with your watch,' Martyn smiled. 'Looking at it won't make the time go any faster. Drink your beer and be patient. George will bring the pictures the minute he has finished them.'

'I can't wait for you to see . . .' Jarvin began when the sound of the door opening made him glance round. 'Joni!' he cried, almost sending his chair crashing backwards as he leapt up in surprise at seeing her. 'Joni, what's the matter? What's happened?' He hurried across the room to where she stood, her right hand still gripping the brass door handle.

She didn't seem to recognise him or the circle of faces looking at her but stared blankly ahead as if she was in some sort of trance. Martyn had been quick to follow Jarvin and realised something was wrong immediately. Gently, he loosened her hold on the door handle and between them they guided her to their table and sat her down. She looked thinner, her clothes were filthy and torn and her face white and gaunt. Her skin was almost translucent and drawn tightly across her cheekbones and there were dark rings of fear around her eyes. Her pale lips were trembling and her teeth were chattering together.

'Martyn, what's happened to her? She looks terrible.'

Martyn watched her for a moment and then moved closer to examine her pupils. They were dilated. Her skin was cold and sweating and when he felt for her pulse he found that it was rapid and thready. He put his ear close to her mouth and listened to the quick, shallow rhythm of her breathing.

'Shock,' he muttered, sitting back in his chair. 'I think she is suffering from severe shock and exhaustion, but I haven't a clue what could have caused it.' He paused and felt the crumpled, dirty sleeve of her denim jacket and looked down at the ragged, muddy hems of her jeans. 'But I'll wager she's been in the river, or in water and mud of some sort.'

Jarvin gripped her arm and shook her gently. 'Joni, talk to me. Tell me what happened!'

Martyn touched his arm and shook his head. 'She's not hearing you – at the moment her body's concentrating on keeping her alive. Leave her with me while you go and get her a hot, sweet cup of tea. Tell the barman it's for me.'

Martyn patiently coaxed the steaming cup of sweet tea to Joni's lips, holding it steady for her while she took the first tentative sips. She swallowed and then blinked her eyes and stared into his face. 'No! No!' she gasped in fright, shuddering violently as she tried to pull away and scattering hot, scalding tea over the rim of the cup and onto his fingers.

Martyn barely managed to keep the cup steady. 'Joni, you're amongst friends now,' he whispered, without flinching and pushed the cup toward her. 'Drink the tea – it will help you. Nobody is going to hurt you. Jarvin's sitting there beside you. You're safe now.'

She hesitated but her eyes were confused: it was as if she didn't know where she was. She turned her head and stared blankly at Jarvin and then recognition gradually focused her eyes. 'Jarvin, thank God I've found you, it . . . it . . . it was . . .' Her voice stuttered and stumbled to a halt: she couldn't get the words out, it was all choked up in the back of her throat in a terrified tangle. Huge tears ran down her dirty cheeks.

'Drink the tea, Joni, give yourself some time. It'll make you feel better.' Martyn smiled as she took the cup in both hands and began to drink. He leaned across to Jarvin and quietly told him to get to the bar and fetch another cup of tea and order something for Joni to eat.

Joni seemed to have recovered a little and smiled weakly up at him as he returned with the second cup of tea. 'It was horrible,' she whispered, barely waiting for him to resume his seat, her fingers gripped the handle of the cup and her teeth chattered as she spoke. 'Those foul creatures . . .' She paused again, her eyes wide with fear as she glanced across her shoulder to the door.

'What creatures, Joni?' Martyn frowned – he couldn't understand why she was still trying to frighten Jarvin. 'Please, start at the beginning, tell us what happened.'

She studied Martyn's face for a moment and then shook her head. 'No,' she muttered. 'I can't do that.' And she began to replace the half-empty cup in the saucer and slowly get to her feet.

Martyn reached across the table and put his hand lightly on her arm to restrain her. 'I don't know what you're trying to hide, Joni, or who you're trying to protect, but you're exhausted. You can't run forever, you know.'

She hesitated, her face wretched with indecision. She looked from Martyn to Jarvin and back again before glancing fearfully toward the door. 'You have to both promise me you won't go to the police. You won't tell them who I am.'

Slowly they both nodded and Joni resumed her seat, pulling it even closer to the table. Her eyes were clouded with concentration as she searched for the right words to explain her misery, to make them understand what had driven her to run away. She pushed the cup around the saucer and then picked it up and drained it in three, large swallows. 'I disappeared from university in November last year.' The words came out in a rush and the relief at finally sharing the secret she had bottled up was obvious in her voice as she continued in a quick, confessional whisper. 'I had to get away. I was suffocating, living my life through other people's expectations. You're so young when it begins that you don't realise it's happening and then one day you look in the mirror and you don't recognise the face staring back at you any more. But then I ran away and my picture was in all the newspapers – they thought I had been kidnapped or murdered. There was a nationwide hunt . . .'

'And you never told anyone? You never told anyone at all that you are all right?' Jarvin interrupted, his eyebrows raised in shocked surprise. 'Not even your mother? Not anyone?'

Martyn frowned and hushed him into silence. He hadn't expected a confession like this. He leaned closer to her, holding her gaze and asked directly, 'Has old Mary's disappearance got anything to do with your fear of the police? Are you hiding anything else? It's important, I really have to know.'

The question caught her completely off-balance. She stared blankly at him and then slowly shook her head. 'No, of course not, how could it? But if I go to the police they'll never believe what I tell them about her murder, they'll find out who I am and then I'll have to face the recriminations, all the awful . . .'

'You're afraid of facing all the pain and suffering you have caused aren't you?' Martyn said softly as he took her hand in his.

For a moment Joni sat perfectly still, looking at him, then her eyes filled with tears. He had touched the very centre of her torment. Suddenly the dam of all that heartbreak, all the suffering she had so selfishly inflicted, broke and she buried her head on his shoulder and wept. Between her sobs she whispered, 'I never meant to cause so much pain, I just had to get away. Once the newspapers got hold of the news of my disappearance the publicity made me feel that I couldn't go back, and every day I left it it got harder, until I knew that I'd never be able to make that journey home. I could never breach the rift.'

'Of course you will, and when you're ready I'll help you to make that journey,' Martyn soothed, giving her his large, white handkerchief and gently rocking her backward and forward, waiting for her tears to subside. He glanced across at Jarvin and found him staring quizzically back.

'Wait a minute,' he hissed, his anger rising. 'Don't you believe her story? Why did you need to ask her about the old woman's death?'

'There are so many loose ends.' Martyn smiled as he tried to placate him. 'I thought she was hiding something about Mary's disappearance. After all she had convinced you that the old woman had been ritually murdered despite the lack of a body or any blood at the scene of the murder. She knew Mary's movements that evening: what else was I supposed to think?'

The clatter of spoons and forks on the table and the arrival of three, steaming bowls of soup brought a halt to the conversation. Martyn thanked the waitress and ordered another round of drinks before motioning to the others to eat. Jarvin couldn't contain his curiosity for long and after a couple of hastily-eaten spoonfuls he asked Joni what had happened to her after she had left the 'Cranes' on the previous evening. Hesitantly she related everything: how the demons had broken into the squat and forced the crowd to abandon the old Dean's Hall early the previous morning. They had decided it had 'bad karma' and that it was time they moved on. There was a new place, a large old house in Greyfriars that they had been sussing out, and they were going to invade it that evening.

'I didn't say anything but I had decided that I wasn't going with them. I wanted to get right out of the city, I was afraid that those demons would come after me again if I stayed around.' Joni paused. 'I've got some friends who run a commune over at Fritton, it's about fourteen miles to the east of the city if you follow the railway line through Buckenham and Cantley. There's a short cut across the marshes if you know the paths and don't mind getting your feet wet. Anyway that's where I intended going after I left here last night. Everything was fine as I made my way through the crowds in the city centre. I was escaping, getting away. It was only when I reached Thorpe Road and left the noise of the city behind me that I began to sense that I was being followed. It seemed so weird, it wasn't exactly footsteps, more a dull scrape and patter of something sharp running across the pavements or the brickwork of the buildings. It was getting closer and closer. I didn't want to find out what it was so I broke into a run and turned away into Stacey Road and then ducked out of sight into a maze of back alleyways. Luckily I know that area fairly well and I managed to find my way into the alley that leads into the road directly opposite a hole in the wire fence above the railway. I squeezed through the hole and slithered down the grassy embankment. I waited for a moment at the bottom and listened. Everything was quiet. All I could hear was the breeze in the power cables overhead. I was sure I had shaken them off so I began to follow the track toward Brundall. I kept a sharp ear open for the sound of the trains, I didn't want to get killed.'

'You were going to walk all the way to Fritton?' Jarvin exclaimed.

'How else was I supposed to get there? I don't have any money and I hate begging lifts.'

'But you hadn't shaken off your pursuers had you?' Martyn asked, urging her to continue with her story.

Joni shivered, her eyes widening with fear as she shook her head. 'No, I hadn't. I had just crossed the viaduct over the River Yar. I had no trouble following the line through Postwick, then I heard them again. I was just thinking I was safe and was about half-way through the tunnel when I heard the scrape of their claws on the gravel, then I heard the shriek of their voices and I knew who it was following me. My blood ran cold. I looked back and saw them, dozens of small, hideous creatures filling the mouth of the tunnel and swarming after me. Then I heard another noise ahead of me. I turned round and there were the headlamps of a train. I thought I was dead – there was nowhere for me to go. I threw myself sideways against the tunnel wall and fell into one of those shallow recesses they must have built for workmen to shelter in. Something tried to follow me, it was clawing at my heels, but it was snatched away. There was a blaze of sparks and the stench of burning flesh as the train ploughed through the creatures. Then suddenly it was gone, one minute a blur of lights and a thunder of noise and then nothing, just me cowering in a hole.

'All around there were screams of agony and tongues of fire crackled in crazy lines across the tunnel roof. It lit up a terrible scene and I could see dismembered limbs and mangled creatures scattered all across the tracks. I didn't wait to find out how many of them had escaped, I just scrambled to my feet and ran towards the end of the tunnel.

Some of them must have survived because I could hear them start to follow me but when I ran out of the tunnel I found I was trapped. The cutting was too steep to climb. Then I remembered that there was only a few hundred yards before the track ran onto an embankment that fell away toward the River Yar.'

Joni fell silent and shuddered. Talking about it had resurrected vivid images of that desperate scramble down the embankment, their howls of pursuit filled her ears and she could still feel their claws snatching at her mane of flying hair and snagging on her jacket as she sprinted through the narrow bank of trees that lined the river bank. She could clearly remember the starlight shimmering on the water as she raced toward it and she could still see the dark, ominous shadows that rippled and danced beneath the opposite bank.

'What happened? How did you get away?' Jarvin's anxious whisper made her jump and drop the soup spoon onto the table with a clatter.

'I . . . I ran straight into the river. I didn't have any other choice, those monstrous things had almost caught up, another yard and they would have been swarming all over me. I waded out through the mud and weeds and when the water had reached my waist I started to swim. The flow of the river is quite strong and it began to pull me downstream, forcing me back toward the bank I had just left where the river bends sharply to the left. I'm not a good swimmer and I was beginning to panic. I was expecting to feel their claws grab my legs and the weight of them on my back would have dragged me under the water. I was sure they had followed me, they were so close when I had jumped off the bank. It was only then that I realised that their voices were some way off. I managed to look back without swallowing too much water and I could see the creatures streaming along the bank between the trees. They were following me as the current took me downstream. Suddenly it occurred to me that they couldn't swim, or they were afraid of the water. Then I saw a chance to get away, if only I could keep in the centre of the river and let the current carry me around the bend toward the opposite bank.'

Martyn listened to her describe how she had dragged herself out of the river exhausted and terrified on the far bank. Joni's fear was real, frighteningly real, he could see it in her face and hear it in her voice. She hadn't hallucinated or invented her ordeal, but what the hell were those creatures? He didn't subscribe to ghosts or fairy stories, he exorcised the fantasies of madness with reason. Jarvin cut across his train of thought with a question.

'What happened to the demons? Did you see any more of them?'

'Yes.' Joni nodded grimly, with half an eye on the door. 'There aren't many places to cross that stretch of water – it gets marshy on both sides after Brundall, so I thought I'd be safe enough if I kept to the bank and I hoped I'd come across a boat I could borrow. I'd hardly covered a mile by crossing drainage ditches and wading through freezing cold channels of mud before I heard their hideous shrieks and saw their grotesque shapes on top of the river bank. I've no idea how they got across but they were almost directly above me. I slipped back into the water and tried to hide where the current had undercut the bank but they must have smelt me out or something because they seemed to have a supernatural way of knowing where I am. Suddenly, without warning, they swarmed straight down, hurling branches and stones at my hiding place as they tried to drive me out.'

Joni put her elbows on the table and rested her head wearily in her hands. 'The rest of the night was a nightmare of hide and seek and eventually I gave up trying to get to

Fritton.' She hesitated, shaking her head. 'No, that's wrong, those monstrous creatures sort of herded me back towards the city. They kept crossing and re-crossing the river somehow. They were always there, always ready to claw at me whenever I tried to get out. I was getting so cold and tired wading through the mud and water. I'd almost got past the point of caring if they caught me as dawn began to break. After that it's all a blur. I remember thinking that if I could just find Jarvin he would know how to get rid of them then the sun came up and I don't remember seeing them today.'

'My God, no wonder you're so exhausted!' Jarvin exclaimed.

Joni was beginning to shiver with exhaustion again and Martyn thought he had better wait to ask her why she thought the creatures were after her. Suddenly the door of the bar burst open. Joni gave a startled gasp and Jarvin spun round, but Martyn rose to his feet, his face split into a beaming, half-moon grin as he waved and called out. 'George, we're over here.'

'These prints are too dark to really see if anything is hiding up in the roof. They don't show us anything at all except for . . .' Jarvin paused and bent closer to examine the photographs. 'Pigeons! It's just a flock of pigeons.' He muttered with disappointment as he shuffled through the thick wad of photographs that George had just given to him. He stopped and looked up at the photographer to thank him for developing them so quickly and then he asked if it would be possible to reprint the darker shots of the roof and make them lighter.

George pulled on his glasses and looked carefully at the prints, then he took the negatives out of the folder and examined them minutely against the light from the bulb that hung above the table before he shook his head. 'No, I'm sorry, you won't get a better definition. I think the problem was that your flash gun wasn't properly synchronised with the shutter of the camera and that split second of time difference meant that there was insufficient light to expose the film properly. There's also a couple of frames out of focus but I've printed them as well since Martyn asked me to enlarge everything.'

Jarvin re-shuffled through the prints slowly, more carefully, stopping when he reached one that looked as though it had been taken through a bowl of dirty water. A second's glance was enough to tell him that it was the one he had taken of the demons' footprints as he looked along the clerestory. 'There! Take a look, that should have proved beyond a doubt that those demons exist. I wish I wasn't such a lousy photographer though,' he muttered and tossed the photograph dismissively to Joni.

She looked at the blur of light and shadow and turned it upside down and back again. It could have been anything. She silently passed it back to Jarvin. Martyn returned from the bar with a drink for George and sat down thoughtfully.

'Hey, Joni, look at this, it's most peculiar. I don't understand, it's . . .' Jarvin's voice trailed off. He had moved the empty soup bowls and the half-empty glass onto the floor before spreading the photographs over the small table top. He was peering down at the stylised carvings of two angels locked in combat. The relief had been cleverly hidden amongst the arabesque tracery at the top of an arcade of medieval stone work.

Martyn watched as a photograph fell off the edge of the table and fluttered to the floor. 'I think it might be better if we took this lot home and spread them out on the drawing-room floor, don't you?'

'Yes, yes, of course,' Jarvin answered as Martyn's hand re-appeared above the table top to place the rescued print on top of the others. Standing up Jarvin gathered the pictures into the large, brown envelope they had arrived in.

George decided to stay in the pub and as Martyn and Jarvin turned to leave they noticed that Joni hadn't made a move to rise from her chair. 'You can't stay there all night, gal,' Martyn said, his face creased with a frown of concern. 'Where will you go after closing time, have you thought about that, young lady?'

'I don't know. I'll find somewhere, you needn't worry about me.' Joni tried to put on a brave face but her defiant shrug was a wretched failure, her eyes gave her away, they were haunted with the knowledge that those creatures were out there beyond the bustle and noise of the pub. They were lurking in the shadows, waiting to hunt her down.

'Worry?' Martyn laughed as he moved toward the door. 'I wouldn't be able to sleep a wink tonight for worrying about you after what you went through. You're coming back with us, no "ifs" or "buts", there's plenty of room to spare, it's a huge, rambling old house.'

Joni heaved a sigh of relief, but still she hesitated to get up and follow them. There was something so kind, so warm and genuine about the doctor and she didn't want those creatures to harm him.

Martyn paused, his hand on the door handle, and he turned back toward her, a welcoming grin spread across his face. 'Come on, Joni, hurry up.'

'But what if those creatures try to get at me during the night? They'll smash up your house.'

'I'm sure the three of us can drive them away. At least we'll be ready.' Martyn laughed as he rubbed his hands together. 'Come on, Jarvin's getting impatient to unravel the secrets in these photographs.'

CHAPTER NINE

Hard Evidence (Unusual Substances)

THE MOMENT Joni stepped out of the 'Cranes' and the door clicked shut behind her all thoughts that she may have given those monstrous creatures the slip earlier in the day, during that frightening struggle up the river, evaporated. She could sense them somewhere close, lurking in the shadows, and she imagined that she could smell their foul odour on the evening breeze. She called out to the others, begging them to wait until she caught them up, and she kept close to Jarvin as they walked across the city into Giles Street where Martyn had parked the car.

'Can't you smell them? They're hiding all around us.'

Jarvin sniffed at the night air for a moment before shaking his head as a diesel cab pulled up and stopped only a few yards from them, obliterating all smells in clouds of blue exhaust fumes. 'No, I don't think so. I'm not sure really!' he shouted above the roar of the cab's engine.

Joni perched rather than sat on the wide leather seat as she peered out of the back window at the deserted streets on the short journey to Bishopsgate. She was expecting to see demons swarm after them in pursuit at any minute and she watched, shielding her eyes against the occasional glare of other cars' headlights, and breathed a sigh of relief as they turned through wrought-iron gates and along the gravel driveway to pull up in front of the main door of Martyn's house. It was an exorcist's house in medieval times, but had been in Martyn's family for the past hundred and fifty years. It was a sturdy, wooden-framed house of whitewashed stone and black, ornately carved beams. It had tall, mullioned windows and stood well back from Bishops-gate, shielded at the front by a row of ancient beech trees and at the rear by a low, flint and brick wall with a small, arched gate which separated it from the cathedral grounds.

'Come in, come in,' Martyn beamed as he unlocked the front door. He led them past a sweeping staircase and along a wide hallway lined with coloured hunting prints, two umbrella stands and a small collection of brass-handled sea-chests. He stopped halfway along the hall to throw open the drawing-room door and switched on the lights before ushering them in, telling Jarvin to draw the curtains and spread the photographs out wherever he liked while he organised some refreshments.

A smile of surprise tugged at the corners of Joni's lips as she followed them in over the threshold. The warm, friendly atmosphere of the low-beamed room caught her completely off-balance. There was a faint smell of wax polish from the wooden floorboards and the deep leather chesterfield and reclining armchairs reflected the soft lamplight in muted hues. A cavernous inglenook with huge, twisted firedogs occupied almost one entire wall and white bookshelves crowded with hundreds of books and pictures filled the other. The wooden floor was scattered with Turkish rugs and there were three coffee tables, strategically placed to catch the sunlight, bearing dozens of exotic plants in orna-mental pots. The room reflected a very private, personal side of Martyn that she hadn't given a thought to before. It had a particularly warm, homely feel and made her realise how much she really missed her own home, how much she had so selfishly sacrificed to 'find herself'.

'Joni. Joni!' Martyn's voice cut across her regrets and made her blink as she looked toward him. There was a soft smile of concern in his eyes as he continued, 'You can have my sister's old room tonight. There's a wardrobe full of her clothes, or at least what the moths haven't eaten. Anyway, follow me up and rummage through them yourself. See if you can find something warm and dry to put on.'

Joni stood awkwardly in the centre of the small bedroom, feeling confused. She looked at him as he stood in the doorway. 'Why? I don't understand why you're doing this, you don't have to help me.'

Martyn was thoughtful as he returned her gaze. He was undecided as to how he should reply: he needed Joni's help if he was to break the cycle of madness that possessed Jarvin. She was obviously a key figure to him: if she said it was all nonsense then that would shake his conviction, but he wasn't sure how he was to approach her and get her co-operation. Martyn wasn't sure how much he could really trust her since she was the one who had originally triggered his chronic delusion. She was scared, he was certain of that, and she was running away, but from whom? Was it from the same people who had destroyed Jarvin's room? What was it that Jarvin had really stumbled upon in that porch and how was Joni tied up in the old vagrant's disappearance? Martyn decided to keep his doubts and questions to himself for a little longer, at least until he knew a little more. He smiled softly and spread his hands. 'There is no ulterior motive. I just wanted to help you and Jarvin. There's nowhere else for you to go tonight and when I said I would help you I meant it.'

Joni suddenly felt foolish for doubting him. 'Thanks. I'm not used to people being kind.'

Martyn laughed and waved his hand toward the wardrobe as he turned toward the door. 'Sort out some dry clothes – take any of them. Coffee will be ready in ten minutes.'

He turned and hurried down the stairs but hesitated when he reached the bottom, then turned towards his study rather than going directly into the kitchen. He crossed the floor of his study and rolled up the top of an oak bureau, switching on the desk lamp at the same time. He quickly found a small key and unlocked one of the inside drawers where a heavy service revolver lay at the bottom under some papers. Alongside it lay a small box of cartridges. He didn't believe in demons or living stone angels but . . . He hummed tunelessly as he carefully loaded the revolver, checked that the safety catch was on and then slipped it, and the spare ammunition, into his coat pocket. He patted the heavy bulge as he re-locked the bureau and switched off the light before moving into the kitchen. He had barely finished making a pot of strong coffee before he heard an excited shout from the drawing-room.

'Well?' Martyn asked, making room on one of the coffee tables for the tray. 'What manner of secrets have you unearthed in those photographs?'

'It's all here!' Jarvin cried, excitedly stabbing a finger at the mass of photographs that were spread out on the floor. 'Everything that Joni told me about the old woman's murder is here – repeated again and again, only there's more . . . much more.'

A rush of footsteps on the stairs and Joni's tight, anxious voice, made them both turn toward the doorway. 'What is it? What have you found?'

Jarvin hesitated, not quite knowing where to start, but Martyn smiled at her and beckoned her into the room. She looked completely different in his sister's striped jumper and faded slacks.

'Everything's here. The demons, the dark angel, there's so much here: take a look at this section of the ornamental screen, and this relief carving from the font . . . where's it got to, it was here a moment ago . . .' His voice faltered as he sifted through the photographs.

'You mean you can prove that what I saw really happened in the porch? It wasn't an hallucination or a nightmare, it really did take place? I was beginning to wonder if I wasn't going mad.'

'Oh yes, yes, of course I can. Here take a look,' Jarvin answered quickly as he found the two photographs he was searching for and held them up for the others to examine.

Martyn studied the picture and then shrugged his shoulders. All he could see was beautiful, medieval tracery. An intricate, interweaving mass of light and shadow.

'No, don't look at the overall design, look inside it,' Jarvin urged.

'Where? What am I looking for?'

Jarvin cleared a space on the floor and laid the pictures side by side, then, with the tip of his pen, he traced around the stylised outline of the angel and the sprawling figure of a monk who lay beneath it with his chest torn open, the shattered ribs and sternum clearly protruding through the wound.

Martyn tried to follow the pen. 'Yes, yes I think I can see the angel . . .' He paused. The pen had moved on and the outline of what could have been the angel's outstretched wings shimmered and then vanished back into the intricate mass of light and shadow. Martyn blinked and rubbed his eyes and then tried again, but the more he stared at the picture the dizzier he became.

Joni blinked and looked away from the photographs. 'No, I can't see anything, and the harder I try to see the angel the sicker it makes me feel.'

Jarvin frowned. He couldn't understand why they hadn't immediately seen the carvings of the angel in either picture.

The bodies below it were more difficult to decipher, more stylised. He stared at the pictures, wondering if it was trying to look at them together that was making it more difficult. 'Perhaps if you just look at the photograph on the right it will be easier.' He pushed the lefthand picture away amongst the others. 'Here, let's try again, I'll trace around the angel's outline again, only more slowly.'

Martyn glanced around as he remembered the coffee. An idea occurred to him. 'No, wait a moment,' he murmured, reaching for the coffee pot and pouring out three cups. 'Let's get what we're trying to see into perspective. Latin was a necessity if you studied medicine – can either of you understand it?'

'Yes, a little,' answered Joni, baffled.

'Of course, it's a fundamental language for archaeology.'

'Good. So we can roughly translate any inscription in English or Latin, or at least grasp at its meaning. But what if it's in Hindu, or some obscure South American language, what then?'

Jarvin shrugged. He couldn't see where Martyn's line of thought was taking them to. 'It would be meaningless to us. We would have to get someone to translate it. But we're not likely to come across anything like that in this cathedral.'

Martyn laughed. 'No, of course not, but it does illustrate the problem Joni and I are having with these pictures. You're familiar with the languages hidden inside those carvings, whereas we don't know what we're looking at or its significance.'

'Oh, of course, how stupid of me!' Jarvin exclaimed, scrabbling through the photographs for something they might be able to recognise, for somewhere to begin. He stopped when he came to the ones that showed the medieval graffiti scratched on the walls of the clerestory. The focus was sharp enough for them to see the symbols to protect against evil that had been etched there.

Martyn examined the picture very closely and found he could easily pick out the signs of the cross and the symbolic drawings of hundreds of eyes that Jarvin indicated but it was beyond the stretch of his imagination to unravel the thousands of other meaningless scratches and see them as demons and horned monsters. 'Yes, I can see some of the more obvious signs but what do they all mean?' he asked as he passed the picture on to Joni.

'Mean?' Jarvin cried. 'Can't you see – they are desperate scratchings by frightened people, a continuous cry for help against an evil they didn't understand, a cry that echoed down the centuries for over six hundred years! They are trying to ward off the winged terror that haunted their lives! The astounding thing was that I could find so many signs etched by so many different hands and in different styles all crowded together on the same clerestory wall.'

'Yes, but surely people have been seeing demons and having visions of angels since the dawn of civilisation?' Martyn argued putting his empty coffee cup back on the table. 'Research has proved that it is mostly due to diet, you know, eating the wrong kind of mushroom, too much yeast in the ale . . .'

'Yes, yes, I've heard all the arguments. They're probably the reasons why anyone discovering a couple of these pictures of the angels or the devils would have attached no importance to them – they are likely to have treated them as mild curiosities,' Jarvin retorted impatiently. 'And normally I would agree with them and dismiss the odd carving or wall painting of a visitation but these are different and far too numerous.'

Joni let their arguing voices fade into the background as

she picked up some of the photographs and looked through them. Suddenly she let out a cry and dropped the pictures as if they had burned her fingers. Both men turned abruptly toward her. 'What is it? What did you see?' Jarvin asked quickly as he retrieved the pictures and shuffled through, stopping as she indicated the one he had taken of the gargoyles on the roof.

'There's some of the creatures that devoured Mary's body and hunted me along the river!' she gasped, trembling from head to foot. 'That's them, I swear it.'

'Demons, where? Let me have a look!' Martyn's voice quickened with expectation. He had never expected to see any real evidence of their story or imagined that they would ever be capable of providing anything to support their ramblings, but he found himself eagerly crowding forward to take a closer look at the photograph. 'Gargoyles!' he muttered, straightening. 'They're only gargoyles and they have been squatting up there on the roof over those gutter spouts and pissing in the drain pipes for the past couple of hundred years.'

He saw Jarvin's eyes narrow as he opened his mouth ready to argue in reply. 'Don't take my word for it,' Martyn continued quickly before Jarvin could speak and he crossed to one of the bookshelves, pulling out a narrow volume bound in dark blue cloth before handing it over. 'There are extensive photographs of the cathedral in RH Mottram's book, *The Glories of Norwich Cathedral*. Here, take a look for yourself.'

The telephone began to ring in Martyn's office and its noisy, persistent tone forced him to answer it at the very moment when the first opportunity to disprove the delusions had presented itself. 'I'll be right back,' he muttered.

Leaving Jarvin with the book, he hurried along the hallway and picked up the phone. 'Martyn Burr here.' The line crackled and then he heard a voice that he vaguely recognised.

'Martyn, Martyn, is that you? This is John Groves, from the museum. I'm glad I caught you in – it's about those samples of stonedust you brought in earlier today.'

'Ah, yes,' Martyn answered, his interest sharpening. 'Have you managed to determine what sort of stone they are?'

There was a slight pause before the analyst answered and Martyn could discern some agitation in his voice. 'You did say that the samples were taken from a statue in the cathedral and the South Porch didn't you? This isn't some kind of a prank is it?'

Martyn frowned. 'No, I wrote on the envelopes quite clearly, they told you where the samples came from. Why, what's the matter with them?'

There was another pause and what sounded like a rustle of paper. 'You're sure some of the students at the hospital where you teach couldn't have swapped those envelopes while you weren't looking? Only these samples would make more sense if you had said they were taken from the floor of a mortuary or an abattoir.'

Martyn felt a cold shiver go down his spine. 'What? Say that again.'

'I analysed the dust particles from the envelope that you labelled "from the porch" first. I think the stone particles are caen stone, judging from the granular appearance, but the odd thing was, I found traces of blood and tissue cells amongst the stonedust. I didn't recognise them at first, partly because I wasn't looking for them but mostly because the colour had been leached out of the cells. To the naked eye they were invisible, that's why I thought it must be the students from the hospital trying to play a joke or something. It's not far from the end of term after all. But I still don't know how they did it.'

Martyn frowned, his mind reeling. 'Are you sure?'

'Oh yes. They're definitely red blood cells.'

'What about the samples from the angel? What did you find there?'

'The darker substance in the other of the two envelopes you brought in also showed up as a heavy saturation of red blood cells, but I can't identify the stone – in fact I haven't got a clue what it is. It's showing up under the microscope as some sort of soft, porous substance with an unusual molecular structure. It doesn't seem to match anything I've ever seen before, but at least your students hadn't bothered to try to disguise the red blood cells at all.'

Martyn tried to keep his voice level as he asked. 'Are the samples of blood compatible? Could they have come from the same source?'

There was a pause while the analyst considered the question and consulted his notes. 'I'm not sure,' he answered slowly. 'I didn't try a cross-match and I didn't isolate the blood group, but from my rudimentary examination of the sample I'd say some of the cells were so old that they appear to have mummified and bonded with the stone, or whatever it is. I'd say it's been there a hell of a long time. That's why I thought the samples were from the floor of the mortuary or somewhere like it.'

'Could they be animal cells?' Martyn asked.

'Oh no. They're definitely human. It's the cleverest prank I've ever seen.'

Martyn felt his knees going weak and he slumped down on the chair beside the phone. 'Yes, well the end of term jokes get more complicated every year. Thanks for alerting me.' Martyn answered slowly, but his mind was racing and he barely heard what John was saying as he tried to encompass the horrific discovery he had just made. 'No, don't throw the envelopes away!' he called down the receiver as he realised what the analyst had said. 'Is there any way you could age and cross-type the samples from the envelopes for me? I'd really like a full report, and it would be good to find out what was used to leach out the colour from the other cells. I'd really like to know how it was done. We've got to try to keep one jump ahead haven't we?'

After John disconnected Martyn slowly replaced the receiver and sat staring at it. So old Mary had been murdered in the porch and someone had gone to a lot of trouble to hide the evidence and plant this absurd story about the stone angel coming to life. They had even drowned the statue in blood to make it seem more plausible, but why? What had the old woman stumbled on to make her assassins go to so much trouble? And why had Joni come back – was it because Jarvin had talked to him? Was it to see if he had swallowed the absurd story? His hand brushed against the bulk of the revolver in his pocket and he was glad he had it with him. He probably knew too much for his own safety already, and if they found out about the laboratory evidence he'd be dead. He sat there pondering what he should do next when something John had said struck home. How could the angel be saturated in blood so old it had bonded with whatever substance the statue was made of? Mary had only been murdered a few days ago so where the hell had it come from? He couldn't possibly believe Joni's bizarre story about the angel coming to life and pouring the blood over its head – statues didn't move – but it coincided with what the analyst had just told him. This whole business was getting ridiculous. There had to be another explanation.

The faint sound of talking drifted to him through the half-open door of the drawing-room. It made Martyn glance anxiously along the hallway. What if Joni had over-heard him on the telephone and contacted her friends to tell them what he had just discovered? He listened intently to their voices but found it difficult to pick out more than the occasional word of their conversation and he breathed a sigh of relief. There was a part of him that didn't want to believe Joni was involved in Mary's murder – he was getting to like the person beneath the hard, street-wise exterior, perhaps if he'd been younger . . . He sighed and slowly got to his feet. Sitting there guessing in the dark wasn't going to provide any answers, at least now he was sure Mary had met her death in the cathedral porch: the blood typing would prove it beyond any doubt. What he needed now was to know why, and then who had done it.

He decided to keep the laboratory report to himself as he pushed open the drawing-room door. 'Just a patient,' he smiled vaguely in response to their questioning looks, but he needn't have bothered to try to hide the nature of the call – they weren't interested.

Jarvin hurried across the moment he entered. 'Look, look at this!' Excitedly, he thrust the open book and a handful of the enlargements into Martyn's hands. Sitting on the edge of the chesterfield he looked at two full-page photographs, one of the Jesus Chapel and the tower and the other of the leaded roof and guttering of the nave and the North Transept taken from the north-west. Then he spread out the enlargements and compared them with the book. That same cold shiver he had experienced only moments ago while he listened on the telephone rippled through his nerve endings. There were more gargoyles perched on the walls and hidden in the shadowy corners in the pictures that Jarvin had taken than there were in the book, he could see that without counting them.

'Well, what do you think about Joni's story now? Now you can see she was telling the truth.'

Martyn was at a loss to know what to say. To acknowledge their existence would mean that he accepted that the angel had anointed itself with blood. His mind was a mass of contradictions: he wasn't sure what he was looking at, which ones were gargoyles and which ones were demons, or whether they were merely decorative pieces of sculpture that had been added since the book was published. He looked across to Joni to ask her to point out which ones she meant and saw her sitting huddled, her knees drawn up to her chin, in one of the armchairs. She was shivering and her face was gaunt and chalk-white with exhaustion.

'You, young lady, should get off to bed this instant. You look just about all-in. These are doctor's orders!'

Joni nodded, her face softening into a half-smile. It had been a long time since anyone had taken this much care of her. Slowly she got to her feet.

'It's easy to tell which ones are the demons. The real gargoyles all serve a purpose – they are all positioned on cornerstones and gutter-spouts. Here, take a look at this picture.' Jarvin nudged Martyn's arm to get his attention as he knelt down on the floor beside the couch and continued, 'I thought there was something odd about those other figures when I was photographing – I even put my hand on one of their heads. I suppose I should have realised what it was then but the two workmen distracted me. The scales felt warm as if from the sun and it was as though it was covered with moss. God, to have been that close!'

Joni paused in the doorway and turned back, her eyes dark with fear, her voice barely a whisper. 'Some of the creatures that chased me along the railway line are there. It's easy to tell which ones – they have severed limbs from when that train ploughed through them in the tunnel.'

Martyn bent forward and studied the pictures again, only more closely. She was right, a lot of the vile figures did have severed limbs. 'Go to bed. We'll talk about all this in the morning. Get some rest now,' he insisted.

Moving across to a cabinet which was set into a bookcase he began rummaging through the top of a drawer for his magnifying glass. He let out a whistle of surprise as he moved the glass slowly across the photographs, magnifying and bringing the severed limbs sharply into focus. They hadn't been broken off and then weathered smooth with the rub of time, they had been sheared through, splintering what looked like gristle and bone, and they stood, gripping onto the stone guttering with their clawed feet, their raw stumps exposed to the wind and weather. He heard Joni's footsteps on the staircase and looked up to the empty doorway. Perhaps he had been wrong all along. Absurd as it all seemed it looked as though Joni had been telling the truth. He studied the photographs again, absently pulling his sideburns as he did so. What he wanted was some real evidence, something he could take to the authorities to convince them. A set of photographs, even with the lab report, just weren't enough on their own.

He scrutinised the photographs of the gargoyles again through the magnifying glass. It was difficult to believe they weren't the real thing, they blended in so well with their surroundings. Without Joni's account of the train ploughing through them in the tunnel and their severed limbs he wouldn't have given them a second glance. Obviously, from the look of their clawed hands and feet, they could have been responsible for destroying Jarvin's room at his lodgings; but why, if they had broken into the Gatehouse to kill him, hadn't they attacked him while he was on the cathedral roof? They'd had the perfect opportunity, unless the proximity of the workmen had saved him.

Or was it the daylight that immobilised them? God, there was so much they didn't know about these creatures. He noticed the scaffolding in one of the pictures, set up against the north-west wall of the transept, and he wondered if it was still there. If it was, they might be able to climb it early the next morning before the workmen arrived and they would try to capture one of the demons. He could probably concoct a tranquilliser that would be strong enough to knock out an elephant. They could snare it like a wild animal – but it wasn't an animal: he might kill it, it might kill them, or it might turn itself into stone and then no one would believe them. He didn't have any idea of their physiological make-up or their tolerance to a tranquilliser: the only thing he knew was that they were carnivorous, they knew that from Joni's account of how they ate Mary's flesh, and he wasn't even sure whether any of them would still be up there when the sun came up.

'There were definitely two angels.' Jarvin's voice cut through his musings and made Martyn glance up.

'What did you say?' He frowned, losing his train of thought.

'There were two angels,' Jarvin repeated, pointing to the spread of photographs on the floor in front of them. 'During the Middle Ages an image of two angels locked in combat keeps recurring. The pictures are very complicated and it will take me a while to unravel their meaning but the white angel suddenly disappears completely after the end of the fifteenth century.'

'That sounds very interesting,' Martyn muttered, returning his attention to the enlargements of the gargoyles. It seemed more important to him to concentrate on getting their hands on one of those vile little creatures than worrying about something that may have happened four hundred years ago. The word 'hands' stuck in his mind and an idea began to crystallise. 'Hands and claws,' he repeated under his breath. Joni had said that the demons were pursuing her through a tunnel when that train had run through them, what if fragments of their severed limbs were still there, lying in the darkness beside the track?

'Jarvin, I've just realised . . .' he hesitated with the sentence unfinished. They couldn't both go rushing off into the night searching for pieces of those creatures along the railway line towards Great Yarmouth. It could take hours to find that tunnel and he didn't want Joni to wake up and find herself alone in the house. She'd be safer with Jarvin there. 'You know with all this excitement I've completely forgotten to visit one of my patients. I'd better attend to it right away!' he cried, quickly rising to his feet. 'Don't bother to wait up for me, I've no idea how long I'll be,' he added as he hurried toward the door.

'Have you got any tracing paper?' Jarvin asked quickly before he left the room. 'Because if I traced the hidden images you'd be able to see them easier.'

'Tracing paper?' Martyn shook his head. 'No, but I think there's some greaseproof paper in a drawer in the kitchen, will that do?' Jarvin barely had time to nod before Martyn had disappeared out of the doorway and through a thickly engraved door at the end of the hall into his surgery.

The doctor could put his hand on a torch with a powerful beam straight away but he couldn't remember where he had put his father's old collection of ordnance survey maps. It was ten years since the old man had died and although Martyn would never have thrown them away all he could remember was that they were in there somewhere. He could remember a large cardboard box and he could see himself putting them on top of the patients' filing cabinet. He looked in the least used one, the one labelled Y – Z, and quickly found the map he was looking for. From Joni's account of her flight he must concentrate on the stretch of line between Postwick and Brundall. There were a number of tunnels there where small roads crossed the track, but there wasn't any way of telling which one: he would just have to search them all. Sighing, he carefully refolded the map and slipped it into his pocket with the revolver.

It was after ten pm and the streets were dark and empty as he fired up the old Silver Shadow and headed out of the city, following the ring road until he branched off onto the A47. The countryside was flat and featureless, desolate fields and dykes, isolated houses and windmills that stood out like bleak sentinels on the paler horizon line. A low, wet mist hung over the watermeadows and the river on his right which shimmered as a pale, ghostly shroud would in the moonlight. He turned off the main road at the signpost to Postwick and pulled up when he reached the bridge. From here he would have to continue his search on foot.

It had been a long time since Martyn had done anything as crazy as this and he felt a little ridiculous as he scrambled up and over the rusty, wire fence that bordered the railway line and wished that he'd had a timetable so that he could check on the trains. He would hate to be standing in the centre of one of those tunnels as the night train came thundering through, and he couldn't imagine how he'd explain away his trespass if a patrolling police officer should apprehend him. He swept the beam of the torch down the steep sides of the cutting and found the black, inhospitable mouth of the tunnel. 'I must be stark, staring mad,' he muttered, almost turning back, but he needed some hard evidence, because there was a part of him, a hidden, darker side of him, that was afraid of the supernatural. He was terrified of the implications such a discovery would have. He needed to prove that whatever had chased Joni along this railway track and now crouched waiting on the roof of the cathedral was from this world and not from some hideous, demon-ridden hell.

He moved the beam of the torch slowly along the bank, searching for somewhere to climb down through the straggling bramble bushes and dense swathes of nettles that grew there. Then he moved the light back toward the tunnel and noticed a winding track that wild animals must have trodden down in the undergrowth and decided to follow it. He had descended no more than a yard before he lost his footing on the wet grass and slithered helplessly down the bank, emitting a yell as he ploughed through the nettles and snagged his clothes, scratching his face on the brambles before he reached the bottom. The torch flew out of his hands, the beam of light erratically stroking both sides of the cutting before it landed with a clatter on the gravel beside the rails. Martyn followed it with a wailing shout, cursing loudly as he emerged through the tangle of bushes, stumbling and grazing the heels of his hands as he sprawled on the stones.

The suddenness of his descent knocked the breath out of him. He crouched there for a moment, gathering his wits and listening to the silence, half-expecting his noisy arrival to have woken the inhabitants of the neighbourhood. But all he could hear was the muted cackle of ducks roosting on the river bank, the rustle of rodents in the undergrowth and somewhere in the distance a dog was barking at the moon. 'I'm not cut out for this sort of thing any more,' he grumbled, tentatively rubbing at the dirt and grit that clung to the palms of his hands.

Climbing to his feet, he retrieved the torch to shine it along the path his rapid descent had cut through the bushes. At least his route back would be fairly easy to find. 'Now let's see what, if anything, remains of these hideous demons.'

He walked slowly forward, keeping to the centre of the track and playing the light from the torch backward and forward across the ground. The darkness inside the tunnel swallowed him up instantly. The moonlight vanished and it became suddenly cold. The echo of his footsteps on the gravel sounded all around him and eerie fingers of river mist drifted in and clung to the floor of the tunnel, swirling around his feet and reflecting back the torch light. There was a rank smell of soot and mouldering brickwork and a dampness that made Martyn shiver. The sound of his own footsteps made him glance repeatedly over his shoulders. He tried to laugh, to shake off the sensation that he was becoming afraid, but the sound stayed with him, haunting him and making him sweep the beam backward and forward faster as he hurried to the patch of light at the far end of the tunnel where moonlight was shining on the railway lines.

There wasn't anything that looked remotely like a demon's arm or claw in the tunnel and Martyn breathed a sigh of relief as he walked out into the moonlight. About six hundred yards ahead of him he could see the black, blind eye of the next tunnel on that stretch of railway line. He took a deep breath and walked on toward it. Immediately he stepped into the darkness of that next tunnel he caught the faint stench of decay and the odour of burnt flesh. A knot of apprehension tightened in his stomach and made him stop and carefully play the beam of the torch over the sleepers and along the rails, carefully looking between them and the walls. The swirling mist was thicker here than the first tunnel and it made the search more difficult but he found the shallow alcove into which Joni had said she had thrown herself. There was nothing on the ground but a pile of broken bricks and a few iron couplings that were used to secure the sleepers. He walked over to the alcove and crouched inside to look back toward the archway he had just entered through. He was disappointed – without those severed limbs he couldn't prove the demons existed.

There didn't seem any point in going any further. He turned back and crossed over to the other side of the tracks to walk close to the wall just in case he had missed anything on the way in. Suddenly something hard crunched against the gravel underneath his left foot. Martyn jumped backward and shone the torch down to where his foot had been and saw the shrivelled remnants of a clawed hand that he had shattered beneath his shoe. He crouched down to examine it more closely, sweeping the beam of light more thoroughly over and between the sleepers and the rails. Then he saw them, at least three or four dismembered limbs. They were so well-camouflaged, lying in the shadows cast by the rails and coloured so like the gravel that he could easily have missed them altogether if he hadn't actually trodden on one. He felt in his pocket for a pair of forceps and a plastic specimen bag that he had stuffed into his jacket before he'd left the house and reached down to pick up a hand that had been severed half-way along its forearm. He shivered and a tingle of fear prickled at the hairs on the nape of his neck as he turned the clawed hand over and began to look closely at it. Even in the stifling darkness of the tunnel and with only the light from his torch he could see it wasn't human, or even from any animal he knew of. There were three elongated fingers and a short, hooked thumb, all of which had vicious talons instead of fingernails. The palm of the hand was covered in a thick mat of hair while the coarse skin, or scales, on the back of the hand and forearm looked positively reptilian.

There wasn't much else he could do in the tunnel other than collect up as many of the severed limbs as he could find and take them back to the hospital, where they had the facilities for a more thorough examination. While he was transferring a hand into the specimen bag he noticed it was brittle beyond the state of rigor mortis. He took out his penknife and gingerly scraped at the scaly skin on the back of the hand; the scales crumbled and flaked away and to Martyn's surprise revealed not layers of flesh and muscle or the anatomy of veins, sinews and bones but a solid, greenish-yellow gravelly substance rather similar to ancient stone. It was so dry that it crumbled into powder at the slightest touch. It explained why, when he had accidentally trodden on it, it had shattered so easily. But why were those severed limbs drying out so quickly? Why had they degenerated into a state of mummification in little over twenty-four hours? If anything, the cold, damp atmosphere inside the tunnel should have had the reverse effect. Unless Jarvin's theories were correct and these demons were hundreds, perhaps thousands, of years old. Being severed from the host must have withered their power of animation, reducing them to ancient, crumbling husks.

A faint, rumbling sound and a whispered vibration in the railway beside him made Martyn glance anxiously behind him. He had forgotten about the risk of being run down by a train. 'Jesus Christ!' he gasped, letting the limb drop into the bag as he saw the cyclops headlamp and huge black shape of the train enter and fill the tunnel. As it thundered toward him, the light from its lamp sent the shadows fleeing before it. He had to get across to that alcove – it was his only chance. He hurled himself sideways, his feet skidding on the rough gravel as he scrambled across the railway lines. He threw himself headfirst into the shallow recess and rolled over, pulling his legs and feet clear of the line seconds before the train screeched past him in a blaze of light and noise.

He lay there dazed and shaking, his heart thudding like a steamhammer as he listened to the sound of the train receding into the distance before climbing unsteadily to his feet. The rustle of the specimen bag made him realise that he was still clutching it in his left hand. The torch lay on the far side of the line where he had dropped it in his mad scramble and nervously crossed the track to retrieve it and shine the beam into the bag to see: but the severed limb had been crushed. All that remained in the bottom of the bag was a fine, greenish-yellow powder, a few matted tufts of hair and broken fragments of the creature's talons. 'It's not much for almost getting myself mown down by the mail train is it?' he muttered under his breath before going down on his hands and knees to search for the other pieces he had seen scattered along the track.

It took him less than fifteen minutes to complete the search and gather up the crumbling remains of two clawed hands and what must once have been the clawed toes and splintered ankles of another couple of the creatures. Unfortunately they had all lain so close to the track that the vibrations of the passing trains had accelerated their degeneration and they were barely recognisable as anything more than withered fragments.

Carefully, he filled the bag and sealed the top before standing up. He'd had enough of trespassing on the railway for one night and he hurried out of the tunnel. The embankment was slightly lower there, and a set of concrete steps led up from a signal tower to a wooden gate. He decided he would rather use the steps than risk damaging the fragile remains of the demons on the steeper ascent on the other side of the first tunnel – it also eliminated the risk of meeting another train even if it did mean a longer walk following the road around to where he had left the car. He had a lot to think about now.

CHAPTER TEN

The Last Pieces of the Jigsaw

JONI HAD found it impossible to get to sleep in the bedroom upstairs. The shadows of the leaves on the ceiling and the rustle they made against the window made her hurry back down to the drawing-room to sit with Jarvin. She suddenly gave a startled cry and sat bolt-upright in the armchair where she had fallen asleep, letting the blanket that she had brought downstairs with her slip unnoticed to the ground. The rattle of the door handle had awoken her. Jarvin looked up tensely, half-rising from where he knelt amongst the pile of books and photographs that were scattered on the floor.

'Martyn!' he cried, his face breaking into a smile of relief as the doctor opened the door and came bursting into the drawing-room. 'I was getting really worried that something had happened. You said you were only popping out to see a patient and you've been gone for hours.'

'I've been demon-hunting.' Martyn grinned, holding up the specimen bag for them to see.

'What? Where have you been? Have you been up on the cathedral roof at this hour, on your own? You must be crazy. Why didn't you tell us?' Jarvin exclaimed, scrambling to his feet and crossing the room to peer closely at the greenish-yellow powdery substance, hair and shrivelled scales, fingers and claws that filled the transparent bag.

'Demons?' Joni's voice was barely a frightened whisper as she shrank back away from Martyn's outstretched hand

and fell back in the chair, her face stark white and her eyes wide with terror.

'Yes, demons, Joni, the ones that chased you along the railway line,' he answered softly. 'I'm not foolish enough to go up onto the roof in the dark and on my own,' he added, glaring at Jarvin.

He carefully deposited the bag of remains onto one of the low tables and pushed the drawing-room door firmly shut. He turned back to face them and looked thoughtfully from one to the other, pressing his hands together as he spoke. 'I think it's time I levelled with you, as they would say in an American film. You see, up until tonight I didn't believe a word of this ritual sacrifice story. The notion that a stone angel could come to life and a horde of demonic creatures would assist it in murdering an old vagrant in the cathedral porch was ridiculous.' He motioned to Jarvin to be quiet and continued, 'I thought you were suffering from a chronic delusional state. Joni's account of the murder fixated your mind on the angel and you have been showing many of the classic symptoms of the disease in your behaviour. I took some scrapings from the statue and the floor of the porch with the intention of proving that there was nothing unusual about the angel. I intended to show you that the murder couldn't possibly have taken place in that porch – stone is porous and some trace of the blood would have remained no matter how thoroughly it had been scrubbed.'

He turned slowly toward Joni. 'Of course I thought you were involved in the old woman's disappearance and when I found traces of blood in the samples that I had taken from the porch it only confirmed it in my mind. After all that was the last place she was seen before she disappeared and Jarvin found you there early the next morning. But what I couldn't understand was why you had gone to so much trouble to invent a sacrificial murder story. There wasn't a body or any visible signs of blood, and you couldn't possibly have known who was going to open the door of the porch that morning – you also couldn't have known about Jarvin's accident or how susceptible it would make him. The whole story was absurd and I really didn't know what to believe.'

'You said you took scrapings from the statue of the angel and from the floor of the porch. What did they show? What made you change your mind about us?' Jarvin interrupted, his voice alive with curiosity.

'On their own they didn't help change my mind,' Martyn answered flatly. 'Both samples revealed traces of red blood cells which came as a complete surprise. The ones that came from the porch had had the colour leached out – as if someone was trying to hide their existence. That merely confirmed my worst fears. I realised that Mary must have been murdered in there – which probably implicated Joni. But there were two odd things about the other sample, the one from the angel; the first was that the analyst couldn't tell me what it is made of, and the second was that some of the blood on the statue had been there for a very long time – so long it is bonding with the stone and mummifying. That is when I began to have doubts, but it was when I heard Joni's account of those demons chasing her along the railway line and saw the photographs of the gargoyles with their severed limbs that I really began to wonder if I'd been wrong all along. I couldn't possibly take both of you with me in case my original theory was correct and if I told you about the samples it would only have revealed to Joni how much I had guessed about her part in Mary's murder.'

He paused for breath and smiled at her with concern. 'Looking at those photographs made me wonder, what if

243

you had been telling me the truth all along? Evidence of the demons' existence might still be lying in that railway tunnel, but I didn't want to leave you here alone while Jarvin and I searched just in case those creatures came looking for you while we were gone.'

'But you really do believe that I didn't have anything to do with that old woman's murder, don't you? Now you must know that I didn't invent those stories about the demons!' Joni leaned anxiously forwards, her knuckles showing bone-white where she was gripping so hard onto the arms of her chair, searching his face for the truth.

'Oh yes, they're real enough. I know that now,' Martyn agreed grimly, rubbing a hand wearily over his face.

It had been a long day and it was a long way from being over yet. He prodded the revolting contents of the specimen bag with the pair of forceps that he had taken from his pocket and frowned. 'But what I don't understand is what those creatures are doing in the cathedral or how they've stayed hidden for so long, or even where they've come from in the first place. And the trouble is I don't think anybody's going to believe what you've stumbled into. I'm still finding it difficult to comprehend it myself and I saw those creatures' limbs lying beside the railway line. Reporting it won't be of any use – I doubt if an analysis of the contents of that bag will reveal anything beyond vague animal-matter and with the little evidence we have at this time we'd be laughed at and then ignored. Statues just don't come to life and demons shouldn't materialise out of thin air.'

He paused and let the forceps clatter onto the table top. 'I've given this . . . this absurd nightmare a lot of thought while I drove back and I'm at a complete loss as to what to do now.'

'We've got to find a way of destroying that angel and its host of demons before they murder again. The answer's here in this room, staring at us out of those photographs, I know it is!' Jarvin spoke with such determination that the other two turned sharply toward him.

'But how? They're not human, you can't just kill them!' Joni cried, her face gaunt with anguish and fear. 'I know they can't be killed, I saw them leap back onto their feet, or what was left of them, and come swarming after me only moments after that train had ploughed right through them. It's impossible, just impossible . . .' Her words faded into a sob.

'No,' Martyn murmured, shaking his head and returning his attention to the bag of remains. 'Their limbs shrivelled and crumbled into dust once they were severed from their bodies. There has to be a way of destroying them even if we have to chop them up piecemeal. But . . .' He paused and turned thoughtfully back to Jarvin. 'But what makes you so sure that the answers are hidden in those photographs? How can they help? I thought they were only scribbled or hastily carved images of what those medieval craftsmen accidentally witnessed.'

Jarvin glanced darkly at the curtained windows and beckoned the others closer to him before he whispered, 'Oh, they're a lot more than that. They tell us exactly how and often where the sacrifices took place. They record the murders in startling detail right back to the twelfth century. And there's something else. I think I've come across something in the archives that makes sense of that manuscript I found: listen to this.'

He slowly read out the rough translation he had made from the damaged manuscript from Bishop Elmphric's reign, which recounted an attack by unknown assailants upon a young mason who was seeking sanctuary beneath the altar. It told how his face had been cruelly clawed 'as if by demons'. 'I made a note of it because it's probably the earliest reference to the demons in the archives and the only written one I've found so far. There is the odd written one that I've found scratched among the carvings, but there's something else much more important in this manuscript that I might have completely misread. I'll need a lot more time to translate it properly. It goes on in some detail about the carving of a miraculous angel. I naturally assumed it was a reference to the dark angel but after studying these photographs I'm pretty sure I'm wrong about that. I think someone has carved another, a white angel, because from early in the twelfth century and for the next three hundred years the images of two angels, sometimes surrounded by raging fires or other forms of chaos but always locked in combat, keep reappearing. And the demons are depicted as helpless onlookers, their claws raised in helpless gestures or else they're covering their eyes. During that period there only appear to have been one or two ritual sacrifices.

'What I can't understand is why Bishop Elmphric, or any other cleric of that period, resorted to having a magical figure sculpted. It's as if they were trying to protect the cathedral from the ravages of the dark angel. But it would have been heresy to dabble in magic – the repercussions of such an act would have shaken the foundations of the Church. I can understand that the Bishop might have commissioned the statue in secret as a desperate measure to stop the killings, but Elmphric dedicated the white angel publicly and in the manuscript he calls it a "miraculous angel". Then nothing is ever heard of it again, at least it's not in the ecclesiastical records. It's as if it didn't exist. It would have vanished forever if I hadn't made the connection when I saw the two angels in these photographs. Here, take a look. I've traced the important parts of the pictures onto the greaseproof paper that I took from the kitchen.'

Martyn couldn't see the relevance between something that

had happened hundreds of years ago and what they were trying to do now but he bent forward and took the tracing, smoothing out the crumpled corners of the flimsy paper as he studied the picture. The two angels locked in combat were instantly obvious – he couldn't see how he could have missed them when he had looked at the photograph.

'Now if we add the most important part of the story you will see that it is telling us exactly when the dark angel was active,' Jarvin murmured, carefully laying a second sheet of the paper over the first.

Martyn rubbed his eyes and peered closely at what appeared to be an intricate design of leaves and berries in the background behind the two angels. There was also a broken spire with tongues of flames curling around it with stylised bolts of lightning in the sky, and at the bottom of the picture he could just make out crude numbers carved amongst the leaves.

'Yes, it's very interesting.' He masked a yawn and straightened his back. 'But I don't see what it's telling us.'

Jarvin frowned with impatience and stabbed his finger at the tracing. 'These medieval craftsmen were trying desperately to tell us what they had witnessed. They were trying to warn us the only way they knew how, telling us about the terror that stalked the cathedral and showing us their joy at seeing the white angel who seemed to be trying to stop the evil. There isn't a line or a mark in their work that doesn't tell us something. The floral patterns of mistletoe tells us it was deep winter, probably soon after Christmas, and the garlands of summer flowers denote the seasons when the angel appeared. In fact, from all these photographs I have already built up a pattern of exactly when the summer sacrifices take place. There is a repeated astrological sign of the moon in the seventh house.'

'What did you say?' Joni suddenly cried. 'I remember, I

remember what he said.' Her voice was full of dread. 'He said that as he called to someone called Samuel! He said exactly what you've just said – "the moon is in the seventh house"!'

'There! It fits with what I've found out. We know exactly when the angel will kill again next summer!' Jarvin exclaimed.

'But you said it struck twice a year. Can you tell when, which day in winter?'

Jarvin shook his head and pointed to the two tracings Martyn had just been looking at. 'No, the interwoven branches of mistletoe have ripe berries, representing winter and there are numerals hidden in the branches, which read 1463. Wait! The collapsing spire, the flames, they might point it exactly. I remember writing something in my notebook . . .' He flicked quickly through his book. 'Yes, the spire was struck by lightning in 1463 resulting in a fire and structural collapse, but I haven't got an exact date. I'll look it up tomorrow.'

'Tomorrow is already today and it won't tell us how to destroy those monsters.' Martyn yawned and rose to his feet. 'And I need some sleep, I've got surgery and then my rounds at the hospital in the morning. You, young lady, should go and get your head down for a couple of hours.'

'No, thanks, I'd rather stay down here.' She smiled, shaking her head. 'I've tried to sleep up there but the rustle of the wind in the trees and the shifting shadows their leaves make across the ceiling made me really afraid. I'll stay here and keep Jarvin company. Maybe I'll sleep in the chair.'

Jarvin was completely preoccupied as Martyn left and he hardly heard the drawing-room door click shut as he immersed himself in the pictures, comparing them with extracts from the pile of old books he had taken down from the bookshelves and cross-referencing them with his notes.

'You know, Joni, there's something so ancient about those demons. They don't appear to conform to the medieval imagery of demons at all. It's as if they're far older. It makes me wonder if they weren't here for a long time before the cathedral was built – maybe as part of some pagan rite or another.'

He laid out the pictures that Martyn had taken of the dark angel and studied them thoughtfully. 'Yes, there were definitely two angels and they were as different as chalk and cheese. But after looking at these photographs what seems odd to me is that the white angel seems to be involved in all the disasters that befell the cathedral. You don't think it could have been responsible in some way, that it might have been trying to bury the dark angel by bringing the building down on it? Surely . . .'

His voice made Joni stir in her sleep. 'Angel, white angel, protect me,' she sighed before drifting away to deeper dreams.

'Of course! I hadn't given it a thought,' Jarvin murmured as he climbed stiffly to his feet.

Her words had made him remember something he had witnessed that first afternoon. He had watched her vanish as she'd clung to that worn, white statue standing amongst the ancient gravestones.

'No, it couldn't be.'

He found himself moving across to the window to draw back a chink in the heavy curtain but the memory of the statue persisted and he remembered how different it had felt. He looked out across the night-dark lawns but the stone wall that bordered them obscured everything except the brooding bulk of the cathedral. He wondered if he could see more from the window of his room. Leaving the drawing-room door ajar he quietly climbed the stairs and crept along the corridor. He rested his fingers on the sill as he gazed out across the cathedral grounds. The lawns looked as soft as dark velvet in the moonlight, the gnarled shadows beneath the yew trees looked blacker than stagnant pools of death. The only onlookers were the ancient gravestones that peopled the lawns in drunken, haphazard rows, their blind faces shining dirty white in the translucent light.

'I must be able to see you from here,' he muttered, craning his neck and searching through the blackened tracery of yew tree branches that crowned the top of the wall.

Away to the right he could see something shimmering in the darkness. He moved along the sill for a better view and saw the statue. It was bathed in moonlight and seemed to glow with a phosphorescent hue that illuminated every feather of its arched wings and etched them against the darkness. The gentle contours of its arms and face, the flowing folds of its robes and everything else that time and the elements had rubbed away had been renewed in startling detail. Jarvin stood in his darkened bedroom transfixed, mesmerised by the soft play of light and shadow on the statue, imagining that the slightest breath of wind might ruffle the angel's feathers or send a ripple of shadow through its flowing robes.

'Beautiful, so beautiful,' he whispered, unaware of the smile that was tugging at the corners of his mouth.

A movement away toward the Erpingham Gate, something running through the shadows beneath the yew trees, caught his attention. He frowned and began to turn but froze, a gasp of surprise escaping his lips. The statue was moving, twisting its head, its beautiful face clouded with anger. Its wings were fanning outward as it looked across its shoulder.

Jarvin crowded forward and tried to open the window. It moved an inch but then stuck. He pressed his face against the cold glass before standing on tiptoe to get a better view.

He could just make out a group of small figures, dark shapes in the moonlight, running and scrabbling across the lawn.

'Demons!' he hissed as they scattered, giving the statue of the white angel a wide berth, and ran on toward the cathedral.

Jarvin gave the window another violent tug and it creaked open. He leaned out as far as he dared and heard the demons' hideous voices shrieking and cursing the statue and then he saw their clawed arms raised in obscene gestures before they disappeared from his sight and vanished beneath the wall. The angel beat its wings so furiously that they became a shimmering blur. It stooped and tried to snatch at the fleeing creatures, its fingers snapping shut on empty air. Jarvin was bewildered. Why didn't it fly? Why didn't it chase them as they began to swarm up the walls of the cathedral and vanish across the roofs?

'Martyn, Joni, quickly, come here, you'll never believe this if you don't see it for yourselves!' he called out, ducking back through the window. 'I think I've found the white angel. Martyn, Joni . . .'

He listened to the silence inside the house for a moment and cursed them softly for not waking up before turning back, his elation and excitement abating. The angel was still again, no more than weathered, petrified stone, its anonymous, blind face staring up at the dark and silent cathedral. It made a sad and solitary figure amongst the headstones.

The cold night air made Jarvin shiver and he moved back to shut the window. As he turned toward the door he realised that he hadn't bothered to put the light on. He grinned and felt in his pocket for the pills that the doctor at Beckonsthorpe had given him and put them on the windowsill. He didn't know how or why it had happened but he wasn't afraid of the dark any more. He yawned as he felt a wave of tiredness sweep over him and remembered that he hadn't had more than a couple of hours' sleep in the last couple of days. He walked across to his bed and sat down, leaning against the pillows and savouring the night. Tomorrow he would take a look at that crumbling statue of the white angel and he would try to find out a little more about Thomas Joseph.

'I have raised thee, fallen angel, out of the ruins to stand once more in glory . . .' he mumbled, the words slurring as Jarvin fell asleep.

'Thomas, Thomas Joseph,' Jarvin murmured softly as he turned the pages of the fifth, huge, dusty volume written about the lives and good works of the wool merchants of the city during the sixteenth century.

He had been searching through them all morning and, at last, he was on to something. He ran his finger carefully down the acres of fine, medieval print.

'Found him!' he exclaimed to Joni who was sitting beside him idly watching the browsers comb through the library shelves in the museum.

'Well? What does it say?' She shifted on the hard, uncomfortable chair, glad of an excuse to move and lean forwards over his shoulder. She tried to decipher the paragraphs that Jarvin was indicating with his index finger but gave up with a shrug of her shoulders. 'I can't make out more than the odd word here and there.'

Jarvin read through the passage, his voice barely a whisper.

'What?' She frowned. 'I can't hear you.'

Jarvin shook his head as he read on. 'There doesn't seem to be anything here to interest us – it's mostly a catalogue of Joseph's good works, details of alms for the poor, donations to the priory for clothes and food for lepers and . . . wait a minute, there's something here!' He fell silent and quickly read on, turning the page before he looked up, his eyes wide with excitement. 'There's an account here of Thomas Joseph's involvement in rebuilding the presbytery vault and part of the spire in 1480, the one that's still here today. It seems that he hadn't only donated a considerable sum of money for the work but he took a keen interest in the building. During the excavations they unearthed the statue of a white angel that had lain buried in the mud beneath the rubble where the spire had collapsed in 1463 and he paid a further sum to set the statue within the cathedral grounds.'

'So, what does that mean? How does this help us?' Joni asked.

'It's more pieces of the jigsaw,' Jarvin smiled. 'It explains the quote on the statue's plinth, it means exactly what it said, "I have raised the fallen angel out of the ruins". It also explains why the statue is so much older than the plinth, it means that the angel was there a long time before 1463, a lot longer. I'm pretty sure now that we've found the white angel that's depicted in those carvings, and more important than that – we've found an ally who can help us to destroy the dark angel and its swarm of demons.'

Joni laughed out loud making readers at the other tables in the library turn and frown at her.

'That's ridiculous!' She giggled, covering her mouth with her hand. 'That worn-out statue hasn't done anything to stop these ritual killings since the fifteenth century, you said so yourself!'

'Yes, yes, I know I did, but that was before I found out the statue still existed and before I saw it move last night. There must be a reason why it stopped battling with the dark angel. There must be some explanation. I wish you'd woken up when I called – you'd have seen it try to reach out and grab at those demons,' he muttered defensively.

'Well, I didn't, and a fat lot of help it was for old Mary!' she replied hotly. 'We're wasting our time here – there's nothing that can help us destroy those monsters.'

'I'm not so sure about that.' He closed the large, leatherbound volume as he rose to his feet. 'There's still so many pieces of the puzzle missing – I can't be sure of anything yet. Perhaps . . .' Jarvin hesitated and then shook his head as he picked up a pile of books and returned them to the desk.

Joni stretched and then turned toward the library door. 'Wait a minute, there's something else I want to try to follow up while we're here,' Jarvin whispered.

'I know your moments.' Joni frowned. 'We've been in here all morning.' She glanced out through the swing doors to the pattern of sunlight and shadow dancing on the museum steps. 'There's a cafe across the road, I'll wait for you there.'

Jarvin nodded briefly and walked back to the librarian's desk to ask if there was anything in the museum that related to the area before the cathedral was built. Maps, documents, anything that might show the whereabouts of religious sites, pagan temples or early burial grounds.

The librarian thought for a moment and then consulted the index system. 'There's an early illuminated document that we think may have come from sometime between the ninth and the eleventh centuries. It refers to a pagan temple but it doesn't say exactly where it is. You'll have to apply in writing to view it though.'

Jarvin fumbled in his pocket and produced the official name-badge that the Dean's secretary had given him, making the excuse that the paper he was writing on the cathedral was due in two days' time. It worked: the librarian beckoned Jarvin to follow him down into a small, dimly-lit room in the basement of the museum.

'The temperature and humidity are kept constant in here: it helps to preserve some of our more fragile artifacts. Please make sure you shut the door behind you.' The librarian spoke reverently, switching on a reading lamp above one of the flat, wooden cabinets on the far side of the room and removing the protective covering. 'The *Hell's Gate Scroll*,' he whispered, stepping back.

Jarvin moved forwards and adjusted the angle of the lamp. He took a sharp intake of breath as he looked down at the illuminated manuscript beneath the glass. It was a complicated and frightening pictorial display of devil-worship with a temple and a bloody altar with a figure stretched out on it. It was devoid of perspective yet executed with painstaking detail, the colours were still so bright and rich. What startled him the most and made his flesh crawl was to see those same demons and a winged figure that looked very much like the dark angel but paler, almost flesh-coloured, except for its face and hands which were the same colour as the blood on the altar. There was a priest in a horned head-dress who appeared to be struggling, wrestling with a monk and soldiers, protecting the angel figure who was hovering over the altar. There were bodies lying around everywhere, in neat rows, with their hearts torn out, being consumed by flames. The picture was almost split in two by a yawning hole in the earth, full of dancing flames and demonic shapes. Amongst the trees were figures armed with swords and what appeared to be a river threading its way around the temple. There was no date; but there was a legend written along the top and bottom of the manuscript. It was in Latin and it would take him a little time to translate it.

'Is that of any help?'

The librarian's voice made Jarvin jump. 'Oh, yes, it is exactly what I was looking for.' He smiled as he looked up.

'You don't happen to have a copy do you? Something I could take away and study more closely?'

'I'm not sure, there were a few photographs taken some years ago. I'm sure the curator won't mind if you borrow one of those if they're still around.' He began to search through a sheaf of papers in a drawer below the cabinet. 'You're in luck!' He pulled out a large folder. 'If you'll just sign your name here on the folder and promise you'll return the picture within a week.'

Jarvin nodded. 'Of course, I'll bring it back as soon as I've translated the legend.' He tried to suppress his excitement but his hand was shaking as he signed his name.

'I think I've discovered where the dark angel and those demonic creatures originally came from.' Jarvin spoke in a conspiratorial whisper as he opened the envelope that he had brought with him from the museum and handed Joni the photograph of the illuminated manuscript. He pulled out a chair and sat down opposite her in the crowded café. 'Well, do you recognise any of the creatures who attacked the old woman in the porch?' he asked, shaking his head at the waitress who was approaching the table to take their order. 'Well?' he pressed, returning his attention to Joni and impatiently drumming his fingers on the table top as she examined the picture.

Joni shuddered and nodded. 'Yes, they are exactly the same. But how could they be, that's not the cathedral is it?'

'No, it's a pagan temple, probably over a thousand years old, but it could have stood where the cathedral is now. Look at the way the river bends around it. Those early illuminated manuscripts were often very accurate maps of an area, if a bit crude. It clearly depicts the destruction of the temple and I hope I'll know more when I've translated the Latin inscription. The librarian said it's called the *Hell's*

Gate Scroll, which I should think refers to the demonic figures dancing around that yawning fissure in the ground, it's close to the altar in the centre of the picture and it's belching smoke and fire.'

'I don't see how knowing there was a pagan temple on the site will help us. Thousands of churches have been built on similar sites. Anyway the things in that picture happened hundreds of years ago.' Joni frowned.

Anger flashed in Jarvin's eyes. 'We won't know the significance of any of it until we have every piece of the jigsaw!' he snapped, pushing the picture back into the envelope and standing up.

'Where are you going now?' Joni asked, swallowing the remains of her coffee.

'Nowhere special, I'm just going to kick up the dust of history and try and find out exactly where this Gate to Hell was.'

Jarvin paused outside the door of the cafe. He had a crumpled street map of the city that he had borrowed from Martyn open in one hand and the photograph in the other. He glanced from one to the other, moved slightly to the right as he looked up to check his bearings and squinted at the shaft of bright sunlight that streamed down through the leaves and branches of the avenue of sycamores lining the street, dappling the pavements in light and shadow.

'The sharp bend in the river should lie due north directly behind the cathedral,' he murmured as he tried to trace the line from where he stood on the map without dropping the photograph.

'What are you trying to do? Here, let me hold the map,' Joni exclaimed, catching it as it slipped from his hands.

'I'm trying to match this early medieval manuscript with the more enduring aspects of the landscape. If you compare the shape of the river it hasn't altered all that much, even though it's probably moved east through silting and dredging quite a lot; and the background of low hills is very similar if you look beyond the city. Try to imagine it without the rows of houses, the factory chimneys and electric pylons. I think the monk or whoever created the manuscript must have drawn it from somewhere quite close to here because it's the highest point and affords the best view. All we need is a couple of clear reference points and we'll find where the temple stood.'

'I'll bet it's where the cathedral stands now, they nearly always built their churches over the old pagan sites. Why don't we start from there?' Joni interrupted.

'No, we can't assume anything, that's the biggest mistake a lot of amateur archaeologists make.'

'But everything in the picture is all jumbled together – the figures are standing on top of one another, sometimes they're even upside down, the altar's above the temple in the air and that gaping Gate to Hell, or whatever it really is, is so close to the bottom of the picture it must be miles from the temple, almost where we're standing now.'

Jarvin laughed softly. 'You're misinterpreting, or rather not reading the images in the manuscript correctly. Remember the monk who drew it probably didn't know anything about perspective: everything was laid out on a flat plane. For him the size and placement of the objects denoted their importance not their actual dimensions, and to show that the altar was in the temple he put it in the sky above the building. The position of the gateway to hell, directly beneath the temple, suggests to me that it lay in the centre of the building and not outside it. But I do agree with you – from the placing of the temple, close to the bend in the river, the cathedral is the most likely place for it.'

Joni studied the manuscript again. 'Well, there isn't anything else in the picture except those trees on either side of the temple and they're standing on top of one another in two lines. If they're meant to give us any landmarks they won't help, they probably died or were cut down hundreds of years ago.'

Jarvin stared at her for a moment and then let out a cry of delight. 'Of course! The trees, the trees, why didn't I think of them?'

Joni frowned, at a loss to understand his excitement.

'Yes, Joni, the yew trees in the cathedral grounds. They must be the ones in that illuminated document. Yew was a sacred wood that was most commonly planted on pre-Christian sites. It's very slow growing so many of the trees are still alive. Take a closer look at the picture – the trees on either side of the temple are older, more established, which would suggest that the site was used for some sort of worship long before the temple was built. But the ones that have been drawn on top of one another leading up to the temple doors are younger, and I think they must have been planted when the temple was built. You know it's funny but I noticed the difference in the age of the trees in the cathedral grounds when I first arrived – it's the sort of thing you would notice in my job, but I didn't give it a second thought.' He paused and carefully slipped the photograph back into its envelope. 'But then I wasn't looking for a pagan temple, was I!'

Joni fell into step with him as they hurried toward the cathedral, threading their way through the early afternoon crowds that thronged the city centre. 'But I still don't see why it's so important to know what was there so long ago, and even if you're right about it there'll be nothing left of it now, nothing that can help us.'

'I'm not sure about that. We don't even know what sort of evil we're up against, what kind of dark magic there is tangled up here.' Jarvin shrugged as they waited for a gap in the traffic before crossing over into Tombland and walking over to the Erpingham Gate. 'I've just got this gut feeling, no this aching knot deep down in my stomach, that I've got to find out everything. We have to know our enemies' weaknesses, it'll be the only way we'll destroy them.'

They reached the shadows in the gateway and stopped to compare the long avenue of ancient, gnarled yew trees that stretched away past the West Door with the photograph.

'That's funny, I'd always imagined they led toward the cathedral.' There was an edge of disappointment in Joni's voice as she looked along the gravelled pathway that led to nowhere.

'I think it did once,' Jarvin answered, taking her arm as he moved her forward out from beneath the archway and into the centre of the avenue. 'If you look at the trees further along the avenue you will see that there are holly and mountain ash planted amongst the yew. I think they were put there to deliberately curve the avenue away from the temple. From where we're standing the pathway curves to the northeast and arrives at the west end of the cathedral. The original avenue would have led due east toward the rising sun.' He slowly turned to the right and walked out onto the lawns. 'I think this was the original avenue,' he called across his shoulder.

Joni hurried out to where he stood, her face tense and drawn.

'Now, if you use your imagination,' he continued before she had time to speak, 'and fill in the gaps between the few straggling yew trees that still remain and the blackened stumps between those old gravestones, you'll see that the avenue leads directly toward the tower into the centre of the cathedral. That's where the temple must have . . .'

'Jarvin! There are two police cars and a lot of people milling about near that building opposite the West Door.

You don't think . . . ?' She paused and anxiously bit her lip, her eyes darkening with fear.

Jarvin drew her back between the trees and onto the gravel path. 'Come on, we had better find out what's happened.'

'No, I can't, I'm afraid!' she cried, pulling against him. 'I can't face the horror of seeing . . .' She swallowed her words and her shoulders began to shake violently as tears trickled down her cheeks.

Jarvin hesitated: a figure in cleric's robes who was standing next to the police cars shouted his name and began to hurry along the path toward them. Jarvin recognised him as the priest who had been sent to meet him on the day he first arrived and he remembered the unpleasant incident beneath the Erpingham Gate.

'Do you remember where Martyn said he'd hidden the key to his house if he was out?'

Joni nodded.

'I'll see you back there later. Oh, and take this with you,' he added on impulse, thrusting the envelope with the photograph in it into her hand.

Joni turned and hurried away, vanishing beneath the archway as the priest reached the spot where Jarvin stood.

'The Dean's been trying to get hold of you all morning. Where on earth have you been? You had better get to your office immediately.'

'I've been working in the museum,' Jarvin offered, but the priest didn't seem interested in listening to his explanation as he hurried him through the knot of people in the doorway and up the stairs toward the small room that Jarvin used as an office.

Jarvin's footsteps faltered as they reached the stairhead and ahead of him was the Dean, his secretary, a police sergeant and two of his constables who had interviewed him and locked him up a couple of nights ago. They were crowding around what remained of his office doorway, their faces grim and set as they turned toward him.

'I want an explanation for all this wanton vandalism, Mandrake!' The Dean's voice exploded with anger as he saw Jarvin appear. His lips were taut; his accusing finger trembled and shook.

The police sergeant put out a restraining hand and held the Dean's arm respectfully as he began to advance along the corridor. 'Perhaps it would be best if you were to leave it to us to investigate the matter, Dean.' He spoke softly, but with enough authority to make the Dean hesitate and turn angrily.

'Investigate? There's nothing to investigate, we've had nothing but trouble ever since the Bishop agreed to have him here. He . . . he arrived rolling drunk, he upset Mrs Sibson and then vandalised the room she kindly let him use; and yesterday he was running about on the scaffolding taking photographs like a demented tourist – drunk again I expect. Now he's smashed up his office. Well, Mr Mandrake, we've had enough of you – consider your employment here terminated. There'll be a letter to your uncle in tomorrow morning's post and I will explain your deplorable behaviour. Now, sergeant, charge him with this wilful vandalism and then get him out of my sight.'

'But I didn't do it . . .'

Jarvin felt a knot of fear and panic tighten in his stomach as he smelt that same odour, that reek of corruption and decay, that he had smelt on the threshold of his room in the Gatehouse after the demons had torn it apart and in the transept the morning after the old woman's murder. It burned in his nostrils.

He walked mechanically towards the doorway, knowing exactly what he'd find, but still his stomach retched. There was a gaping hole in the roof, the walls were scored and smeared with a foul slime and his desk and chair were smashed into a thousand, splintered pieces. Amongst them there was a fragment of Bishop Elmphric's manuscript about the miraculous angel and the other documents that he had borrowed from the archives. Everything had been torn to ribbons and covered in the slime.

'I could never have done this – it was the demons,' he whispered, stepping back hastily. 'I saw them crossing the cathedral lawns last night . . .'

'Demons? Alcoholic demons you mean, the ones inside your head: they caused all this damage. Look! Look at what you've done, Mandrake. I want you out, out of this cathedral now!' The Dean took a step towards him and snatched the name badge from his lapel.

The police sergeant quickly intervened. 'Exactly where were you last night? Can you account for your movements after the cathedral closed, Mr Mandrake?'

'There! I told you he was guilty!' the Dean cried as Jarvin hesitated to answer.

Jarvin was looking down through the ruined doorway at the mess strewn across the floor of his office. He was sure something was missing, but what?

'What did you say?' he asked, looking up and focusing his attention on the question.

'I can vouch for Jarvin, he was at my house all evening, officer.' Martyn's calm voice from the stairhead cut across the Dean's accusations and made him spin round with a look of surprise on his face.

Martyn strode along the corridor and looked in at the wreckage, then stepped back, wrinkling his nose at the disgusting odour.

'Interesting,' he murmured, before turning toward the Dean. 'I can assure you that Jarvin was with me all evening.

He didn't leave the house until this morning when he went to the museum. I'm letting him use one of my spare rooms until he gets sorted out.'

The Dean's face was livid and his mouth opened and closed like a goldfish. 'Out!' he managed eventually, spitting the word at Jarvin and gesticulating with a quivering finger. 'I want you out of this cathedral now!'

Jarvin felt Martyn's hand gently tug at his sleeve. 'Come along, there's nothing more you can do here.'

'I didn't do it. I would never have done anything like this, you've got to believe me,' Jarvin tried to explain, but the Dean had already turned his back on him and was issuing instructions to have the room thoroughly cleaned once the police had finished with it.

'Will you be staying on with Dr Burr now?' the sergeant asked as he followed them along the corridor. 'We'll need to be able to contact you if there are any further questions.'

'Yes, yes, officer, he'll be staying with me for now,' Martyn replied.

'Joni was worried and thought you might need some moral support.' Martyn smiled by way of an explanation of his sudden appearance in the middle of the Dean's accusations as they crossed the cathedral lawns and entered the house through the arched doorway at the end of the garden.

Joni looked up as they entered the kitchen door, a smile of relief on her face as Jarvin nodded to her despondently and slumped down in a chair at the kitchen table.

'He's back safely,' Martyn murmured as he hurried through into the hall.

'Those demons – they've destroyed the office I was working in – the Dean blames me, he wouldn't listen to a word when I tried to tell him . . .' Jarvin paused, buried his head in his hands and sighed. 'What are we going to do now, Joni? If I try and go into the cathedral he'll probably have me arrested on sight. All the documents from the archives I've borrowed have been destroyed, all my notes, everything.' He sat up suddenly as he remembered what was missing from his office. 'They took the carrier bag, those newspapers and the rusty old baked bean tin that belonged to the old woman. They took the only scrap of evidence we had that she was ever in that porch! We'll never destroy them, it's hopeless, utterly hopeless!' He threw up his hands in a gesture of helpless finality.

'You can't give up, Jarvin!' Joni cried as a cold shiver travelled up her spine. 'If they knew that you had hidden Mary's things in that room they must know that I saw them at the sacrifice, and that you know all about it now, too. It's only a matter of time before . . .'

Her voice faltered to a halt as Martyn reappeared in the kitchen doorway. He had caught the thread of their conversation and saw the fear mirrored in Joni's eyes. 'I came across something today that I thought you might find helpful.' He walked across to the table and laid a rather battered book that had been covered in brown wrapping paper in front of Jarvin.

Reluctantly he turned the book around, drawing it toward him as he opened the cover and read the title page. 'Angels! It's *A Dictionary of Angels* by Gustav Davidson! Where on earth did you get it?'

Martyn grinned. 'There's a secondhand bookshop that I often browse through near the market. I went in this morning and asked if they had anything on angels. Will it help?'

'Help?' Jarvin frowned, flicking through the pages of the book so fast that the thousands of names and descriptions became a blur. 'I don't know – I'd need a name, somewhere to start. No, wait a minute, that photograph of the Gates of Hell – there might be a name in the legend. Joni, where did you put it?'

Joni grabbed the picture from the dresser and handed it to Jarvin. He studied the Latin inscription that ran along the top and bottom while the other two watched and waited. 'It's a description of the sacking of the temple and the blood sacrifices that were carried out, it also tells us about the yawning pit full of devils. Ah, yes, here it is – the angel's name is Sammeal.'

Something about the name stirred a memory for Joni. She frowned and her thoughts raced as Jarvin began to leaf through the dictionary.

'Here it is, listen to this. "Sammeal, Satanil, Satan, Ser, Salmeal, a combination of *Sam* meaning poison and *el* meaning angel in rabbinic literature. Sammeal is a chief of the Satans, the angel of death. He is the prince of demons and a magician, the angel who guards the Gates of Hell".' Jarvin paused for breath and Joni opened her mouth to speak. 'No! Wait a minute, there's more!' he cried, silencing her with his hand. 'It says here that his residence is in the Seventh House, which coincides with the time of the summer sacrifices; and further down the page it says, "the dogs shall howl and the ice break when the shadow of death stirs in the Gates of Hell". That must mean the midwinter sacrifice. The dark angel kneeling in the South Transept has got to be Sammeal, hasn't it?'

'No, you're wrong.' Joni's voice made them both look up sharply. 'Hearing you speak its name has triggered my memory. It was all so horrible I suppose I'd shut it out but now it's all coming back. The dark angel called out to Sammeal as he prepared the sacrifice – I think he was trying to raise him.' She fell silent, the shadow of fear showed darkly around her eyes.

'What?' Jarvin gasped as he stared at her.

'Think, Joni, think! Try and remember, did the angel say anything else, anything at all?' Martyn urged.

Joni shuddered and wrung her hands together. She shrank back until her shoulder blades were pressing hard against the dresser. The room seemed to have darkened around her, the late afternoon sounds of birdsong in the garden and the distant hum of the city was muffling into an eerie, haunted silence. 'I don't know,' she whispered. 'I'm not sure. Its voice was more of an echo, a cry, a howl of anger and despair. Just remembering it fills me with dread and makes me go cold in the pit of my stomach. It was so horrible . . .'

'Try, you must try,' Jarvin insisted.

Joni huddled against the dresser. There were beads of sweat glistening on her forehead, yet she shivered, her knuckles whitening as she clenched her hands and cast her mind back to that dimly lit porch. 'Bloodstone!' she whispered. 'I think it called out, "I abad . . . abor – something – I anoint the bloodstone" and then it squeezed the old woman's heart over its head and the blood trickled down into its hair and across its forehead and face. Oh, God, it was horrible, so horrible . . .' And she buried her head in her hands and wept.

Martyn put his arms around her shoulders and comforted her.

'Aba, Ababa . . .' Jarvin murmured to himself as he searched through the dictionary. 'Abachta, Abaddon . . .'

'That's it!' Joni cried, looking up in horror. 'That was the name it called itself!'

'"Abaddon, the destroyer, the angel of the bottomless pit, the blood-red angel of the Apocalypse, the hooked-winged lord of all demons",' Jarvin slowly read out before he looked up at the others with a gleam of triumph in his eyes. 'Now we know its name, the description of its hooked wings fits exactly. It's got to be that figure kneeling in the South Transept!'

'What's in a name? Knowing what the thing's called can't

help us destroy it can it?' Joni frowned.

'It might,' he answered thoughtfully, studying the picture of the Gates of Hell more closely. 'I think we've stumbled on the last few pieces of the jigsaw, secrets we're not supposed to know. Secrets that the creature has murdered for in order to keep them hidden for almost a thousand years.'

A sudden noise, a distant rumbling sound, made them all jump.

'It's only thunder,' Martyn said, loosening his tie. 'We need a good storm to clear the air, it's been so humid for the last couple of days.'

'I think the angel is the altar from that temple!' Jarvin cried out. 'Here, look at that picture again. Abaddon called itself the bloodstone didn't it? Well, in the picture the angel is joined to the altar, it's a part of it. Or perhaps it's in the process of metamorphosis as it tries to escape from the monks destroying the temple. Yes – it says something here beneath the picture. I'll try to translate it.'

The others crowded forward anxiously, oblivious to the afternoon shadows lengthening and deepening into evening, while Jarvin poured over the Latin text. He muttered to himself under his breath and scribbled rapidly on the notepad beside him.

'Listen to this,' he said at last, raising his voice to be heard over a longer, deeper rumble of thunder. 'That monk in the illuminated manuscript, the one striking the high priest, is St Felix, the Bishop of East Angles, and those soldiers are the Knights of the Holy Order of Dunwich. They were on a holy crusade, searching for a whole village of people who had mysteriously vanished when they came upon this pagan temple hidden in a grove of yew trees on a bend of the river. It seems that they caught the high priest, Sammeal, in the middle of a mass sacrifice, but unfortunately they were too late to save most of the victims. You can see them in the picture scattered all over the ground with their hearts torn out.' Jarvin indicated the corpses and then continued, 'From what I can make of the text and the position of everything in the illustration, Sammeal was performing some sort of evil blood-magic, ritualistic murder. He was trying to transfer the life force, or energies, of his victims into the altar, literally saturating it with blood. That's why it is called the bloodstone. I think he was trying to open the Gates of Hell to release the demons from the pits of fire and raise Satan.'

'It looks as if he almost succeeded,' Martyn commented darkly as he pointed at the demonic figures dancing in the flames that were issuing from the yawning hole in the ground.

'I don't know, there's more here. St Felix was convinced that he had killed Sammeal and destroyed the evil – at least that's what it says here. He struck the high priest twice with his crozier and he fell headlong into the flames with demons hanging on to him, screaming a curse on the bloodstone as he fell. The altar exploded into a ball of crimson fire and out of the flames a pale, flesh-coloured angel with hooked wings appeared. It hovered for a moment over the dying flames and then vanished into the sky. The Knights of Dunwich sacked the temple and burned it to the ground, trampling and sealing up the Gate of Hell with their horses' hooves. St Felix appeared in the centre of the smouldering wreckage and struck the ground with his crozier and then a holy spring burst up to wash away all traces of the evil.'

Joni looked at the picture for a moment and then turned her hands up in a hopeless gesture of defeat. 'But I don't understand – if the bishop and the Holy Knights have destroyed the evil then why are the sacrifices still happening?'

'Because they didn't destroy it,' Jarvin answered flatly.

'I think they misinterpreted the metamorphosis of the altar. The transformation of the bloodstone into an angel was not good triumphing over evil: it was the black, bloody heart of the magic escaping. I'm certain now that the figure kneeling in the transept was once the altar in that pagan temple, and the ritual sacrifices it performs are its efforts to resurrect Sammeal.'

'But I don't understand.' Joni frowned. 'What happened to the angel? It couldn't wander around after the temple was sacked and razed to the ground . . . the cathedral wasn't to be built for another couple of hundred years and how did it get into the building once it was completed anyway? It couldn't just have flown in through an open window could it? Surely someone would have noticed if it had just arrived.'

'I really don't know.' Jarvin shrugged. 'There could have been any one of a dozen minor cults using the site for worship during those years. There might even be records of it hidden away somewhere. The angel could even have become a central figure in their beliefs, but we'll probably never know. I don't think that the statue would have had any trouble getting into the cathedral. Try and imagine the place in the eleventh century, a huge medieval building-site, a forest of rickety, wooden scaffolding with hundreds of masons, priests and carpenters living and working there. Think of the noise, dust and confusion. Everything had to be brought in from outside – there would have been a procession of carts full of stone and timber and some with food for the workforce, fleets of barges would have been hauled along the canal which was especially dug behind the site, and people would have been continually unloading the cargoes. Nobody would have noticed the kneeling statue of an angel arriving on any of those carts or barges amongst all the other religious effigies that would have been delivered. Once Abaddon had established its presence and become a part of the place there was nothing to stop the bloody rituals starting again in earnest.'

'Of course! That's why the laboratory report said that the blood cells and scrapings I took from the angel appeared to be so old, so ancient that they are mummifying with whatever it is that it's made of. That statue has been saturating itself with the blood of its victims for centuries.'

'I think it's done more than that,' Jarvin corrected Martyn grimly. 'My guess is that the black magic that Sammeal was invoking when St Felix banished him into the fire-pits of Hell has endured and stayed alive in that angel and that each blood sacrifice it's made has fed its power, making it incredibly strong – so strong that I doubt if there's anything we can do to stop . . .'

'Dynamite!' Martyn interrupted, his lips curling back into a menacing grimace. 'We've got something those medieval craftsmen didn't have: modern technology. We could blow the angel and his horde of demons into a million tiny pieces.'

'No!' Jarvin frowned, slowly shaking his head. 'I don't think that would destroy the magic: it would merely fragment it, and who knows what damage that would do? It would scatter an almighty evil all over the city.'

'I don't care . . .' Joni began as a louder peal of thunder drowned out her voice.

The room grew suddenly darker as the black thunderclouds boiled up to hide the setting sun. A gust of cold wind stirred the branches of the holly trees that grew outside the kitchen window, stroking and scratching their spiky leaves against the glass. The breath of wind died away, the leaves rustled and were still, but the scratching sound persisted, growing gradually louder and louder. An odour of corruption and decay began to fill the room and the kitchen door began to shake, the handle rattling violently.

'Demons!' Jarvin hissed, half rising from his chair as

something struck the door, making it bulge inwards.

'Joni, get back, get out of here!' Martyn shouted, but it was too late.

The door exploded, showering them with splinters of wood and glass.

Lightning flashed and cracked in the dark sky above the cathedral, momentarily illuminating the angel which hovered above the doorway. A mass of hideous, demonic creatures rushed through the gaping hole.

'Seize her!' Abaddon hissed.

A gale of stinking air churned up by the beat of its wings tipped over cups, plates and vases, sending them crashing to the ground and scattering Jarvin's photographs everywhere.

Joni screamed and tried to scramble backwards towards the inner door to the hall, but the demons were upon her before she took three steps. They clawed and scratched at her arms and legs, overwhelming her and bringing her crashing to her knees. She tried to fight them off. In desperation she grabbed hold of the chairs and table as they dragged her across the kitchen floor toward the broken doorway.

'Jarvin, we've got to stop them!' Martyn shouted, snatching up a heavy stone pitcher that stood on the dresser and using it as a club.

He tried to beat the demons off, bringing it down with all his strength on their horned heads, shattering it into a thousand pieces. Two of the demons turned on him, snarling and cursing, biting at his ankles and tipping him up, sending him sprawling backwards across the kitchen floor.

Jarvin looked around for a weapon and grabbed the back of his chair with both hands. He tried to swing it above his head to strike at the creatures, but three of them were clinging onto the legs as he lifted it up and they swarmed down over the seat, along his arms and clawed at his face, momentarily blinding him.

Another tangled itself between his legs and he toppled forwards, crashing against the table, his breath knocked out of him as he too fell to the ground.

It was all over in a matter of seconds. The demons and the angel were gone before Martyn and Jarvin had managed to stagger to their feet. Joni's frantic screams became fainter and fainter.

CHAPTER ELEVEN

Hell's Gate

MARTYN WAS the first to scramble unsteadily to his feet. 'Joni!' he cried as he heard her voice fading and the gate in the garden wall clatter to the ground.

He ran to the ruined doorway, slipping and sliding on the thick trail of slime that the demons had left on the kitchen floor. Behind him Jarvin groaned and struggled to his knees.

'Jarvin!' he cried, urgently. 'For Christ's sake, man, get up. Those filthy creatures have captured Joni, I think they're taking her towards the cathedral! Come on, we've got to get after them now. Quick, before they disappear, come on!'

Jarvin groaned again. Everything was spinning. His head felt as if it had been broken open. He felt for the table and clutched onto it for support as he climbed unsteadily to his feet. The room seemed darker, the familiar objects blurred. He tried to blink and rubbed a hand across his eyes, wincing at the pain as his fingertips touched the raw wounds the demons had gouged around his eyes. He cursed under his breath as he forcefully wiped away the trickles of blood that were oozing into his eyes, using the pain to focus his concentration. He blinked again and saw Martyn silhouetted in the doorway against the erratic fingers of lightning that were stroking the thunder-dark sky.

'Jarvin, come on, those bastards are getting away.' He

grabbed at Jarvin's sleeve as he reached the door.

'No, wait!' Jarvin hesitated. 'We can't chase them empty-handed, we need something, anything, a hammer, a spade, anything we can find to attack them with.'

Martyn remembered the revolver in the pocket of his jacket that he had left hanging in the hall and he made a run for the door. 'There are some tools in the garage!' he shouted over his shoulder.

Jarvin threw open the door to the garage and snapped on the light switch. He searched the untidy shadows behind the big old car. Behind him he heard Martyn's footsteps on the gravel.

'I think they're on the righthand side.' He played the beam of the flashlight onto the darker side of the car.

Jarvin ran around to the other side of the garage and fell onto his knees, scrabbling at the jumble of forgotten, rusty tools that had accumulated there over the years.

'Come on, they're getting away!' Martyn cried impatiently, his voice rising against the rumbles of thunder. 'Just grab anything you can use to hit them with – I've got my gun.' Martyn waved his revolver in front of him, then turned and ran across the lawn.

Jarvin gripped the handle of a sledgehammer in his right hand and a rusty pitchfork in his left and sprinted after the doctor.

It was beginning to rain, large, isolated drops, splattering onto his cheeks and forehead as he ran through the arched doorway into the cathedral grounds. He stopped, uncertain about where the demons would take her. 'Which way? Can you see them?'

Another crash of thunder and a searing flash of lightning showed Martyn the answer. 'Over there – they're running toward the South Transept!' He pointed the gun toward the dark bulk of the cathedral as the flash of lightning momentarily picked them out and threw their hideous shadows across the lawns.

Something moving in the sky away to Jarvin's right made him look round. 'Wait!' he shouted as Martyn began to run after them. 'The white angel – look at the white angel.'

Martyn skidded to a halt and turned just in time to see Abaddon swoop out of the darkness to attack the white angel from behind.

'Look out behind you!' Jarvin shouted.

He didn't know what made him do it, but he changed direction and began to run across the lawns, leaping and stumbling over the forgotten headstones towards the statue. The solitary, winged figure had been leaning forwards on its plinth, wings outstretched, silently shaking its raised fist at the demons as they fled with their prisoner. It must have heard Jarvin's warning shout because it twisted its shoulders and threw up its arms in an attempt to protect itself and deflect the full force of Abaddon's attack, but it was too late. With a bone-jarring crack the dark angel struck, sending the white figure sprawling forwards in a cloud of dust and broken stone feathers.

Abaddon snarled a curse and flew around behind the statue again, striking another brutal blow at the back of the angel's head and driving it to its knees before clawing and gouging at the leprously worn face with its blood-dark fingers.

Jarvin came to a skidding halt less than ten yards from the embattled angels.

'Thomas Joseph, you fool!' he cried. The reason for the white angel's disappearance from the cathedral was suddenly clear. The angel's feet were buried in the mortar of the plinth: it was hopelessly trapped! Thomas Joseph had inadvertently handicapped the only real deterrent there was against Abaddon's evil when he had discovered the white angel lying in the mud and ruins of the collapsed tower and had set it up on the plinth for his own glorification in 1480.

Jarvin threw his pitchfork onto the ground. He knew he had to try and free the angel before Abaddon succeeded in tearing it to pieces, but how? He took a step forwards when he suddenly heard Martyn's voice shouting to him against the noise of the storm.

'Jarvin, they're taking Joni to the porch. For God's sake, man, come on or we'll lose them in the cathedral!'

Abaddon's head snapped up at the sound of Martyn's voice and a fork of lightning lit up the lawns as he saw Jarvin advancing towards him. Abaddon's cold, pitiless eyes focused on him. 'You dare to challenge me?' it hissed, its lip curling into a murderous sneer.

Jarvin felt a knot of panic tighten in the pit of his stomach. He clenched his hands into fists and found he was still clutching the sledgehammer. He gripped it securely with both hands and raised it defensively. 'I know all your black secrets, Abaddon, and I'm going to send you back to Hell!' he shouted defiantly as he ran forwards.

Suddenly he saw a way to free the white angel. If only he could smash the slab of mortar that held it trapped onto the plinth – if only he could get there before Abaddon swooped down and tore him limb from limb . . .

Abaddon snarled and flung his weight against the white angel, sending it toppling sideways and trampled on its fractured wings. Then it rose menacingly into the air above Jarvin. Martyn watched the dark angel's shadow fall across his friend. The angel lunged. Martyn swore and took aim, firing twice at the dark, winged shape. Jarvin ducked instinctively as he heard the shots and ran faster. The bullets whined over his head and struck Abaddon, ricocheting off his glistening, rain-soaked skin, but the sudden impact made the dark creature curse and veer away.

Jarvin seized the moment and leapt forward. He covered the last giant stride with his sledgehammer raised high above his head. 'Angel of Miracles – I'm freeing you!' he shouted as he brought the hammer down, striking the mortar on the plinth between the angel's buried feet so hard that the wooden handle shattered into a thousand splinters in his hands.

The mortar cracked and fell apart from the force of the blow. Jarvin let out a scream of pain as the broken hammer flew out of his hands. He staggered backwards and fell to his knees, his arms numb and burning from fingertips to shoulders.

Somewhere above him in the stormy darkness he heard a scream of rage and the hum of Abaddon's wings getting louder and louder as it renewed its attack.

Jarvin looked up, blinking at the force of the sudden downpour, and watched the white angel struggle. It was crouched down, tearing at the fractured slab of mortar. First one foot appeared and then the other and then it rose into the air, frantically beating its rain-streaked wings, soaring above Jarvin's head to intercept Abaddon. Fragments of blood-soaked stone and particles of dust mingled with the rainstorm to shower down on him as the angels clashed.

'Jarvin, get up! For God's sake come on! Those demons are getting clear away!' Martyn shouted, urging him onto his feet. 'You've freed the angel, there's nothing more you can do here, come on!'

Jarvin scrambled up and ran after Martyn, catching him up half-way across the lawn. 'That angel – the white one – was carved by the mason who was attacked by the demons,' he gasped as they ran toward the door of the porch. 'I saw it all in brilliant images as I struck the mortar. The angel's name is Shateiel, the angel of silence. It's called the miraculous angel because the mason, Geothrick, carved it after he was blinded by the demons. It's been trying to bury the dark angel beneath the ruins of the cathedral from the moment the mason finished it. It's used storms and freak hurricanes, it's used fire and earthquakes to try to destroy Abaddon's evil magic, and it was weakening the magic each time it denied it the ritual sacrifice. The trouble was, each time Shateiel brought the building crashing down to bury Abaddon, the workmen dug it up; until Thomas Joseph interfered by setting it onto that plinth. From that point on, Abaddon has been gaining in strength and power. We've got to stop it. We've just got to, Martyn!'

A sudden noise behind them made them both duck and throw themselves onto the wet gravel as Abaddon, snarling and cursing, fought to break free from Shateiel's grip, their wings beating against the entrance. Suddenly the dark angel escaped and flew in through the porch door and into the South Transept.

'Come on, we've got to find Joni and get her out of there!'

As they ran in through the porch door, the floor of the transept trembled and shook beneath their feet.

'Remember those photographs I took of the tell-tales I put in the tower walls to prove that the tower wasn't safe? Well, the tower's moving so much that they've broken. We've got to be quick – the tower, the spire, everything could come crashing down at any moment. It'll bury us alive!' Jarvin's voice echoed in the dark vastness of the cathedral.

'Hush, listen!' he called, bringing them both to an abrupt halt.

'Which way? What can you hear?' Martyn hissed. He'd been running so hard all he could hear was his own rasping breaths and the blood pounding in his ears.

Jarvin took a step forward and hunted the darkness with

his eyes, searched it with his ears as he listened between the deep rumbles of thunder and drumming rain on the steep roof. The water was gurgling into the gutter-spouts as the floor of the transept continued to tremble beneath his feet. Far away and very faintly he imagined he could hear Joni's tortured screams from somewhere in the bowels of the earth.

'Hell's Gate!' He gripped Martyn's arm. 'Of course! Why didn't I think of it before? It's got to be here somewhere – it's probably directly beneath the cathedral and these convulsions in the ground are why the tower is on the verge of collapse. It's the perfect place to hide the bodies from all those ritual sacrifices, but where exactly is the entrance?'

He took the flashlight from the doctor and slowly swept the beam across the floor.

'What's that smell?' Martyn muttered as they moved carefully forward across the floor.

Jarvin sniffed and felt his spine tingle. It was like the foul odour that the demons had left behind them in the Gatehouse, his office and in Martyn's kitchen; only now it smelled far older, more rank and musty with decay. He remembered he had smelt something like it here in the transept before, the day after the old woman had been murdered in the porch.

'Wait!' he whispered, playing the beam of the torch along the right-hand side of the transept and pausing briefly on Abaddon's empty plinth. Loops of broken chain hung down, almost touching the ground. Some blacksmith must have once tried to prevent the killings many years before, and failed. 'Keep a sharp look-out for the angel, it could spring out on us from anywhere.'

'I think there's something on the other side. I saw something move!' Martyn hissed.

The torch-beam flickered wildly up into the vault of the

283

roof. There was a whirr of wings high up in the lantern of the tower and the sound of stone grating on stone and then louder noises of falling masonry as the angels fought amongst the tiers of supporting arches.

Jarvin steadied the beam of light and brought it down along the righthand side of the transept, sweeping it across the floor. 'I can see a flickering light behind us, half-way along the wall,' Martyn whispered.

Jarvin quickly moved the light along the wall until it illuminated the blank, bricked-up archway that had once led into the ancient transept chapel. 'There! Look at the floor in front of the old archway. A slab of stone has been moved aside – the light I saw was the reflection of flames.'

'It must be the entrance to Hell's Gate. I'll bet that's where those demons have taken Joni!'

'Then we'd better get after them before it's too late,' Martyn urged, removing the spent cartridge cases from his revolver and reloading as he ran across the transept.

Jarvin followed on his heels, glancing anxiously up to his left to the lantern of the tower as the sound of falling masonry grew louder.

'They're going to bring this whole place crashing down on top of us if we're not very quick.'

The claustrophobic fear of being buried alive again re-awakened in his subconscious.

The floor of the transept shook violently, making them both stagger as they reached the lip of the dark entrance. Martyn came to a sudden halt and Jarvin stopped beside him as a hot, stinking gust of air full of the haunting sound of lamenting, wailing screams stopped them both in their tracks.

'Good grief, what on earth's that?' Martyn gasped, clamping his handkerchief over his mouth and nose against the fetid stench that threatened to overpower them.

'I don't know – it could be the echo of all those tortured souls, perhaps the residue of Abaddon's sacrifices trapped in the Gates of Hell,' Jarvin answered uncertainly, his voice muffled as he held his sleeve over his mouth. With his other hand he played the beam of the torch over the twisting flight of stone steps that led away from them down into the bowels of the earth.

'The sound of a load of ghosts isn't going to stop me. I don't really believe in ghosts – come on!' Martyn began to descend the steps, full of determination.

Jarvin hesitated. Claustrophobia tightened in a band of panic across his throat. He tried to swallow and shut it out as memories of being buried in the Egyptian tomb flooded over him.

'Jarvin, come on, what's the matter?'

Martyn's voice cut through the torment inside his head as beads of cold sweat began to trickle down his forehead and wet the palms of his hands. Jarvin shuddered and gritted his teeth. He'd beaten the claustrophobia before when he had been in the police cell and again in the darkness of his room, he had to do it again, now: Joni's life depended upon it.

'Nothing!' he muttered thickly, forcing the emerging phantoms in his head back into the darkness of oblivion.

He couldn't find the courage he needed to open his eyes, not yet, but he took his first, faltering, downward step, keeping his hand upon the rough stone wall as he felt for the next step. He felt naked, so alone, unarmed and helplessly afraid.

'Take my arm, I'll guide us,' Martyn whispered softly. He had to calm Jarvin down: he couldn't make this journey on his own. The limit of his own courage was running out.

'Jarvin, you must try and open your eyes. Focus your mind on anything else but the darkness. Talk out loud if it

285

helps you, watch the bright beam of the torch and we'll be out of here in no time, no time at all,' he urged as they worked their way down the slippery steps.

A noise above them, the sliding, grating sound of the stone slab that covered the entrance being dragged back into place, made Jarvin open his eyes and try to scramble back up the steps in panic. A terror of being shut in the swallowing darkness overwhelmed him. Above them Abaddon's sneering face appeared in the closing gap.

'Die slowly, you fools, you helpless fools. Perish in the black, choking fires of Hell!' His voice rose in a cruel, pitiless shriek of laughter as he struggled to close the entrance.

'No . . . no!' Jarvin screamed.

A sudden rush of cool, fresh air, the smell of rainwashed grass and night flowers, filled the closing gap. Abaddon's laughter turned into a snarling curse. There was a scuffle of footsteps and the whirr of white wings in the darkness above the entrance, then the heavy stone slab rocked violently backward and forward. Suddenly with a shattering crack it split into thousands of tiny pieces.

'Look out!' Martyn cried.

He pulled Jarvin against the wall just before the shattered rock cascaded down the stairway. Shateiel had broken the magic spell that had been woven into the stone. It vanished forever in a blaze of stinging, bitter, hot sparks.

The white figure appeared momentarily at the top of the stairhead to grapple with the dark angel. There was such power, such a strength of purpose in him: he had to destroy the evil. His certainty quelled the terror that was strangling Jarvin's courage. 'Come on!' he shouted as he started forwards down the steps. 'Shateiel will keep the way clear at least until we've rescued Joni. Come on. There isn't a moment to lose.'

They rounded the sharp twist in the stairs and there their

steps came to an abrupt end. Ahead of them a vast crypt opened out, a forest of thin, twisted columns that had been clawed and gouged from the ground beneath the cathedral. The spires of stone held up the low roof of the crypt and everywhere there were stone coffins and desecrated tombs. The remains of robes and vestments clung to skeletal figures that hung from the ceiling and the stench of death was overwhelming. The air was thick with its swirling, stinging vapours.

'Come on, we've got to find Joni,' Jarvin whispered, but his hand trembled as he lowered the beam of the torch and swept it slowly across the floor.

'Oh, my God, it's a mass grave,' Martyn gasped as the beam of light illuminated hundreds, perhaps thousands, of skeletons lying there.

They were so jumbled together it was impossible to see which bones belonged to which. Some glistened with a fragile whiteness while parts of others were still grimly bound together with blackened, withered strips of skin, gristle or flesh. Here and there the light picked out a staring eye or a tooth. The rotting remnants of cloth, hassocks, wimples or monks' robes were everywhere, but in amongst them were the remnants of leather jerkins, battered metal helms, armoured boots, shoes and simple wooden sandals that still clung to many of the gruesome skeletal remains.

Wherever Jarvin moved the trembling finger of light it revealed more bones, more evidence of the ritual slaughter that had thrown those bones into careless heaps or stacked them in haphazard, glistening, sickening piles that stretched away as far as the torch-beam reached.

'I think all the rib-cages have had their sternums smashed open exactly like the victims in that illuminated manuscript,' Martyn whispered.

Jarvin shuddered. Suddenly a yawning crack split open across the floor immediately in front of them. Flames roared up and licked greedily through the tangled mass of bones, shrivelling the sinews and making them perform a lurid, rattling dance of death. Fragments of fat that still clung to them crackled and spat, sending up a choking, thick, yellow smoke. The light of the flames illuminated the vastness of the crypt and behind the flames Martyn caught a glimpse of the swarm of demons dragging Joni up across the endless heaps of bones.

'She's over there! Over there to the right. We've got to get across the flames somehow!' Martyn's voice echoed through the low crypt.

One of the straggling demons stopped and turned its horned and scaly head toward the sound and looked back, gesticulating wildly as it saw them beyond the fire. It let out a warning shriek that drove the swarm of hideous creatures scrambling faster than ever over the mounds of bones and away into the inky darkness.

Joni caught the faint echo of Martyn's voice. It made her twist and fight harder against the vicious claws that held her captive and she managed to raise her head high enough to see the two of them silhouetted in the light of the flames. She screamed out their names and kicked and struggled in a desperate effort to break free, but the demons gripped her arms and legs more tightly, their claws cutting painfully into her flesh as they ran faster.

'Damn, they've seen us!' Martyn shouted angrily. 'We'll never catch up with them if we can't get across this infernal fissure.'

'This stuff must be from the fire-pits of Hell – it's reacting against us, stopping us from chasing those creatures!' Jarvin shouted back.

He tried to approach the fiery crack again and find a place

to jump across only to be driven back as the flames roared up.

The floor of the crypt trembled and shook violently as an earthquake rippled through it, making the piles of gruesome remains rattle and jump. Pieces of bone, fragments of coffins and the relics buried inside them, loose rocks, earth, stones and clouds of dust began to shower down as the roof of the crypt began to collapse.

'We're going to be buried alive!' Jarvin shouted in terror, staggering backwards as the floor moved beneath his feet.

He would have fallen amongst the heaps of bones if his flailing hands hadn't grabbed at something that hung down from the crumbling roof above his head. A long, thin, metal-bound staff or pole found its way into his hand and he clung on as he regained his balance. He shone the torch up to see what it was, and then gave a startled cry and let go.

'What's the matter? Come on, there's something odd over there. Shine the torch over, there's a cloud of steam billowing up further to the left, it looks as though there might be a way across.'

'No, wait a second, look at this. I think I've found St Felix's crosier, the one he used to banish Sammeal all that time ago.' Jarvin steadied the beam of the torch on the long, thin shaft of iron-bound wood that protruded from the rock and earth of the roof above him.

'That's crazy! You're wasting precious time, come on! There's a waterfall or something away to the left. I think we can get across over there . . .'

Martyn's voice trailed away into a sickened gasp as he retraced his steps through the piles of bones and looked up into the dusty beam of light at the remains of an ancient stone tomb that must have sunk down through the ceiling of the crypt hundreds of years ago. A withered, skeletal hand hung down through a gaping hole in the tomb, its blackened, ringed fingers death-locked around the curved, ornamental, bronze head of the staff. The ground beneath the tomb was clear of bodies and a circle of at least three feet wide was left where the iron-bound tip of the crozier almost touched the ground.

'I know I'm right,' Jarvin whispered, giving the staff a tug to try to free it. 'Look at the ring on the middle finger of his hand – it bears the same motif and heraldic design that was drawn on that manuscript about Hell's Gate. It's got to be the same. Don't you realise the power that this staff had to . . .'

Joni suddenly let out a series of tortured screams that made the floor buckle and heave beneath their feet and the flames roar up out of the pits of Hell.

'Jarvin, they're trying to tear her apart. Come on, we've no time for this!'

Martyn made a dash for the waterfall and the way across to where the demons had stopped on a steep slope of bones about twenty yards away. They were cursing and jabbering, fighting over her, trying to pull her in a dozen different directions at once, mauling and clawing at her arms and legs, ripping through her clothes and tearing at her wrists and ankles until they were a mess of bloodied flesh.

The Bishop's withered fingers shivered as she screamed and momentarily eased their death-lock on the staff.

'Help us!' Jarvin cried as he gave the crozier another tug, but the fingers wouldn't yield. The soul of the Bishop couldn't have understood him, and his ghost wouldn't have understood the language even if it could have heard him.

He cried out again in sheer desperation, this time in Latin, evoking all that was good and pure in an attempt to triumph over the evil. A whispered sigh came from inside the tomb, a murmured echo of an intonation, and a sweet smell of ancient incense wafted over him. He knew, somehow, that he had received the Bishop's blessing to use the crozier against Abaddon and it now slipped easily from his blackened fingers. He grasped the staff gratefully in his right hand and followed Martyn, running and stumbling through the mounds of bones.

The sound of dripping and tumbling water grew louder. Ahead of him the ground was clear of bones and a solid column of wet, glistening rock reached up to touch the roof of the crypt. A steady shower of sparkling droplets cascaded down all around it. The yawning, fiery chasm in the floor stopped well short of the strange waterfall. Jarvin frowned as he looked up and then realised that it must be the overflow from the baptismal Font of Tears, the holy spring that St Felix had created in the very centre of the Gates of Hell.

Another violent tremor shook the crypt, bringing a rain of loose earth and stones crashing down. Jarvin remembered that the font was almost in the centre of the tower and that they were probably directly beneath thousands of tons of rubble and stone.

The terror of being buried alive paralysed him. The core of Jarvin's sanity screamed inside his head, shouting at him to move, to rescue Joni and get out of there before it was too late.

Three sudden, loud explosions drowned out the roar and crackle of the flames as Martyn fired into the swarm of squabbling demons. The sound of the gunshots echoed throughout the claustrophobic crypt.

'Jarvin, for God's sake, help me. There are too many, help!'

Martyn's desperate shout was almost lost amongst the creatures' wild, demented howls as they attacked, threatening at once to overwhelm him, but it was enough to break the binding spell of fear that had gripped Jarvin. With a savage, avenging shout he leapt forward, scrambling up and over the mounds of bones, the phantoms of his terror quelled and temporarily forgotten. Wielding the crozier like a spear he stabbed and skewered at the milling mass of hell-creatures as he attacked.

The armoured tip of the ancient staff grew white-hot in his hands as it seared through the demons' scaly skin, sending up clouds of bitter, stinking, acrid smoke. They screamed with pain and scattered, dropping Joni in terror as they ran.

'Get out – make for the steps – there's a place by that waterfall, close to the chasm!' Jarvin shouted as Joni scrambled unsteadily to her feet.

Martyn managed to break free, crushing a demon's skull with the gun barrel, and he grabbed at Joni's arm as the demons surged back, screaming and clawing for their blood.

'Look out behind you!' Jarvin shouted as two large, double-headed monsters leapt up at them out of the roaring flames.

Martyn spun round and fired twice, point-blank, into the creatures' chests. The impact of the bullets drove them backwards, tumbling them over and over, shattering and crushing the carpet of bones before they crashed to a halt against the glistening column of rock beneath the waterfall.

There was a moment of utter silence as the demons swarming around them hesitated in horror while the two creatures were drenched beneath the curtain of water. They began to howl, uttering desperate cries as they clawed frantically at the wet ground in an effort to get out, but they were powerless to escape. Their claws shrivelled and their fingers and toes began to melt.

Slowly, everything that was in contact with the water began to dissolve. Their screams of pain became strangled, choking gasps as yellow, bilious slime frothed out of their mouths. Blood gushed from their eyes and noses and the scaly hide that covered their bodies began to bubble and blister. Rapidly their hideous forms began to collapse and melt into a reeking, writhing, shapeless mass that boiled away across the ground and slowly poured over the lip of the fiery chasm. The flames roared up and licked angrily across the roof; the floor of the crypt buckled and convulsed as new fire-cracks opened and the demons surged forward once again to attack.

'It's the water from St Felix's spring. It's holy water, it destroys them!' Jarvin shouted, hooking a creature on the end of the staff and hurling it into the waterfall. 'Force them into it – use anything you can, just drive them into the water. Gather it into your hands, throw it over them as you run for the steps.'

The demons attacked ferociously, clawing at their legs in a desperate attempt to stop them reaching the water but Jarvin beat them back until Joni fell exhausted onto her knees at the edge of the curtain of water. Now she understood why the demons had been afraid and why they hadn't been able to follow her into the river, and she knew they couldn't touch her now. She cupped her hands and felt the chilling coldness as she filled them, then leaned forward and let the water splash onto her head and trickle down her face. She sensed Martyn beside her and heard him gasp for breath as he reached the safety of the waterfall and then she heard Jarvin shout, urging her to her feet.

Suddenly a thunderous rumbling shook the crypt and loose rocks and earth fell to the ground as the ceiling began to come down.

'Get out! Get out! The cathedral's going to collapse at any moment!'

'Come on, keep close together and throw the water at the creatures' faces. There's not a moment to lose, quickly!'

Martyn cried as he rushed at the mass of demons that were swarming to block off their escape.

He scattered the water he had collected in his cupped hands and the creatures' snarls of rage turned to howls and shrieks of pain as the holy water hissed and burned, dissolving the scaly skin that covered their faces and melting their red-veined eyes so that they vanished into oozing sockets. Blinded, they writhed and helplessly trampled and clawed at each other as their surge carried them relentlessly forward.

Jarvin stabbed and slashed at them frantically with the crozier, but the sheer weight of their numbers and their demonic fury was driving them back toward the fiery crack. Jarvin's foot slipped as he trod on an ancient metal helm and he would have fallen if Joni hadn't grabbed his arm. He glanced quickly down as the helm rolled away amongst the brittle bones that they were trampling beneath their feet.

'Use the metal helmets, the funeral urns, anything!' he shouted suddenly. 'There's a lot of them lying on the floor – fill them with the water.'

Joni ducked down just a foot away from the demons' claws and scrabbled desperately amongst the tangled mass of gruesome remains. She snatched and pulled free two of the battered, rusty helmets, a heavy stone vase and an altar cup and then leapt back beneath the safety of the waterfall, shuddering and trembling with the horror of it all. 'We're never going to get out of here!' she cried above the blood-curdling howls and screams of the seething mass. 'For every one of those monsters we destroy a dozen more are leaping up out of the flames. It's hopeless, utterly hopeless!'

'No! We mustn't give up – we must fight our way out of this infernal place before Shateiel brings the tower and the spire down to seal it up. Fill these vessels and be ready for a last desperate dash for the steps.'

The crypt shook and the floor buckled as billowing clouds

of earth and stones fell from the crumbling roof. The rumbling thunder of falling masonry filled their ears.

'Now! Throw the water across the creatures' heads and then run through them as their flesh melts. Run for your lives!' Jarvin shouted as the falling debris choked the flickering light of the flames.

Dimly, a pace ahead of him, Jarvin saw the other two break through the milling chaos, kicking out at the distorted bodies of the demons, tearing themselves free from their flailing claws as with one, last mighty effort Martyn reached the steps and clambered up, pausing briefly to pull Joni up after him.

Something made Jarvin hesitate and look past them up the winding stairway as he caught a sound above the sounds of torment, a noise, a vibrating hum that struck terror into the pit of his stomach. He barely had time to shout the angel's name before Abaddon filled the entrance to the crypt, stirring up a gale of hatred in the screaming demons as he flew down through the Gate of Hell. His wings fanned the leaping flames into a white-hot frenzy and left a blazing trail of sparks where they struck the rough, stone walls.

'You shall burn, burn in the fire-pits! You shall shrivel to nothing for daring to try and defile my magic!' the angel snarled, its face distorted with fury, its eyes pin-points of murderous rage as it swooped down and reached out to snatch at Martyn and Joni and hurl them into the roaring flames.

'Look out, Abaddon's above you!' Jarvin shouted.

Martyn heard the shout and felt the wings' downdraught as the angel's black shadow engulfed them and then he threw himself forwards onto the steps dragging Joni beside him. The stone feathers of Abaddon's wings grazed painfully over their heads and shoulders, tearing through their clothes. The dark angel hissed and cursed and tried to turn in the low crypt but its wings snagged on the crumbling roof. Jarvin ducked as it flew over his head and then spun round and instinctively raised the ancient staff, forcing the angel back further into the crypt as Abaddon landed.

'You helpless pryer into the secrets of my magic ritual! You shall be the first to feed the flames of Hell! You shall burn for daring to meddle into powers of darkness far beyond your comprehension.' The dark angel hissed and spat the venomous words, its harsh, grating voice striking fear into Jarvin's heart as it landed heavily on the carpet of bones, splintering and crushing them carelessly beneath its feet and heedlessly trampling on the milling mass of blinded demons as it turned toward him.

Advancing, it came with a menace of hatred that made Jarvin stagger backward and let out a strangled cry of sheer terror. Fear turned his guts to water and his knees to jelly. He wanted to run, to throw the staff away and flee for his life but he couldn't move. The angel was towering over him, mesmerising him, freezing him like a trapped animal, and it was moving closer and closer. Its hooked wings were brushing against the low roof, bringing down an avalanche of rocks and earth in its wake; then it spread them, and the shadowy shrouds of death that dwelt beneath them began to smother and overwhelm him.

A triumphant sneer of hatred split Abaddon's lips as it reached out to grip the crozier and snap and crumble it as easily as a stalk of straw between its blood-dark fingers. 'Nothing can harm me, you fool, there is no escape from the Gate of Hell. You are mine to torment forever.'

Jarvin's feeble hands trembled and shook as they held onto the staff. He wanted to offer it to the menacing figure, to beg and plead for his life, but he stood still and held the crozier between them. There was a rush of footsteps up the steps behind him and he heard Martyn's voice shouting at him, urging him to hurl the staff at the dark angel and run, get out while Shateiel guarded the entrance to the crypt.

'Come on, Jarvin, move, it's what the white angel wants you to do!'

But something inside Jarvin refused to let go and he grimly stabbed at the angel as it threatened to engulf him. Abaddon's face contorted with rage. He snarled and grabbed at the crozier with both hands, emitting a tortured scream as the armoured tip blazed between his fingers.

The angel's blood-saturated, stone hands hissed and bubbled and it leapt backward, the muscles in its arms convulsing into knots as it tried to let go of the staff but its hands were locked together, the skin of its fingers fused and wet. The livid blood of the countless victims it had sacrificed over the years was beginning to ooze and weep through the bubbling blisters that were creeping up its arms and weakening the magic. Abaddon threw back its head and a wailing scream of agony, something it had never known in the thousand years of torture and death it had inflicted upon others, poured out of its mouth. It thrashed its wings wildly, scattering and crushing the blinded demons that milled around its feet, and then it charged at Jarvin, threatening to hurl him to the ground.

Jarvin staggered and almost lost his footing beneath the dark angel's furious onslaught but somehow he hung on to the ancient staff. Somehow he found the courage and the strength to drive Abaddon back underneath the waterfall, to make him the prisoner of the crypt, to cleanse the bloodstone and wash away the evil forever.

'Jarvin, come on, we can't wait a moment longer – the cathedral's collapsing!' Martyn's voice was shouting from the top of the steps, his voice becoming fainter as Joni grabbed him and began to drag him out of the transept and into the rainy night.

'Get out, get out while you can!' Jarvin shouted back. His voice echoed up across the Gate of Hell and across the transept. 'I have to stay here, I have to force this evil creature back into the holy water. Nothing else matters – it's the only way we can destroy it forever. Take Joni and go, run before it's too late.'

The dark angel screamed and cursed as it fought desperately to break free. It cried out for the serpents from the fiery pit to swarm up and drag its attacker down into the flames. Writhing tentacles rose up out of the fire and snaked through the mounds of bones. They squirmed towards Jarvin's legs and curled around his ankles. Abaddon wrenched at the crozier, brutally twisting it so that the ornate bronze head of the staff that had been cast in the shape of two, curling, intertwined fern leaves cut and tore the soft skin on the palms of Jarvin's hands to ribbons. He gasped and gritted his teeth against the pain, refusing to let go of the slipping staff as the blood oozed between his clenched fingers and dripped down onto the shiny tentacles that were clasping and tightening around his ankles, beginning to pull him away toward the flames. Droplets of his blood splattered on the scaly serpent's skin and shrivelled it away to nothing.

'I will destroy your evil forever!' Jarvin shouted into the angel's face, throwing all his strength against the towering dark creature as it screamed and spat at him.

Nothing else mattered now: he had to force Abaddon relentlessly backward, step by tortuous step, and keep him beneath the misty, shimmering curtain of water.

The angel frantically beat its wings until their hooked tips scraped and scoured across the low roof and his heels began slipping on the carpet of bones in a last effort to stop Jarvin's relentless onslaught, but the power of its magic was weakening.

'All your evil will be washed away, purged for all eternity!' Jarvin cried, giving Abaddon a last savage push that made the angel lose its balance and stagger. First its wings and then its head and shoulders, followed by its glistening torso splashed beneath the waterfall.

Abaddon's body convulsed; its mouth became a howling, distorted cavern of pain and the rending sound that issued from it shook the crypt and sent a violent tremor up through the fabric of the cathedral, tearing it apart as the water from the Font of Tears, St Felix's holy spring, began to wash away the evil magic. Rivers of sacrificial blood ran down between its dark feathers, streaking its screaming face and running down its chest and legs. It oozed out of the porous stone in a bloody tide that flooded away, sweeping the refuse of its ritual slaughter towards the fiery doorcracks of Hell itself.

The continuous rumbling sound of thunder was directly above Jarvin's head, telling him that the cathedral was collapsing on top of them, but the sound was now being drowned out by Abaddon's screams. The lantern of the tower swayed and split apart, jagged cracks raced up the sides of the soaring spire as it slowly toppled and began to fall across the transept, its slender beauty illuminated by the electric storm sweeping over the city. The forest of stone ribs that supported its vaulted roof fractured and rained down huge blocks of masonry capitals, piers and columns of stone as it sealed the Gates of Hell forever and cut off Jarvin's only means of escape as it sent up thick, choking clouds of dust and debris.

Through the thickening dust storm, just as the rubble began to spew down the steps of the crypt, he thought he saw a glimmer of light, a last chance of escape, a way to save himself. He was about to turn, to make a desperate dash, to let go of the ancient crozier and make a rush for the closing entrance at the top of the steps but the dark angel staggered forwards and almost broke free of the shimmering curtain of water. The flames briefly roared up, feeding the magic and forcing Jarvin to turn back and drive the shivering, bloody creature back beneath the water.

'Why can't you die, damn you, why can't all the magic be washed away?' he shouted as tears of hopelessness began to well up.

There was no escape. He was never going to get out, he knew that now. Millions of tons of suffocating earth and stone were already crushing down on top of him and the roof of the crypt would collapse at any moment. It was growing darker as the fires sank into the floor. He looked down at the figure of the angel, its body almost bleached white: it was shrinking, dissolving away.

Then, it became nothing: he had finally destroyed the evil. A churning terror overwhelmed him: he was utterly alone, abandoned in the dark.

The roof of the crypt began to creak and settle. Every nerve and sinew in his body was tense with waiting, holding his last breath, when suddenly he heard the sound of footsteps behind him. He turned. 'Shateiel!' he cried as he saw the white angel rushing toward him out of the darkness and he knew he had not been abandoned to die alone.

The angel of silence gathered him into its open arms and drew its wings down over his head.

At once Jarvin felt the silky touch of the angel's skin and flowing robes as its arms enfolded him. The terror of being buried melted away: he wasn't afraid any more. He lifted his head and felt the soft rain beating down upon his face and smelt the balmy fragrance of a summer's night as the roof of the crypt finally collapsed in a roar of thunder that sealed the Gate of Hell forever.

*

EPILOGUE

Joni awoke from her recurring nightmare with a cry. The images of the demonic creatures swarming all over her crowded the darkness. The roar of collapsing masonry echoed in her head and her tongue was dry with the bitter taste of stone dust. She blinked and sat up, gripping the bedclothes tightly while the images of her desperate rush to get out of the collapsing building gradually melted away into the moonlit silence. She slipped out of bed and pulled on her dressing-gown before crossing to the window that overlooked the cathedral grounds and gazed out at the bare, skeletal bones of the new spire etched in albescence against the starry sky. Time had not dimmed the memory or allowed her to forget one moment. It was all still so vivid, as though it had happened only yesterday.

She sensed a movement in the darkness behind her and felt Martyn's arms gently encircle her. 'Are you watching for them?' he asked softly.

Joni smiled in the darkness and shook her head. She didn't have to wait or watch for them: Jarvin and the white angel were always there, somewhere on the edge of sight, walking together in the moonlight and dwelling in the shadows beneath the avenue of silent yew trees.

☐	MAGICIAN Raymond E. Feist	0-586-21783-5	£6.99
☐	SILVERTHORN Raymond E. Feist	0-586-06417-6	£4.99
☐	A DARKNESS AT SETHANON Raymond E. Feist	0-586-06688-8	£5.99
☐	THE SILVER BRANCH Patricia Kennealy	0-586-21248-5	£4.99
☐	THE ELVENBANE A. Norton/M. Lackey	0-586-21687-1	£5.99
☐	MASTER OF WHITESTORM Janny Wurts	0-586-21068-7	£4.99
☐	THE DRAGON AND THE GEORGE		
	Gordon R. Dickson	0-586-21326-0	£4.99
☐	BLACK TRILLIUM May/Bradley/Norton	0-586-21102-0	£4.99

All these books are available from your local bookseller or can be ordered direct from the publishers.

To order direct just tick the titles you want and fill in the form below:

Name: _____

Address: _____

_____

Postcode: _____

Send to: HarperCollins Mail Order, Dept 8, HarperCollins *Publishers*, Westerhill Road, Bishopbriggs, Glasgow G64 2QT.

Please enclose a cheque or postal order or your authority to debit your Visa/Access account –

Credit card no: _____

Expiry date: _____

Signature: _____

– to the value of the cover price plus:

UK & BFPO: Add £1.00 for the first and 25p for each additional book ordered.

Overseas orders including Eire, please add £2.95 service charge.

Books will be sent by surface mail but quotes for airmail despatches will be given on request.

24 HOUR TELEPHONE ORDERING SERVICE FOR ACCESS/VISA CARDHOLDERS –
TEL: GLASGOW 041-772 2281 or LONDON 081-307 4052